BLACK CLOUDS IN MANILA
Book 1: Fight or Flight
(Inspired by True Events)

by

Tessie Jayme

Website: www.blackcloudsinmanila.com
BlackCloudsInManila@gmail.com
Gold Canyon, Arizona 85118
Copyright © 2014

BOOKS BY TESSIE JAYME
(As of 1/2014)

NON-FICTION

BOOK OF YES
(A Reinterpretation of the
Ten Commandments for the New Millennium)

I DREAMT I WAS NAKED
(How to Interpret your Dreams)

FICTION

ATOP PEGASUS

BLACK CLOUDS IN MANILA:
Book 1: **Fight or Flight**
Book 2: **A People Undefeated**
Book 3: **After the Ashes**

SCIENCE-FICTION
(Forthcoming)

PEACE WARRORS OF THE GALAXY:
Book 1: **Journey to Lyrica**
Book 2: **Companions in Lyrica**
Book 3: **The Challenge of Lyrica**

DEDICATION

With much love and appreciation to my family:

Parents:

Francisco and Paciencia Jayme

Siblings:

Valentino
Amabelle
Lucibar
Evangeline
Nemesia
Idelia
Nelia
Ophelia

AUTHOR'S NOTE

Writing this novel has long been a dream of mine since my teenage days when I would listen to my mother telling me stories of her life in the Philippines during World War II. She had a knack of making everything so on-edge dramatic and suspenseful. Of course she was always the *"bida"* ("hero") in all her stories, because like most people, she did tend to see herself at stage center in most situations.

Interestingly enough, when my older brothers and sisters spoke of what they remembered about our life in the Philippines, they tended to confirm my mother's stories... including her heroic tendencies. The "saving the neighbor's piano" incident is a true event. She knew how to take charge, all right.

After the war, because my father, in essence, was a member of the U.S. Army, he had the option of having his family with him in America. He took this option. We moved to America when I was six years old and my father was stationed in Fort Riley, Kansas.

When he ultimately retired from the U.S. Army and stayed home full time with us, he told me his portion of the story. He even showed me the notes of his life during the war... for posterity, he said. The incident in the novel about saving the Mayor's son is based on his notes.

There's a specific event which launched me on the path of writing. I have always felt *simpatico* with my mother. For instance, when she told me her *kaluluwa* story – the incident where a white face with red eyes looks in at her through the outhouse window – I could see the *kalululwa* scene in my mind's eye exactly as she told it. I have witnessed her at her most vulnerable, and I have seen her persuasive charm at work in accomplishing goals on behalf of her children. And, yes, I have seen her luck take effect… including her Keno win in a Lake Tahoe casino which provided the down payment for our house in California.

The specific event which placed me on my path as a writer occurred when I was 12. I had accompanied my mother to pay our delinquent electric bill. In America, she often brought one of her children with her when she ran errands because we spoke and understood English better than she did. We reached the payment window and, in her broken English, she began to explain why we were late in paying the bill. The woman behind the window was older, tight gray curls over a wrinkled pale pink face and stressed-out blue eyes. Before my mother had spoken seven words, the woman interrupted and impatiently explained she didn't care why the payment was late. She launched into her memorized standard reply which the whole room could hear.

Standing beside my mother, I witnessed the woman treating my mother like a stupid, inferior version of humanity.   I was furious with this old lady.   My mother was neither stupid nor inferior. I told myself then and there that I would learn how to speak English so well no one would ever treat me in the way this woman was treating my mother.

Yes, I ultimately did well in school, and yes, people have generally treated me with respect in all its variant levels. Of course, meanwhile I fell irrevocably in love with words. How could I not? Putting the right words together in just the right way... there's no power like it. Words can educate, elucidate, illuminate. They can create and conquer nations. They structure people's belief systems and define a country's economy and government. They can destroy or create relationships. And, in a challenging wonderful way, words grouped together in a special way can move people to laughter or tears.

Writing. Well, when the words and the scenes just flow, it's a high beyond description. When it's not flowing at all, but the need to express is there... it's a bummer. My fellow writers will have other brilliant words for it when the pen isn't flowing, and yeah it's all that too.

In this novel, I've written about events which intrigued and fascinated me, educated me and illuminated me, and brought me to laughter and tears. If it doesn't do these things for you, I hope you at least find some other value for it.

ACKNOWLEDGEMENTS

Many years have passed since I first felt the dream of writing this novel. There was so much research to be done, and so many stories to tell which would give a broad overview of how a country and its people survived during a devastating world war.

With patience, dedication and lots and lots of help, I finally done did it, and I herewith acknowledge that help.

First and foremost, never-ending appreciation and gratitude to my parents in heaven and my eight siblings, to whom my book is dedicated. In sharing their *"recuerdos"* with me, they have provided a rich bounty of inspiration for this novel.   Sibs, please forgive the liberties I have taken of your recollections, but remember that this is a fictional work, where I am describing imagined scenarios and not biographical information.   I mixed in fictional people and situations with events from your real memories in such a way that you may not recognize them as yours, but your sharing of those memories was nevertheless crucial to my writing process, and thus you all have been a crucial part of this work. I love each and every one of you beyond expression.

Among my siblings, a special thanks to my older sister, Nem, who not only supplied her memories, but also did additional research to ensure that the cultural, economic and political aspects depicted were as accurate as possible.   In addition, her experience in Philippines during her stint as an American citizen working at the American Embassy there imbued her with savvy and knowledge which added texture and accuracy to the story. Also, much gratitude to my eldest brother Val, who witnessed many relevant events that occurred in this phase of Filipino history.

Then there is the astonishing contribution from my daughter Arielle, whose editorial comments proved to be of epic proportions. She created a practical worksheet with her notes, which not only graded each chapter's suspense ranking, but which suggested tension-building anecdotes and scenarios. She gave her precious time unsparingly, and her commitment to making this work better and more exciting succeeded brilliantly.

Next, there is no way in heaven or hell that I could have written this work without word processing, the internet, Wikipedia, or my beloved 1977 Time-Life Books series of World War II.

When the Time-Life series first came out, I signed up for it immediately, and I received a book a month until I had the whole set. I knew that the brilliant compilation of events and the superior writing within those books would someday save my life. This series of books have answered so many questions, filled in so many holes and provided me with such a rich source of material, that the word "Thanks" just doesn't do it. In fact, words don't exist that can begin to describe how much I love and appreciate those Time-Life publishers. I've tried not to outright plagiarize their books, but at least 80% of the italicized narrative portion were paraphrased from these books.

Word processing: OMG the time I've saved editing and rewriting and replacing names and dates... thanks to the brilliant techno minds that makes that possible.

Wikipedia, Google, Ask.Com and all you other Internet sources: I have just one word to say to you: "loveyouloveyoulove you." It's a new word I've created just for you. It has saved me so much time to have these sources so handy. So many times while I was describing a scene, I simply didn't know what kind of trees grew in the Philippines, or how many miles one barangay was from another... but then I typed in some words in the search bar and voilà, there was a link to the answer. I love books and I love libraries... but I'm relieved I didn't have to make those trips to the library and then search through the aisles of books.

Also thanks to the Internet, I was able to access a website which connected me to the Provincial Governor's office in Aklan for some specific information I couldn't find anywhere else. Thanks to Carlito S. Marquez for helping me out with important info.

Finally, special acknowledgement to Evangeline Cenizal ("Cuz Vangie") who sent me maps and a Tagalog dictionary. She also read my early drafts and gave me essential comments and suggestions about Filipino things.

Whatever writing I did, I happily acknowledge that all those listed above made the end result more comprehensive and much improved in every way.

Thanks, everyone.

INTRODUCTION

I want to tell you a story of ordinary people living their lives during extraordinary times and all the extraordinary things they did.

It's about a family's journey through life – all its challenges and adversities and all its joys and achievements. Life does not find its value in whether experiences are bad or good, or right or wrong. Those are judgments.

Life finds its value in the experience of it, whether harshly grounded through mortar and pestle, or passionately infused through pathways of the heart.

I didn't witness all these things I'm about to narrate, so I hope you'll bear with me and allow my imagination to take flight to the very heights where vision is all-encompassing.

I trust that because you yourself have had moments of being extraordinary, you will understand and identify with the various scenarios and events which you're about to read.

And so our story begins...

TABLE OF CONTENTS

CHAPTER 1
VENTURISSA (VISIONARY)
Cebu, Philippines, (1922-1930)

Venturissa Villa was born a few weeks premature and her parents considered her a lucky child to have survived a difficult childbirth performed by the ministrations of a local midwife. Thus, they named her "Venturissa" to suggest that the greatest luck would always accompany her throughout her life.

Her mother and brothers called her "Rissing" while her father usually adhered to the more formal "Rissa", unless he was feeling especially tender, at which time he would allow himself to call her the less formal "Rissing."

Her mother, Guadalupe, died of breast cancer when Rissing was 11 years old. She still had her father, Julio, an older brother, Benito, and a younger brother, Mario. The death affected her greatly and influenced her character in powerful ways.

For one thing, she lost a source of feminine grace and motherly warmth; secondly, now surrounded by three strong-minded men, she herself learned how to be strong-minded and faithful to her personal convictions. It also shaped her in ways that would be crucial to her survival in later years as a mother and wife.

She learned how to use feminine wiles to get what she wanted from men, and in order to stay on a par with her brothers, she learned how to be practical and shrewd about planning for the future. With their constant talk about freeing their country from the U.S. annexation, they taught her to develop a passion for revolution.

From her father, a Roman Catholic Spaniard who chose to live in Cebu with his Filipina wife, she learned to have faith in the unseen forces heralded by Catholicism. She never veered from her devotion to Santo Nino, the patron saint of Cebu.

Also from her father, by example, she developed high standards that would influence her expectations of others in her life.

In raising her, her mother had provided a gentle guidance that taught by example. Her mother took pains to always be clean and neat in her attire, hair combed and arranged in an attractive manner.

She taught Rissing the traditional tenets inherent in being a Filipina... that there were responsibilities and obligations that came with being a woman.

There was a neat and organized household to maintain, meals to cook, servants to oversee and guide through their various responsibilities. Before her mother died, she had already learned these things, as well as how to cook simple meals for her father and brothers.

By the same token, Rissing took for granted that Papa fulfilled his end of the bargain, providing for their necessities, and, most of all, being the solid and dependable foundation husbands and fathers were supposed to be.

If he never displayed tenderness or warmth to her, at least he was there whenever she needed him, and she firmly believed that he loved her and would always be there to protect her.

His style tended to be dictatorial and inflexible, and she accepted this as a matter of course because she had no experience that it was supposed to be any other way.

After her mother died, she really felt the harshness of her father's style. He reprimanded her sharply if her blouse wasn't tucked in properly at the waist, for example, or if she hadn't ironed out the wrinkles from her ankle-length skirt.

If she joined in the rambunctious play of her brothers, a sharp "Rissa... *cuidao*" from him, accompanied by a stinging glance, was enough to remind her to assume a more ladylike demeanor.

Still, as much as she loved and respected him, there were days when she huddled in her room, crying at the hopelessness of ever pleasing him. He presided over her homework and required her to come home with top grades. He read passages from the bible to her, and they would discuss the meaning of such passages, until he was satisfied she understood their meaning.

Papa tended to function according to the letter of God's scriptures, rather than according to the intent. Rissing was more flexible. As far as she was concerned, if a person acted in good faith and generally followed the Ten Commandments, then one was in God's grace. The rules didn't have to be followed exactly the way God commanded.

Of course, she never argued with her father. That was impossible to imagine, much less act upon. Still, silent in protest against his rigid tenets, she nevertheless harbored more flexible beliefs deep in her heart.

Keeping such feelings to herself and inundated with philosophical thoughts most 11-year-old girls were hardly concerned about, she came across to others as a quiet, self-possessed young girl, and she differed markedly from her schoolmates.

Rissing's father was the overseer of a large banana *hacienda* in Cebu, and so they had a nice wooden house, a few horses for their use, pigs, chickens and a garden. His income also afforded his family with somewhat better living conditions than the majority of other natives of Cebu.

This added to Rissing's distance from her female peers in the area... most of whom were daughters of the land workers. Being mestiza, with refined features and light skin, she was quite beautiful and that also intimidated and caused jealous resentment from potential female friends.

In addition to the different way her father raised her, he also taught her to consider herself "superior" to native Filipinos because of her Spanish heritage from him.

In fact, according to her father, she was even superior to the daughters of the *hacendero* of the plantation, Don Rogelio, because they didn't have the Spanish heritage she possessed.

This was understandable, since the Philippine Islands were under Spanish rule for nearly four centuries and it was a sensible attitude to consider oneself inferior to those who "ruled." To her father, it was reasonable to assume Spaniards were superior to Filipinos.

Of course, Papa didn't pursue the idea of superiority when it came to the Americans. Following his line of thought, one would then have to assume that the Americans who triumphed over the Spaniards were even more "superior."

It was implied, nevertheless, and Filipinos carried conflicted feelings of admiration and resentment for the Americans. The Americans had conquered the Spaniards in the Spanish-American War of 1898, and that was to be admired, since it "freed" the Philippines from Spanish rule.

However, in the post-war negotiations which ensued, Spain in effect "sold" the Philippines to the United States, handing it over to America for the sum of U.S. $20,000,000.00, which the U.S. later claimed to be a "gift" from Spain.

That meant, ultimately, that the Filipinos were still under supervision by a higher authority, and thus still under "rule" of sorts... which generated their resentment.

At this point in her life, however, Rissing didn't think much about Americans. Her immediate world was her father, who used a strong hand in guiding her beliefs, and who raised her to be socially conscious of her "superiority."

Thus, Rissing was always aware of her class status among others. This blocked her from a feeling of equality among her female social peers.

The outcome of her upbringing meant that in all of her childhood years, Rissing didn't have any female friends. Basically, circumstances made her a loner, and while this endowed her with a self-reliance and independence that would serve her well all her life, it had its disadvantages.

So Rissing went to school and, as in all school environments, was exposed to the intrigues and gossip and rumors that young children hear and repeat among themselves.

One rumor was that the thickly wooded forest behind the plantation was occupied by *"kaluluwas"*... spirits or beings who weren't human. People said that if children went into the forest, they were either eaten or overcome in some way and never came out again.

Other people insisted it wasn't a kaluluwa in the forest but an *"aswang"*... an evil creature who would kidnap you in the dark of night, cut you up in little pieces, cook you and eat you. It was like a vampire, but worse, because it didn't just suck your blood... it ate you.

People warned that if you're ever offered strange food, you could test to see if it was *aswang* food by dripping lemon juice on the meat. The lemon juice would make the piece of meat in the broth turn to whatever part of the body it was... but you'd have to look fast and hard because that sight would only last a few seconds.

Young as she was, her unique brand of intelligence enabled her to reconcile beliefs and ideas which would otherwise be contrary to Catholic tenets.

For example, she believed in forces and powers which Catholicism taught were works of the devil. She was superstitious and believed housewives' tales and sayings which tried to explain the unexplainable. So she believed these rumors about the *kaluluwa* and the *aswang.*

Hungry for the non-judgmental acceptance she couldn't receive from her father, and often feeling outcast among her social peers, she was ripe to befriend anyone or anything who would accept her unconditionally.

In this frame of mind, she was more than ready for the bizarre experience which transpired a year after her mother's death.

In the 1930's, most homes in the provinces – and even in more civilized cities – had no running water for flushing toilets, so most homes had outhouse accommodations located a short distance away from the house.

Rissing hated having to use the outhouse at night. It meant taking a lantern with her, and when she'd been younger, Papa would usually walk her to the outhouse and wait until she was done. By the time she was tall enough to maneuver herself into the outhouse seat opening, however, she was granted all the privacy she wanted.

One night, she was sitting in the outhouse doing her business, thinking of whatever it is 12-year-old girls think about when sitting in the outhouse, and she happened to look up at the window. In the flickering light of the candle, a narrow, white, translucent face with big red eyes was staring at her through the window.

She wasn't afraid. She was curious. It didn't look human. The face disappeared within the blink of an eye.

Of course when she came out, the creature was nowhere to be seen. At first she wondered if she'd just imagined it, but no... she remembered exactly the shape of the narrow face, the big red eyes, and the thin-lipped mouth.

Thanks to the stories and rumors under her belt, Rissing realized – when that white face had appeared at the outhouse window – that she had just seen a *kaluluwa*. *Aswangs* looked like normal people, but *kaluluwas* were strange looking... so this one was definitely a *kaluluwa*.

It hadn't killed her when she was vulnerable, so she decided it wasn't dangerous to her. Plus, she felt confident that her inherent "luck" would protect her, and she resolved to befriend it.

She knew she couldn't tell her brothers and father about it, because they would only tighten their protective noose around her. She had no friends she could confide in, so it was a secret she clutched to herself.

On a Sunday morning, after attending mass and enjoying a lunch of *arroz valenciana*, her Papa's favorite dish, she covered a small plate of *biku* with a napkin and entered the infamous forest.

It was early afternoon so the sun was shining brightly, and she could hear birds chirping and see them flying from tree to tree. She felt safe and unafraid.

She didn't want to get lost, so she was careful to memorize unique landmarks along the way. As she proceeded deeper into the woods, the trees were clustered closer together, and so it became darker.

As less sunlight filtered through, her courage began to falter. After all, the forest was a big place and how would she know where to find the *kaluluwa?* And what if she found another *kaluluwa* who wasn't so friendly? What if she ran into a *kaluluwa* who was the type which ate little girls?

Not that she was so little anymore. At 12 years old, she was already having her monthlies and her body was becoming more womanly. But, still...

Yes, something was calling to her. She didn't know how to explain it, other than that it was as if there was a string tied around her which was pulling her closer and closer to itself.

After half an hour of walking, she came upon a grove of Aglaia trees. The bark of the Aglaia was grayish-white and the pale green leaves were small. To Rissing, the trees were dainty and pretty.

From behind a tree the *kaluluwa* stepped out. It was very tall and thin. Its skin was so translucent she could see the reddish trails of the veins running along its chest and limbs. It wore a type of cloth around its privates, but was otherwise naked.

Its breasts weren't like a woman's, so Rissing assumed it was male. The hair on its head was thin and wispy, the longest strands being shoulder-length. The creature moved with a fragile grace, and Rissing thought it strangely beautiful.

She remained as still as possible, and the creature itself didn't move. They looked at each other for some time.

Then Rissing, moving slowly so as not to frighten the creature, unwrapped the plate of *biku*. She extended the plate to the creature and laid it on the ground.

Then, keeping her head turned enough to watch the creature, she began to walk away. When she lost sight of it, she began to run, checking carefully first for the landmarks she had memorized.

After a few minutes of running, she leaned against the trunk of a tree to catch her breath, and when she had rested enough, took off again.

She hadn't been afraid entering the forest, resolved to find the creature. Now that she had found it, her heart was beating like a pounding drum inside her chest, and she was so scared she was shaking.

After half an hour of running, it occurred to her she couldn't find her landmarks any more, and that she should have exited the forest edge long ago.

Now she was beginning to panic. If she couldn't find her way back home, she'd be lost in the forest. She wouldn't have water or food, and she would die. Or, before she died, maybe some evil *aswangs* would find her, kill her, and then eat her.

She tried retracing her steps, looking for her landmarks. She must have circled and gone back and forth for another 30 minutes before finally, she gave in to her fear, sat down at the trunk of a tree and cried.

She cried for while, not knowing what else she could do to save herself. If she started yelling for help, who knew what creatures would come to get her.

She cried for a long time, and finally the tears had run out of her. She sat under the tree, her face streaked with tears, her long black hair unkempt and tangled from brushing against branches, and her clothing in disarray.

If Papa were to see her now, he would criticize and lecture her for the rest of the day. She tried to summon up the courage to get up and try again. She knew it would be certain disaster if she gave up.

Putting her hands together and closing her eyes, she prayed for Santo Nino to use his powers to help her find a way back home.

Not long after, a gentle howling caught her attention, like a strong wind echoing through the branches of a tree. She turned her head and saw the creature, standing quite still several yards away. It was making the wind-howling noise.

She stood, somewhat comforted by its appearance. It made a hand motion, and Rissing understood that to mean, "Follow me."

Without hesitation she followed the creature. After a while, she recognized a landmark, and then another, until finally she was at the exact location where she had entered the forest.

Excitedly, she ran out of the forest and all the way home. She didn't look back once to see if the creature had stayed to watch her or if it was already gone.

Fortunately, her brothers were out doing their chores with Papa, so she had a chance to wash her face, change her clothes, and fix her hair.

By dinnertime, she was composed and quite herself again, though very thoughtful, because she couldn't forget what she had just seen and experienced in the forest.

After a week, she wondered if she might have imagined the whole thing. Who would believe her if she told them? When she used the outhouse, she always checked the window to see if the creature might be looking in.

To her complete disappointment, that never happened.

After the ninth day, her curiosity got the best of her, and she took a walk to the place where she had entered the forest.

Even from a distance, she could see something white on a lower branch of a tree. When she reached the tree, she saw it was a napkin – her napkin – tied around the branch. The plate she had left for the creature in the forest was at the foot of the tree.

She left the napkin and took the plate. When she got home, she found some chicken coop wire, twisted and bent it to create a box. The next day, she made *biku,* put a portion on a plate, wrapped it with a napkin and took it to the napkin-tree. At the foot of the tree, she placed the plate, covering it with the chicken-wire box so animals wouldn't eat the food.

Two or three times a week, after school was over, Rissing went to the napkin-tree, retrieved her plate, and placed a newly filled plate under the wire box. It wasn't always *biku...* sometimes it was just freshly made bread on which she had spread some *santol* marmalade.

In the fourth week of her visits to the napkin-tree, as Rissing placed a plate containing a slice of fried banana fritters at the foot of the tree, the creature came out from behind a tree.

Moving slowly and gracefully, it sat on the ground, facing Rissing, picked up the plate and began delicately eating the fritters. Rissing watched in fascination.

The creature had long fingers which placed small pieces of the sweet fritter into its mouth. Its eyes never left Rissing as it ate everything on the plate.

As Rissing gazed into its eyes, she could hear thoughts in her mind. At that point, she stopped thinking of him as "it"... she began to see him as a "he." She sensed so many things from him. It was as if his mind was talking to hers.

She could sense feelings from him... that he liked her long black hair... the thickness of it and how it fell behind her back and around her face. He liked her brown eyes and the expressions which changed her face. He liked that she wasn't afraid of him.

She tried to think similar feelings to him. That she liked how different he looked, and that he was so graceful in his movements. That she trusted him never to hurt her.

When he had finished eating the fritters, he slowly extended the plate to Rissing, and she took it just as slowly, careful not to touch him.

After that, it was as if she could sense his presence at the tree, and, interestingly enough, he appeared only at those times when she had the opportunity to go to the tree.

She never sensed his presence at night when she was asleep, nor during family gatherings, when she was reading with her father, or playing games with her brothers.

It was either coincidence, or this creature was very adept at reading her mind and sensing her from afar.

At school, something new began to happen. Boys started to hang around her, talking about nothing, wanting to spend time with her... wanting to walk her home.

Three boys walked her home one day. They were best friends and sometimes got rowdy, but she was used to boys being boys and it didn't bother her.

When she got home, her father was working in their garden, and he stood up to watch her as she came into the gate. She suddenly felt self-conscious, wondering how he would react to these young rowdies being rambunctious around her.

She waved at him and shouted, "Hello, Papa!"

He didn't wave back. Still saying nothing, he lifted his hand and pointed out the gate. Even the boys knew what that meant. They stopped in their tracks, took a last look at Rissing, and raced out the gate and down the path.

That night, her father asked her to talk with him in his study.

Julio Villa was a very religious man. He treasured his special relationship with God and was a devoted Christian. He raised his family to respect and live by the traditions of that religion. The idea of a baby coming into the world, Son of God, to save humanity appealed to him. His belief was that martyrdom was a sacred and honorable way to accept one's commitment to the betterment of mankind. Selflessness was a powerful goal to attain.

However, as fervently as he believed in the tenets of Catholicism, he saw gross abuse by the Spanish Friars of its Filipino congregation. They confiscated land from farmers, claiming these lands as their estates.

Several women at the plantation had even complained to him of sexual abuse by the priests. When he had taken it upon himself to approach the Bishop to complain on their behalf, the Bishop had denied any wrongdoing by his clergy, and that disillusioned Julio so powerfully, he left the Roman Catholic Church.

After his wife died, he became a member of the Iglesia Filipina Independiente, a Christian denomination very much in the tradition of the Catholic Church.

However, it absolutely rejected the spiritual authority of the Vatican Pope, and abolished the celibacy requirement from its clergy, allowing marriage among the priests, many of whom were apostate Roman Catholic priests.

Two years after his wife's death, Julio himself became a priest of the IFI. He had even persuaded the plantation owner to donate land and funds to build a tiny church to serve the people in the immediate vicinity. Here in this tiny church, he served God the best way he could, incorporating spiritual responsibilities into his other responsibilities as Overseer of the plantation.

At the time he asked his daughter to visit him in his study, he was only beginning the realization of his dream to become a priest, but his mind and character already had a priestly bent.

"Rissa, you're a young woman now, and I've done my best to raise you as your mother would have done." Indeed he had. While of Spanish mind and spirit, his religious beliefs gave him a humble perspective of respecting one's authoritative religious superiors, one's community and one's current culture.

From her father's tone, Rissing knew something important was going to happen. A change of some sort. A change she might not like. Her heart began to beat in anxiety.

She felt a dread that she had never experienced before... not even in the forest when she had become lost looking for the *kaluluwa.*

She didn't know what she had done wrong. But Papa was not a trivial man, and if he wanted to talk to Rissing, then it must be something really serious.

She couldn't help herself. Tears built up in her eyes and began to roll down her face, "Papa, what have I done? I'm sorry if I've done something bad."

For a moment it even occurred to her that he had discovered her meetings with the creature. As much as she had come to love the creature, she would stop meeting with him if that was what Papa wanted.

He stood up from his chair and looked solemnly down at her.

"*Iha,* I don't think the school you're going to is right for you anymore."

"But it's the only school in this area."

"Yes. Which is why from now on, you'll stay at home."

She was relieved. He hadn't discovered her meetings with the creature.

Papa sat back down. He was a handsome man with strong Spanish looks... an aristocratic nose, a thin, ascetic face, and very penetrating brown eyes. His hair was fully gray now, but it only made him more handsome. She loved him with all her heart because she knew that he was only trying to protect her.

"Rissing, you're a very pretty young woman. This school you're going to... I don't like the habits you're picking up there."

For a moment she wondered if it had anything to do with the boys who had walked her home earlier that day. It could be that he considered her too good for them.

"You're smart and you have all the skills of a wife. You know how to read and write, and you're good with numbers. You don't need that school any more."

Rissing was confused. Papa had always told her that it was a sin to waste one's mind. She did well in school, primarily because Papa himself supervised her homework. As self-contained and isolated as she felt among her peers, she had still managed to find her niche.

"When I can, I'll find time to show you how to do accounts, and we'll read books together. But, soon, you'll get married, and Elena says you are very talented in sewing and crochet. You already cook well, but perhaps you'll continue to get even better if we let you make meals for us once in a while. Elena is getting old and she could use your help in the kitchen."

Rissing was astounded. All her studies, all the preparation of her mind to become a housewife and mother?

She hadn't really thought about it, but now, it seemed to her that being a housewife and mother would create such a limited, small world to live in.

Something in her craved adventure. What was the point of having the greatest luck if all she did was stay home to keep house? Despite being a loner, she enjoyed being on the social periphery of others.

While she had no close friends in school, many of her schoolmates liked asking her for advice when they had problems. Somehow she always knew what to say to them when they didn't know how to deal with dilemmas. She understood things about people and situations, without really knowing how she knew.

As an example, she knew the *kaluluwa* loved her and would always be looking out for her, using his power to save her in times of trouble. She couldn't explain how she knew this, but it was a solid knowledge that influenced how she interacted with him.

In the same way, she just knew things about people. There was one incident when a classmate who had never talked to her before approached her and ask her opinion about why her mother kept getting angry with her.

Somehow Rissing had "known" that it was because the father was being mean to the mother, sometimes hitting her, and the mother was just releasing pent-up frustration and fear on her daughter.

At the same time, Rissing had "known" that the father was being mean to the mother because they had no money saved and he had just lost his job. She had told this classmate, "It's not you, Lucia, it's your mother. She's worried about your father who's going through a bad time."

Unbeknownst to Rissing, she had, in fact, acquired a reputation for being a problem-solver... another factor which intimidated her peers. Rissing's close relationship with her father had imbued in her the same solicitous and counseling nature he possessed. It wasn't enough to see a problem. One had to try to do something about it.

So, apparently in this instance, her father had foreseen a problem, and he was trying to do something about it. She accepted her father's decision. She had been raised to obey and honor him, and it never occurred to her to question him in anything he decided. And she trusted him with all her heart and soul.

From that time on, she was kept so busy she hardly ever found time to be by herself. If it wasn't Elena, the housekeeper, and Manuel, the houseboy, with her, it was her Papa or one of her brothers. And that's how circumstances prevented her from ever visiting her creature again.

Papa allowed her to finish 7th grade, and after that her time was spent perfecting her cooking skills, her sewing, crocheting, and home-caring craftsmanship. Her father also spent time showing her the books he maintained to oversee the workings of the plantation.

She accompanied him a few times when he met with people to arrange sale of the bananas the plantation harvested. By watching him, she learned leadership skills... how to be firm and authoritative, without losing sensitivity to other people's points of view.

She learned how to negotiate in a way which left the other person feeling satisfied with the business transaction. She learned that no matter one's station in life, it was only good business sense to treat clients and customers with respect and good will.

In relative security and comfort, Rissing grew into a beautiful and resourceful woman, strong-minded, wise and gifted with insights about human nature which augmented her already useful people skills.

When she was 19, her father became ill. Her older brother Benito, now 21 years old, had joined the Philippine Division of the U.S. Army and was stationed in Fort McKinley. She was the oldest family member at home now, accepting responsibility for her younger brother, Mario, now 17 years old.

Months before her father's death, he had begun to rely strongly on his second-in-command, Pedro, who had taken over most of the physical responsibilities of his job. Papa still made the decisions, and he still maintained the books.

After several weeks, Pedro began meeting with her father daily, and that was when Rissing that her father wasn't getting better.

The doctor always looked grave after visiting with her father, but whenever she questioned Papa about it, he would say solemnly, "*Iha*, I'm in God's hands. Do you think He would let anything bad happen to me?"

At 19, despite a pointed domestication imposed on her since she was 12, her mind still worked, and what she thought was, "*God taking you to his home in heaven isn't bad, Papa, but it means you'll die and leave me.*"

She tried to accept this impending loss, but she found herself caught in overpowering moments of grief.

During one such moment, she slipped out of the house and ran to her childhood meeting place with her *kaluluwa.* She hid behind the trunk of the tree where they used to meet, and she cried beneath that tree, mourning the loss of her creature, and most of all mourning the soon-to-be loss of her father.

At one point, she saw in her mind's eye the red-eyed creature hovering over her, one white hand resting on the crown of her head, but when she opened her eyes, she was alone after all. Nevertheless, that imagined touch calmed her, and she stood up, straightened her back, and returned home to her dying father.

Yet, there was something about that experience which forced her to grow up... to stop feeling sorry for herself and instead focus on making her Papa's last days as happy as possible. She attended to him devotedly and quietly.

Then came the morning when he called her to his bedside. "*Iha,* I would like to be outside, to look at the sky, to sit on a rock in the river and let the water wash me clean."

So Rissing and Mario helped their father get into a small cart pulled by a *carabao.* Rissing sat beside her father, while Mario walked beside the cart as it slowly trundled its way towards the river.

At the river, the morning sun shed its light over the trees onto the water, dappling the surface of the water in rippling shadows.

The day was warm, so they took off Papa's shirt, and Mario got into the water with their father, gently washing the old man's arms, legs and chest with the precious soap purchased from a local woman in the village.

Rissing sat by the shore, watching the serene look on her father's face, admiring the soapy bubbles float downstream until they evaporated in the morning air. She spread the towels over the cart, so they would absorb the heat of the sun while they waited for Papa to finish his bath.

In the cart, wrapped in the sun-warmed towels, Papa smiled at Rissing. Ill and fragile, he was at his most gentle, and Rissing knew his death was very close. "Iha, I have a taste today for *arroz valenciana.*"

"As soon as we get home, Papa, I'll make some for you."

Her eyes met Mario's. Mario wasn't as handsome as Benito, taking more after their Filipina mother than their Spanish father, but Rissing liked looking at him because of his gentle expression.

While he might be less handsome than Benito, he was, in Rissing's view, the more intelligent of the two. His character was serious and quiet... very much like their father's.

His dark hair clustered in wet clumps on his head and around his face, and his clothes were wet from the river, slowly drying on his body from the warmth of the sun. He looked older than his 17 years, because of the sadness in his brown eyes.

Mario nodded once at her, and looked away. She saw tears sliding down his face, and so she knew he knew.

At home, Rissing rushed to the kitchen to prepare her father's favorite dish.

Papa lingered just long enough to swallow a spoonful of Rissing's *valenciana...* and then he smiled, "*Que deliciosa, iha.*"

And then he died.

* * * * *

CHAPTER 2
VICTORIO (TOWN HERO)
Kalibo and Malinao, Philippines, 1930

Malinao, like many other small towns all over the world, bred its share of heroes. The most compelling heroes are those who are not aware that they are strong, courageous and heroic. Sometimes they are unsung.

More often, their deeds are sung for a day, a week, or a month, and then they disappear from the news radar, although their lives forever after are vividly colored by that inherent quality of courage which comprises heroism.

Victorio Santos, a member of the Philippine division of the U.S. Army stationed in Fort McKinley, was such a person. Getting into the Army had been hard, taking months and months of patient waiting.

It had taken him a year to save enough money for fare from Malinao to Manila, where the recruitment office was located. The U.S. Army accepted applications for new recruits only if there were vacancies. There hadn't been vacancies for a long time.

In Manila, during the long wait, he had lived with relatives and supported himself doing odd jobs – houseboy, manual work, anything that was available. After five months, a vacancy opened up and he finally became a member of the U.S. Army.

On leave in Malinao, Victorio was in full dress uniform, decorated with all his swimming and shooting medals. He was proud of his accomplishments, because it seemed to him they were so hard won. He thought he deserved this time off from a daily routine of training and exercises and hard work.

"Hey, Torio, What should we do when we get to Kalibo?"

Torio turned to his fellow soldier, José, "I don't know anyone there."

"That doesn't sound right. I thought you had relatives in every *barangay* in the Philippines." José turned to his cronies in the truck and they all chuckled.

Everyone knew Torio had 9 brothers and sisters and hundreds of aunts, uncles and cousins who lived in all parts of the Philippines. Of course, most families in the Philippines were large. The common view was that if a man had no money, his wealth could still be measured by how many sons and daughters he had to help with the farm or family business. Still, everyone knew that Torio's family was even larger than most.

"Not in Kalibo itself."

The truck hit a rough spot on the road, and a man who'd been asleep on the bench across from them fell off the bench. Swearing, he dusted himself off and got back on the bench. In seconds, he was asleep again.

Torio and José looked at each other and laughed.

Shouting outside interrupted their laughter. "Manong Rodolfo is drowning! He can't swim." Other people started to shout excitedly.

The soldiers in the truck crowded around the opening at the back of the truck and looked out.

One of the men said, "I hate flood season. That river's taken a lot of good men."

Torio saw a man bobbing up and down, arms flailing, being swept away by the strong current.

Torio jumped down from the truck and undressed quickly down to his underpants. He ran to the edge of the bathing hole where people were gathered, pointing at the man caught in the currents.

One skinny boy was pushing his muscular friend towards the river, "Go on, Virgilio! You're always bragging you're a good swimmer!"

"He's the mayor's son, *tanga!* What if I don't save him? Everyone will be talking about me!"

Another young man had taken off his clothes and looked ready to jump into the river. A little girl was hanging on to his arm, "No, Papa! You'll drown! Remember when Mariano Talango drowned last year?"

Torio didn't say anything. Gauged his chances. He knew that he'd make better time if he entered the river at mid-point, instead of from the bank. Fortunately there was a bridge spanning the river at its narrow point.

He ran across the wooden bridge, wide enough to hold carriages and oxcarts, but used primarily by pedestrians wanting to get to the opposite side.

He chose a spot in line with the man flailing in the water.   Climbed over the railing. And dove in.

The water accepted him easily and without resistance, so he knew his diving form had been right.   He took a few seconds to adjust to the character of the water.

His concentration was focused on only one thing... using the water to get to that man who needed his help.   He felt himself caught by the currents, but he wasn't worried.   The current was taking him to where the man was. His body adjusted to the currents and keeping his head above the water, he moved his legs and arms into a fast front crawl.

Of all the competitive strokes required when he did competition swimming, his front crawl was the fastest.   He loved to do the butterfly and breaststroke when he wanted to concentrate on form, but front crawl would take him faster than the other two strokes to reach the boy.

He had spent many hours in the Army swimming pool, training along with other members of the U.S. Army Swimming Team. He could do a mile in 23 minutes.

Arne   Borg,   who   held   the   world's Freestyle record at that time, had done a mile in 19 minutes... which meant Torio was only 4 minutes slower than Borge.   While he admired Borg, his true hero was Johnny Weismuller, who won the Olympic Gold Medal in 1924.

There was a raw power about Johnny Weismuller which spoke to him. He could understand passion, commitment... wanting something so badly that a man will do whatever it takes to accomplish a goal.

When he swam between 6:00 and 8:00 every night at the pool, it was Johnny whose face came up in his head... who spoke to him and encouraged him to try harder, to take one more lap, to push himself beyond personal endurance.

Now it looked like that kind of discipline might pay off. Torio was a good swimmer and he knew it.

At 28, his body was young and muscular and at home in water. Water liked him. It didn't resist him or test him or reject him. He could move like a fish in water if he wanted to.

Just a few yards ahead, he saw the man still fighting the currents. That was a mistake. The current was too strong and there was no way he could win.

When he reached the man, he shouted, "I've got you. Hang on to my arm."

Gasping and choking, the man nodded and grabbed his left arm, but the current tugged the man away from his hold and Torio watched the man disappear... as if a giant hand had pulled the body under.

Torio dove after him... found him... and locked his left arm across the man's chest, using his right arm to maneuver them to the surface. Another strong current pushed against them and Torio nearly lost his hold.

This time, instead of heading for the surface, he went with the current, using its energy to build up speed, and then using that speed to twist away from its hold.

They were free.

When they surfaced, he grabbed the man's arm and began a sidestroke towards the nearest shore he could see. He had to give the man credit. Afraid, exhausted and fighting for breath, he wasn't giving up. He was kicking and using his free arm to help their movement towards the shore.

Except there was no shore where Torio and the man ended up. Once they felt ground under their feet, Torio helped the man make his way along the rock-strewn shore. It wasn't much of a shore... no sand, no dirt... nothing but big boulders and then a sharp ascent up the mountain flanking the lake.

The man was retching on the ground, his insides convulsing at the water he'd swallowed. After some moments, he held his stomach tightly, his body shaking uncontrollably.

Now Torio got a better look at the man. No, the person he had rescued was really not quite a "man" yet. Maybe a teenager... on the verge of becoming a man. He was lean... but not in a weak or fragile way... but in a small-boned kind of way.

The teenager pushed himself up to his feet. Torio moved to help him, but the teenager shook his head, wanting to assert whatever self-control he could. He extended his hand, "I'm Rodolfo Guapo."

"Victorio Santos." They shook hands.

"Thank you for saving my life. Without you, I would've been... I would've been..." It was too much. Rodolfo broke down, turning away from Torio to hide his face.

Torio understood. He slapped Rodolfo lightly on the back and gave the boy a quick nod.

He turned away to give the boy some privacy, taking the opportunity to check out the terrain. They had arrived at the foot of a steep mountain. As far as he could see, it was the same on both sides of where he stood.

He knew this area. The Belan River, which had gathering holes along its banks for bathers, flowed down into a lake bordered on one side by mountains. The lake itself was very deep, even during dry seasons when the Belan River was otherwise dry enough to walk across. During flood season, as now, the strong currents created strong waves and tides on the lake.

It would have been better had they landed on the other side of the lake, where the road to Kalibo followed the winding path of the Belan River.

As it was, unless they wanted to swim across the lake, which to Torio was not an option since Rodolfo didn't know how to swim, they had no choice but to go up the mountain in order to reach town again.

Not an easy climb.

Rodolfo had reached the same conclusion.

Torio said to him, "Guess we'll have to climb."

Rodolfo nodded, "I'm ready when you are."

The prospect of a climb didn't scare Torio in the least since part of his training in the Army included hiking and climbing. He had some concern about Rodolfo, though, but he wasn't about to tell him that.

"Okay, just follow what I do."

Each choice he made, then, factored in whether Rodolfo could handle it. On his own, he would have chosen more difficult or longer reaches to get a foot or hand hold. For Rodolfo's sake, he made easier choices. The mountain was by no means sheer, and there were plenty of bushes and rocks which were sturdy enough to support them, but he made sure Rodolfo was secure below him before moving on to the next choice.

It took three hours of cautious climbing, with many stops to rest. On his own, he could have done it in half that time, but he chose his way carefully.

Rodolfo never complained. He only slipped four times, but each time, he managed to find purchase quickly so he didn't slide back down the mountain.

Torio liked the teenager's stoic determination. He liked the way Rodolfo tried to keep his dignity... and the way he accepted responsibility for his own fate.

At one rest stop, Rodolfo met Torio's gaze unflinchingly and said, "I'm lucky you're a good swimmer, Victorio."

"Swimming isn't that hard. If you want to learn, I could teach you while I'm in Malinao. My leave is over in two months."

Shaking his head, Rodolfo gave a long sigh. "My father will say it's a waste of time."

That was something Victorio didn't understand. How could learning something useful – something which made the body healthy and the heart happy – be a waste of time?

"My father wants me to be a lawyer, so most of the time I'm studying books preparing for college. My mother is more lenient and she lets me hang out with my friends sometimes." Sighing again, "After today, though, maybe she won't let me do that anymore."

At the top, groups of people were waiting for them. A woman ran to Rodolfo and hugged him tightly. A man standing behind her did the same while the woman turned to Torio.

"*Salamat sa diyos!* Thank you, thank you. I'm Flora Guapo. Thank you for helping my son."

Her eyes were large and liquid... filled with warm emotion. When Victorio met those liquid brown eyes, he suddenly understood what "beauty" was. No, he didn't fall in love, nor did he become weak-kneed and tongue-tied.

He just felt this warm appreciation of something a person couldn't describe as anything but beautiful. Torio instinctively knew she was a woman of impeccable heart –

the kind of woman who always said and did the right thing at the right moment.

"Tatay, this is Victorio Santos."

Like his son, Mr. Guapo was small-boned and slim. His face was narrow and strong, with clear dark eyes and thin lips. He looked vaguely familiar to Torio.

"Victorio, thank you for helping my son. It's... how can I show my appreciation? Can I ask you... are you free to join my family for a late lunch? Please."

Torio clasped his hand and nodded to accept the man's profuse thanks. Of course Mr. Guapo and his wife were grateful. Who wouldn't be? But he didn't think he had done anything unusual. He was a swimmer and the situation needed a swimmer, so he had no choice. He had to act.

When the father turned back to speak to his son, Torio felt someone tapping him on the back. "Good job, Torio!" A grinning José handed him his clothes.

"Thanks." Relieved, Torio busied himself getting dressed. He was dirty and sweaty from the long climb, but he could always take a shower later.

"Did the others go on to Kalibo?"

"They waited long enough to make sure you two were safe. There's an old man whose house overlooks the lake. He saw you jump into the river.   He said you moved like a snake in the water... so fast and smooth.   He watched until you and Rodolfo went ashore."

"Who told his parents?"

"His friends ran to Rodolfo's home to tell his mother. Then they ran to his father's office." Whispering, he leaned in closer to Torio, "It's Saturday, but he was at the office because he's the Mayor."

Glancing at Rodolfo's father, he realized why the man was vaguely familiar. Now, he recognized Tan Manuel Guapo, Mayor of Kalibo. Torio was going to have lunch with the Mayor's family.

"They were asking a lot of questions about you."

"I'm sure you had plenty to say."

"I told 'em about your big family."

Torio chuckled. He didn't mind being teased about his family. He himself wanted nine children.

It didn't take long for word to spread about Torio saving the Mayor's son.

From that day forward, whether he liked it or not, Victorio became Kalibo's town hero. The news of his deed even spread to the neighboring municipality of Malinao, where his parents and other relatives lived.

Instead of staying with his parents in Malinao, where some of his brothers and sisters still lived, he stayed with Tia Delfie, one of his paternal aunts, and she complained that when he accompanied her to market, it took twice as long because everyone had to stop him and tell him what a great thing he did.

Personally, while he was flattered by the attention, he thought it was nothing but an overblown glorification of a simple act. If he hadn't jumped in to save Rodolfo, someone else would have. Still, he had been the one to jump into the river, and it would have been rude to say anything but "thank you" to the well-meaning people who wanted to prolong the celebration of a life saved.

When he returned to Fort McKinley, it was more of the same. Apparently, Tan Manuel had sent his commanding officer a letter. His unit gave him a parade, as did his battalion. That was okay. After all, he had won many awards representing his battalion's swimming team, and so they wanted to honor his swimming feat. It was also entered in his service record, and that he appreciated.

It all died down after a while.

Of course, what he hadn't factored in was the fact that the Mayor was a shrewd judge of character, and while he may have exaggerated the facts somewhat, he had indeed seen to the core of Victorio's character.

Time and events would test Victorio's heroic mettle, and while he didn't know it yet, Torio easily lived up to all of Tan Manuel's premature accolades, even while he surrendered to other human failings.

* * * * *

CHAPTER 3
VICTORIO & RISSING
Makati, Philippines, 1930 - 1932

After her father died, Rissing and Mario no longer had a place at the plantation in Cebu.

They were dismayed to discover that aside from clothing and personal articles, their father had actually owned very little. The house they lived in, the garden they maintained, the chickens, pigs and horses – all these things actually belonged to Don Rogelio, who provided these things for the use of the Overseer of the plantation.

Their father had assured them that Don Rogelio had promised to look out for them, but that entailed Rissing becoming a maid at his home, and Mario working as a laborer in the fields. This didn't appeal to them. They decided instead to make their way to relatives in Manila.

Mario and Rissing buried their father in the yard behind the little church he built, packed whatever personal possessions they had and left for Manila.

Don Rogelio was kind enough to pay for their passage to Manila, as well as giving them 10 pesos each for spending money. They also found money hidden in Papa's money box, which Mario insisted Rissing keep.

Rissing's possessions, then, consisted of about 70 pesos, as well as half a dozen rings and necklaces which her father had gifted to her mother. She had no idea what things cost in the outside world, nor how long her money would last.

As they left the plantation behind, Rissing looked sadly at the forest and sent goodbye thoughts to her *kaluluwa,* knowing she would never see him again, and swearing that she would never ever forget him.

He had been her only true friend during a time when she desperately needed someone to support and understand her. This being, whatever... whoever he was, had filled an emptiness in her heart in a way no one else had done.

Her tears fell as she looked at the forest, and then she thought she saw a white figure hovering at the edge, waving goodbye to her.

She waved back, sobs wracking her body. Her tears were as much a farewell to this dear friend as they were for the plantation, the scene of so many precious childhood memories. Mario took her hand and squeezed it. He was a man, though, so he kept his tears behind a dam which held them back.

They stayed with their Tia Violeta, their mother's sister in Makati, which was south of Manila. Fort McKinley was in Makati, so Benito often came by to visit them from Fort McKinley. As soon as Mario was old enough, he also joined the Philippine Army, and Rissing was alone.

Rissing hated her stay with Tia Violeta. Her aunt had six children of her own, ranging from 14 years old to 3 years old. From the moment Rissing arrived, she was treated as the poor relative come to help Auntie and Uncle in their home.

She cleaned house, looked after the children, cooked, sewed, and was at the beck and call of everyone in the house. Tia Violeta and her husband, Tio David, treated Rissing as their maid and servant. She had no time to herself, shared a bed with the two youngest girls, and on weekends, instead of getting a little rest from the hectic week, she was required to attend the *sari-sari* store which they owned. She received no salary for her time, and when she got home, she was still required to cook and clean house.

She endured this life for eight months, and then one night, as she was walking from the outhouse to the main house, Tio David pulled her into the bushes and groped at her breasts and the place between her thighs.

He smelled of *tuba* and unwashed clothes. His hands were dirty and calloused. He was whispering things to her and acted as if she should be thrilled at his attentions. All she could think of was that Papa had not raised her to be treated in such a demeaning way.

All the frustration of her life since her father's death roiled inside her heart. She hadn't complained at becoming the house servant, treated with contempt and pity and insensitive cruelty. She had placed her pride on a shelf because she knew, without question, that pride had no place in her current condition. She had accepted the need for humility and acquiescence when such feelings were so alien to her. But... now this... to be fondled by her own uncle as if she were nothing but a whore for his needs... it was too much.

She bent her arm at the elbow and made a fist, punching him in the eye. He yelped and released her and she ran into the house, into the kitchen, where she picked up a crying Alicia and hugged the child close against her breast, patting her on the back.

When Tio David entered the kitchen a few minutes later, rubbing his eye and glaring at her, she ignored him.

The next morning, at the earliest sign of dawn, she left the house, her meager belongings in her suitcase. Not wanting to spend her precious pesos, she walked all morning until she reached Fort McKinley.

There, Benito met her in the visitors' lounge, and she told him what Tio David had tried to do.

Benito arranged for her to stay with a woman he was seeing, and after a week, the army provided a housing unit for him in Fort McKinley so his sister could live with him.

Mario had been sent for special training at some undisclosed location, so for now, it was just her and Benito.

Rissing felt bereft and pummeled by life. Though she knew Benito would try his best to take care of her, he was only a private and wasn't making enough money to provide for a second person. Gone was the feeling of security and safety her father had always inspired in her. Her brothers loved her and would try to care for her, but she didn't want to be a burden to them. She was now 20 years old – a young woman old enough to make her own way in life. This she resolved to do.

As it turned out, the powers-that-be at Fort McKinley had determined to woo the Filipino populace by presenting a democratic attitude to them. They decided to sponsor a para-military program which would prepare young girls, as well as young men, to prepare themselves for a military career. Thus, a Junior Unit was formed at Fort McKinley.

Though it was not what her upbringing prepared her for, Rissing joined this Junior Unit. She considered herself as hardy as her brothers who were both in the military in one form or another, so why not?

Besides, what other choice did she have? She refused to accept a role where she'd end up as the indigent caretaker of an aunt or uncle's children. Being the impoverished relative of a cousin wasn't what she'd choose for herself. Never again.

She was smart enough to know she needed a partner to make her way in life, but she much preferred the help of a husband to the help of a reluctant relative.

Meanwhile, she kept house for Benito, sewed his torn socks and shirts, and did his laundry.

During Junior Unit drills and exercises, she paid close attention to her instructors and saw the efficacy of that training. Just as she had seen the wisdom of learning the lessons her father had enforced on her, she saw that the para-military training she was learning was teaching her survival skills... to be self-reliant and resourceful.

She learned the importance of studying her environment and taking advantage of the terrain as a means of survival... to use whatever was available for her own purposes.

Little did she know that in the years to come, during the challenges which World War II would throw at her, this training was to save her life and the lives of her children many times over.

There were twelve males and two females in her squad, and none of them liked her.

They considered her arrogant, with an attitude of superiority. Perhaps she was, but she was still in survival mode, focused on adjusting to her new circumstances and desperate to find any opportunity to better her condition in life.

She had no time to play the games necessary to survive in a society of lazy, jealous and petty youngsters. She was only a few years older than most of them, but she felt decades more mature and centuries wiser.

Then, salvation came. Victorio Santos entered her life.

* * * * *

In Malinao, Torio had become engaged to Emilia Lin. This was an arrangement set up by their two families. Torio, who believed in the influence of the zodiac signs, had consulted his Astrology book and learned that Emilia, a Taurus sign, would make a good partner for him, as he was born in September under the sign of Virgo.

He met with her and liked her. She wasn't beautiful like Flora Guapo, Rodolfo's mother, but she was educated, intelligent and loyal. In fact, her loyalty was an obstacle.

When he suggested to her they get married immediately so she could accompany him to his assignment in Fort McKinley, she said she wouldn't be ready to get married for a few years.

She was a teacher and was supporting her brother and sister, and she wasn't willing to leave them behind until they were old enough to be on their own.

Even while respecting her loyalty and strong sense of responsibility, Torio knew he wasn't ready to take on the support of her siblings, so after some discussion, they agreed it wouldn't work out for them.

This meant that when Torio arrived at Fort McKinley, he was a 29-year-old bachelor and free to look for the perfect wife. He was somewhat concerned, because he had promised his mother he'd be married by age 30, and so he was running out of time. It didn't help that there weren't too many marriageable young girls hanging out at Fort McKinley.

A few days earlier, a fire had burnt down a section of the housing units and Torio had been assigned to supervise clearance of the rubbish.

He wasn't the type of man who'd tell others what to do without lifting a finger himself, so after a few hours, he was as sweaty and dirty as the rest of his clean-up crew.

During a short break, he watched a group of youngsters breaking up after their drill maneuvers. There were about a dozen of them. Two of them were young girls. One was tall and skinny and walked with a stoop... probably self-conscious about her height. She was taller than many of the young boys. Another girl wasn't so skinny or tall. She walked alone, lost in her own world, back straight... she was a proud one.

A muscular youth ran to catch up with her, grabbed her arm to stop her. She freed herself from his grasp and walked away quickly, ignoring the youth. The youth watched her for some moments, then ran to catch up with her. He grabbed her arm again. This time, when she tried to wrest herself free, the youth didn't let go. He pulled the girl against him.

So quickly Torio could hardly believe it, the girl used her free hand to fist-punch the youth in the face. The youth released her and Torio was up and running towards them before the youth could grab her again.

"*Huy*! What's going on here?"

The youth backed away from the girl, one hand rubbing his jaw.

"She... she punched me."

Torio nodded and turned to meet the girl's eyes. He was surprised at how beautiful she was. He could tell she was mestiza, her Spanish blood evident in the creamy pale brown of her skin, the slender elegance of her nose and the full moist lips of an innocent young girl.

Except her eyes... they were like a tiger's eyes. Fierce. Proud. And wild. He felt a thrill inside him. This was a girl who would never be a victim of life. Whatever happened to her, she would stand up to it. She would hold her own and not surrender to anyone or anything which tried to diminish her.

He thought to himself, *"She's the one. She's perfect for me."*

Turning back to the youth, he said, "Go on. I won't report you to anyone."

"Me? She's the one who..."

"She was only defending herself. Go on."

He didn't blink as he stared into the youth's eyes. Because of his swimming, he was bigger and more muscular than the young boy, but the boy's fists were clenched and he was angry. Torio prepared himself for an attack.

It didn't come. Instead, the youth blustered, "I just wanted to talk to her. That's all." And the youth turned and shuffled away from them.

Torio stepped away from the girl, giving her space. He sensed she had strong territorial lines... that a person could not assume anything with her. Her trust had to be won. Her respect earned. Her heart would not be given easily.

"I'll walk you home."

"I can take care of myself."

"I know." He smiled at her. She didn't smile back, but she nodded.

He let her lead the way to the housing unit she shared with her older brother. It was only ten minutes away, and neither one of them said anything during the entire walk. Torio felt that words would have diminished the rich potential of their meeting. Besides, so much was going on in his head he didn't have time to worry about words. Walking beside her, he felt the strength of her character, the permanence of her resolve and dignity.

He felt as if something momentous had just happened, as if their paths had somehow become one, and his heart pounded at the possibilities. She had already captured his admiration, and he felt that she was exactly the kind of woman who could command his heart.

As for Rissing, she couldn't explain how she knew, but she felt with all the passion of her being that she was walking beside a man who understood her. Who respected her. This man wouldn't grab her arm and try to force himself on her. He wouldn't try to impress her with braggadocio words or actions.

He would just understand her and let her be the Venturissa Villa she was born to be. She didn't stare at him directly. In fact, she held herself aloof, not wanting to make herself available to him spiritually, emotionally or mentally. Yet, she was aware of him.

Beneath the dirt which smudged his face were fine features. Somewhere in his past she suspected he had Spanish blood... not as pure as her father's, but it was there in the refinement of his profile. His alert eyes took in everything, and apparently he had the perception to make an intelligent deduction of facts placed before him.

Rissing's perceptions were more generated by her intuitive sixth sense rather than intelligent deduction. Where this young man would be able to outline the bits and pieces which comprised the whole of a situation, she herself would come to an immediate conclusion based on her intuitions and sensory intake.

She knew, first of all, that she was walking beside a man, not a callous youth still confused by the complexities of life. She sensed he possessed the type of determination and strength of character which would guide him unerringly to accomplishment of all his goals.

From the manner of his rescue, she already knew he was quick to make decisions and take actions. She liked his sense of calm... as if he could handle any situation placed before him.

Petite as she was, he was taller than she and taller than her brothers. Strength exuded from his face and body. He was good-looking and had a respectful air about him, someone who knew his place in the world.

Of course he was only a soldier and from the looks of him, a working-class man. Yet, beneath the sweat and dirt covering his face and clothing, she was sure he was a man of principle and texture. There were layers of character about him which piqued her curiosity.

Would her father have liked him? Probably not. Her father had believed no man was worthy of her. She herself had come to believe the same thing.

Yet, she was a woman now and had to make her own choices based on what she herself wanted. Did she want a pedigreed man who would see her as an inferior? Or did she want someone who would recognize her own superior character and treat her as an equal.

Most important of all, she sensed that aside from her brothers, he was the only man she'd met so far who made her feel secure in herself and safe from the ugly realities of the world.

At her door, she turned to him and thanked him. He smiled again, nodded and walked away.

They hadn't even introduced themselves. They hadn't spoken one word to each other during the walk to her home. And yet, they felt a connection as profound as if they'd been lifelong friends.

* * * * *

As a one-time principal of a small provincial school, Torio's education was often more advanced than most Filipinos he met. He recognized that his education had afforded him opportunities to expand his mind in ways that were beyond measure.

One of the books he'd found on sale in a Manila market had to do with Astrology – the study of planetary effects on human personality. What an extraordinary idea... that planets from the heavens – so small and distant they couldn't even be seen with the human eye – would have an effect on people.

He took it home and read it. Then he put it to the test. It turned out to be so accurate that whenever he met a new person, he'd take out the book and try to figure out the person.

The bits of knowledge he acquired about people were so helpful that this book became one of the more important source of guidance that he turned to at significant times in his life. More important, even, than the bible, although he considered himself a devout Catholic, like most Filipinos.

The first astrological sign Torio checked, of course, was his own. The description for Virgos (born between August 23 and September 22) fitted him to a "T".

He liked to analyze people and situations and then use that information to his benefit. He liked to be organized in his thinking and he enjoyed making plans for the future. He was practical, discriminating and methodical.

He didn't know what astrological sign the young fist-puncher was, but he suspected she would be a sign compatible with Virgo. Virgo was an earth sign, so he'd get along with another earth sign... Taurus or Capricorn, but he'd also get along with a water sign... Scorpio, Pisces or Cancer.

Earth with earth was comfortable because there would be a lot of personality aspects in common; earth with water was also good because they mixed together to make clay, a solid material to build with.

By the time Torio had returned to his crew to resume clearing up the burnt rubbish, he had already decided that he would court the proud, fist-punching girl. He would do all the right things to win her trust and heart.

It took two more days for Torio and his crew to complete their work. During that time, Torio kept an eye on the Junior Unit, watching to make sure the muscular youth didn't bother the young girl. He himself made no move to befriend her. Rather, he talked to his buddies, trying to get as much information about her as he could.

He discovered that her name was Venturissa and she was the younger sister of Benito Villa. She didn't have a boyfriend, mostly because her older brother chased away anyone who dared to approach her.

Torio knew he had to behave with the utmost integrity and with clear intentions to commit.

Four days after the fist-punching incident, Torio took meticulous pains with his appearance, making sure his fatigues were neatly pressed, his fingernails clean, and his boots polished.

He had persuaded one of his buddies who had already achieved the rank of "Sergeant" to write an introductory letter to present to Benito. His own rank was "Corporal", which was higher than Benito's rank of "Private," but he thought it was more appropriate for someone else to write about his positive characteristics.

It was a simple letter, affirming his good character and praising him for his various skills and feats, including saving Rodolfo Guapo's life the previous year.

In an early evening of January, 1932, with letter in hand, he made his way to Venturissa's home. Back straight, facial expression pleasant but serious, he knocked at her door.

Her brother Benito opened the door and looked at him. Torio nodded his head in greeting and handed the letter to Benito.

Benito read it quickly, studied Torio, and then challenged him, "What makes you think Venturissa would be interested in meeting you?"

"I don't know if she will. I'd like to talk to her and see if..."

"We've already met, *Manong.*"

The door opened wider and Venturissa stepped out beside her brother. "Please come in."

Torio looked at Benito, who nodded. He brushed past the scowling brother, plucked the letter from his hand and entered their home. Smiling at Venturissa, he extended the letter to her, "Sorry I didn't introduce myself before. My friends call me Torio."

"And I'm Venturissa. My friends call me Rissing."

Rissing read the letter. When she read the part about his swimming out to save the mayor's son, she knew she hadn't been wrong about her initial assessment of him. Her heart began to beat faster in excitement.

She glanced quickly around the room and was relieved to see it was neat and orderly. It was small, with room for a small table and two chairs. She offered him a chair and took the other one, facing him. She gave Benito a look and he went to an alcove in the back and began putting dishes away in an upper shelf.

Nevertheless, Torio felt his presence intruding on his intentions. How could he share personal thoughts and feelings with Rissing when her brother hovered like a hawk in the background. He didn't want to talk small talk. He wanted serious talk which would define her for him, like a map where the important landmarks were located.

Rissing sensed his nervousness even while he presented a calm expression to her. She had just made *biku* that day, and she stood up, "Would you like some *biku?* I made it this afternoon."

"Yes, thank you."

She went to the kitchen alcove where she nudged her brother aside and placed a slice of the dessert on a dish. She glared at Benito before returning to Torio just a few steps away.

With this offer, Torio knew she was interested in him. By offering her something she had made, she was displaying her skills to him, just as his letter had presented his skills to her.

It was delicious. He hadn't had *biku* in months. Not since his last leave when he and his buddies had visited a *sari-sari* store. Cooking was not high on Torio's list of a wife's must-have skills. After all, that was a learned skill.

To him, it wasn't so much what a person could do or what a person looked like that was important. It was more important that a person was smart enough to learn from experience, to possess the character to make decisive choices, and to have the ambition to achieve a high standard of living for herself.

While he ate, he scanned the little room and noticed the white doilies which decorated the backs of the chairs they were sitting on, as well as on the table.

So she could cook. She could crochet and had the initiative to try to make her living space prettier and cozier. She was probably an accomplished homemaker in many ways.

Finally, beauty wasn't a requirement on his list. In his experience, beauty generated trouble in one way or another, and most definitely trouble was something he didn't want in his life.

And yet, he couldn't deny she was beautiful. Her black hair, thick and with a hint of waves, reached her waist and framed a face of creamy perfection. Unlike most Filipinos whose noses were wide and rather flat, her nose was an elegant length above delicate nostrils. Her lips were kissably soft.

Oh, yes, he liked her. He more than liked her. He was excited at the idea that she exceeded his expectations of what his wife should be.

After Benito finished his work in the kitchen, he pulled a stool to the table and sat beside Rissing, looking down at Torio across the table.

Then he proceeded to ask Torio about his background... where he was born, what his parents did for a living, how many brothers and sisters he had.

Torio understood what this was about. Refusing to be intimidated by the third-degree treatment, he answered Benito's questions in a way which made his story humorous and entertaining.

Rissing was charmed by his easy ability to talk about himself and his life. She liked him too. Whether she more than liked him wasn't clear to her yet.

When Benito hinted it was time for him to leave, he stood up easily and allowed himself to be led to the door. "May I visit again soon?"

Benito shrugged, "Maybe next week."

Rissing walked past her brother at the door and followed Torio outside, a few steps away from Benito's hearing.

Torio turned his back on Benito and leaned forward to whisper to Rissing, "Would you marry a man if he was only a soldier?"

Rissing's brown eyes looked down thoughtfully, then lifted up to meet his own with a blazing intensity. "I might. If he's the right one."

Torio nodded. He knew he had approached the doorway leading to her heart. It was open to him, and possibly he would reach the innermost chambers; but that might take more time.

This wasn't a problem for Torio. Another characteristic of astrological Virgos is patience. And, yes, Torio was patient.

* * * * *

Over the next few months, he visited whenever he was off duty. He would bring her flowers or small gifts... practical gifts, because he was, above all, a practical man. A shawl to keep her warm against cool evening breezes. A flower-decorated *abaniko* to fan herself cool during the hotly humid days.

And once, when she mentioned that she had run out of sweet rice to make *biku*, he brought her a package of sweet rice from the base commissary.

They had first met in January, and by early April, Torio and Rissing were in love. By then, Torio had confirmed that she was a

Taurus, an earth sign very compatible with Virgo.

Tauruses were extremely loyal and steadfast, level-headed and practical. They were also stubborn and Torio was concerned about that, but he himself could be stubborn so he decided they would probably disagree and fight about some things, but eventually their basic compatibility would resolve all issues.

He had also been studying marriage manuals so that he would be familiar with how to act as a husband and head of household. After all, if a man knows where he's going, isn't it practical and smart to study the requirements of the journey so that he would be at his best?

Meanwhile, their courtship wasn't an easy one. Benito's constant presence had become frustrating and irritating to the couple during his visits. In addition, Torio resented it. After all, hadn't he proven he was an upstanding young man who fully respected Rissing's innocence?

He couldn't even hold Rissing's hand without Benito's sudden intrusive appearance beside her. Only when she pulled her hand away would Benito return to a discreet distance behind them.

Once, at her house, when Benito left them alone to visit the *kubeta* at the other end of the house, Torio dared to pull Rissing into his arms and kiss her. When he released her, she was flushed and aglow, eyes shiningly bright as she looked up at him.

He saw happiness in her face and her trembling hand against his chest told him he had somehow won his way into the innermost chambers of her heart.

For Rissing, that kiss was the defining moment of her decision to marry Torio. Her body had thrilled to be in his arms... to be held tightly against him. Her heart had begun to beat so strongly she thought it would fly away from her body and leave her behind.

She would be 21 years old on May 10th, only four weeks away. She was a woman ready to begin her own life, except she was still tethered to her older brother who was so overprotective as to keep her a prisoner from her heart's desire.

She had asked Benito why he disliked Torio so much. Benito had answered that it was not a matter of like or not-like. It was a matter of honoring their father's wish that Rissing marry only a man worthy of her. In his opinion, Torio was not that man. Not necessarily a bad man, but certainly a man who simply wasn't good enough for his sister.

She had tried to tell Benito that she was quite capable of coming to her own conclusions as to what type of man Torio was. She didn't need the protective presence of an older brother to make assessments for her. He said he respected that, which was why he did allow Torio to visit her.

He didn't tell her so, but his belief was that Rissing would ultimately come to agree with his low opinion of Torio.

He'd done some investigating on his own and had discovered that while Torio was generally admired and respected for his athletic skills, he was also known to be quite a gambler and drinker. In addition, he was reputed to have a quick temper.

Indeed, Benito perceived Torio as totally wrong for Rissing. As their father's son, he knew what was right and what was wrong when it came to his unmarried, innocent sister. And it definitely would be wrong to leave Rissing alone with a man who was nearly 10 years older than she.

He was convinced that Torio was a man of sexual experience and God only knew where his lustful longings for Rissing would lead him. No, he would not leave her alone with Torio if he could help it.

Still, Rissing was a woman who knew what she wanted. And she wanted Torio. She wanted her life to begin. She no longer wanted to be defined as Papa's daughter raised according to the highest standards of his Spanish upbringing and heritage.

And she no longer wanted to be seen only as a sister who needed to be protected by an older brother. What she wanted – with all the stubborn determination of her Taurus spirit – was to be Torio's wife.

Her father had often lectured to her that she should save herself for a man of high class – one of superior intelligence and heritage who could provide a privileged and pampered lifestyle for her.

But life was life. She would be 21 years old in a month and it was time for her to be herself and only herself. There were no high-class men in sight. Only soldiers. And she had decided that Torio was the best of them.

She trusted him. There was a gentle patience about him which reminded her of her *kaluluwa* (whom she'd named "Kal" to herself).

Most of all, she loved him. Her mind, body and spirit came alive when she was around him. And her heart soared with hope and possibilities when she thought of the life they would have together. She sensed that he would bring her the greatest luck possible in life.

She knew Torio was conducting his courtship patiently, respecting Benito's spoken and unspoken rules in his quest to win Rissing's heart. However, it was time to speed things up. She was a bright and resourceful woman. Surely she could find a way to make use of her assets to maneuver Torio to act decisively and swiftly.

On his next visit, she wore a short-sleeved *baro* over her long skirt. It showed off the pale skin of her arms which had become toned after the Junior Unit's many months of drills and exercises.

She had slimmed down as well, losing the fatty softness of her teenage years. Her hair was freshly washed and hung in long waves to her waist. She looked in the mirror and saw a lovely, ripe young woman, yearning for her life to begin.

And that's exactly what Torio saw when he arrived that evening. Benito was just outside the open door talking to some friends passing by the house. It allowed Torio to watch Rissing closely as she moved about the small room.

He found himself mesmerized by the grace of her movements... by the creamy paleness of the underside of her arms... as she reached up to open a high shelf in the kitchen. He smelled her newly washed hair as she stopped beside his chair before the table.

As she bent to place a dish of banana fritters before him, she sighed.

"What's wrong?" he asked.

"Nothing."

She touched his neck gently, brushing away some imaginary hairs above his collar. Torio shivered, his body suddenly alert and aware of her nearness.

"Just... sometimes I wish..."

"What?"

"You know, that we could spend more time together."

"Benito won't let me come more than three times a week."

"He's just protecting me."

"Why? What am I going to do to you? Assault you? Force myself on you?"

Rissing touched his arm gently. "Sssssh. Don't get upset." From where she stood beside him, she placed the second dish of banana fritters across the table in front of her own chair, and as she leaned forward, her breast brushed against his arm.

Torio nearly jumped at the contact. He looked at her, wondering if she had done that on purpose. She smiled innocently at him and sat down at her chair across from him.

Something was going on. His mind raced at the possibilities of what she was up to. Was she trying to seduce him? Not that they could do anything about it if she was. Unless...

He knew her well enough to know she wasn't going to suggest anything aggressive or inappropriate to him. She was raised to obey the male head of household... in her previous life, her father, and in this case, her brother.

Immediately Torio realized she was trying to manipulate him to make the suggestion himself. Since what she wanted him to suggest was what he wanted as well, he spoke up, "The only way we could be together is if we run away."

Her eyes widened and she stared unblinkingly at him. She couldn't believe how easily she had maneuvered him to make this suggestion. At this point, she didn't realize it wasn't so much that he was easily manipulated.

Rather it was because he had concluded she was open to the idea, and he decided he might as well take advantage of the opportunity.

Outside, they could hear Benito laughing with his friends. Several voices were trying to outtalk each other, so in the hubbub of talk and laughter, she leaned towards him, "Do you really think...?"

"I'll figure out a way. We'll wait until after your birthday. You'll be 21 then. What can he do?"

Rissing extended both her hands and grasped Torio's hands. His responding grip was tight and filled with resolution.

Her heart soared in pride and excitement. This man was no coward. He had only needed to know that she was willing to do this.

When Benito came inside and closed the door behind him, Torio and Rissing were sitting sedately in their chairs, quietly eating their banana fritters.

* * * * *

CHAPTER 4
FAMILY BEGINNINGS
Makati and Manila, Philippines, 1932 - 1941

Torio made his arrangements. He got a 10-day pass beginning May 17th, the day after Rissing's birthday. He contacted his Nanay Nita in Manila and she agreed to let him and Rissing use a spare bedroom in her home there.

Nanay Nita had led quite a wild life herself. Torio knew that if anyone would sympathize with his dilemma, it would be this aunt.

She was the black sheep of his father's family... 5 years younger than Tia Delfie with whom he had stayed in Malinao. She defied rules, conventions, and traditions. She did what she wanted to do and that was that.

At 53 years old, she was as happy-go-lucky as she had been at 23 when she had run off with a childhood friend. She and her husband were still very happily married, though they hadn't tied the knot until their only son, Ikoy, was already 12 years old. Everyone assumed they were married from the beginning, but Nanay Nita had confessed to Torio that actually, their marriage didn't become legal until much later after they had begun living together.

Their son Ikoy had died at the age of 18 of some illness or disease which the doctors had never been able to determine. His organs had started to fail until everything just stopped working.

Nanay Nita had often helped Torio out in the past. During the many months of waiting to get into the army, he had stayed with her and Tio Ramon. She was a motherly woman, warm and nurturing, loyal and supportive. Everyone called her Nanay Nita... even the neighborhood kids who liked to drop by for her *santol* marmalade.

Tio Ramon was a successful photographer, launched in his career by the fact that one of his photos of Senate President Manuel L. Quezon had been published in the Manila newspapers in the early 1920's. His success provided for their mid-income home not far from Manila Bay.

To prepare Rissing for their revolt against Benito's dictatorial reign, Torio had written an outline of his plan which he'd given to her.

It showed the exact time he would pick her up while Benito was on duty on May 17th, indicated the approximate duration of their journey to Manila, and the projected time of their arrival at Nanay Nita's home.

It showed that two days after their arrival in Manila, they would be married by Father Antiguo in the Holy Chapel of Santo Nino at 10:30 in the morning. After his 2-week leave was over, they would return to Fort McKinley where he had already requisitioned and received approval for a housing unit for himself and his new wife.

He had instructed her to memorize the information and burn the piece of paper afterwards. However, Rissing was sentimental and found she didn't have the heart to destroy this precious piece of paper which demonstrated to her how thoroughly organized and committed her husband-to-be was. She pinned it to her under blouse against her heart.

In the weeks before their planned escape, Torio had made it a point to put away his winnings from the poker games he and his buddies played during their off-duty hours. Torio was a skilled poker player. Many of his buddies had tells which gave them away, but he was good at keeping his expressions bland and unreadable. Since his decision to run away with Rissing, he had changed his game habits.

While he was known to keep playing until he ran out of money, now he quit when he was ahead. It was hard because he liked gambling. It was a rush to wait for his cards, figure out his best strategy for winning the game, and then wait to see if his cards were good enough to vanquish his competitors.

However, despite protests from his buddies, and even when the night was still young and more winnings were possible, he disciplined himself to quit after a big win. They would need money to finance their escape, and he refused to be caught empty-handed when it was time to make his plans become real.

Four weeks before the big day, Torio had $76 in his pocket. For a soldier making $11.85 a month, this was a big amount. Fortunately, they would be staying with Nanay Nita and Tio Ramon, so their housing expense was eliminated. However, there was traveling expenses, food and anything else that might come up.

Then, too, he needed a ring. One of his gambling buddies had received a "Dear John" letter, and the ring he had bought for his would-be fiancée was still in his possession. It was a two-ring set comprised of the engagement ring, which hooked onto the matching wedding band. The central diamond was small, but it was a real diamond.

The buddy had spent six months' paychecks – nearly $73 — to buy the rings, but he was willing to give it up to Torio for half that amount. And, to make things easier, the guy was willing to take weekly installments for the payoff.

So now Torio had a ring, a priest to perform a wedding ceremony, and a place to stay for a two-week honeymoon.

Torio wasn't surprised when Benito had refused his request to visit Rissing on her birthday. Mario was coming to visit, and Benito had made it clear to Torio that Rissing's special day was reserved for family and only family.

Undeterred, when Torio arrived to pick Rissing up on May 17th, the day after her birthday, he handed her a small box. Inside was his gift to her – the engagement ring he'd purchased from his buddy.

Eyes glowing in happy acceptance, Rissing stood on tiptoes to kiss him, putting all her heart and soul into it. He worked the ring onto her finger.

It wasn't a snug fit, but Rissing said it was ideal… factoring in weight fluctuation. She didn't elaborate, but Rissing knew that women often had water retention when they were pregnant and their rings tightened on their fingers. They wanted a big family so she anticipated her fingers would change size many times.

At first, their big escape was a resounding success. Everything fell into place according to Torio's plan. They arrived in Manila half an hour earlier than his schedule, and that was good. They took a *calesa – a* horse-drawn buggy – to Nanay Nita's house, where they were welcomed with open arms and big hugs.

Nanay Nita was a round woman with short gray hair that sprang from her head in bouncing curls. Her eyes were black sparkling beads on a sun-browned, round face. Arthritis had deformed her fingers somewhat, but it didn't hamper the use of her hands at all. She exuded a positive, happy energy in everything she said or did.

"*Naku! Maganda talaga si Rissing.*"

Tio Ramon was a little heavier and grayer than when Torio had seen him a few years before. He wasn't bubbly like Nanay

Nita, but he was just as generous and expansive.

"All young brides are beautiful. And I'll bet this young bride is hungry too."

"I hope so. We've got pork *adobo* and *pinakbet* for dinner."

After Rissing's luggage was deposited in the extra bedroom, and Torio's bag was placed atop the *papag* in Tio Ramon's office, they sat down to a late dinner.

Wooden carvings were on display throughout the house. A mirror with a wooden frame of carved *carabaos* hung on the wall behind Tio Ramon's seat at the head of the table.

Tio Ramon's work was also on display: large framed photographs of pastoral scenes hanging on the walls: people planting rice, with thatched-roof huts in the background; farmers hoeing their fields beneath a hot sun; and children playing games on an empty street beneath tall coconut trees.

Torio had always loved Nanay Nita's house. However, he had never really paid it much attention in the past. Now, when he looked around, he saw it through Rissing's eyes, and he was glad that it was a warm and cozy place, filled with memorabilia which affirmed his aunt and uncle's love of home and country.

Because she was indeed very hungry, Rissing ate the delicious meal Nanay Nita had prepared. She knew it was delicious because Torio happily said so, and anything made with love is delicious to those eating it... but at the pit of her stomach was a little fear which neutralized some of the deliciousness.

Rissing had to admit she was scared. Not of Torio, of course. And not of her daring decision to elope with the man she loved. Rather, she had realized during the bus trip to Manila that she had left behind the piece of paper outlining the escape plan which Torio had so carefully prepared for her to memorize... and which she was supposed to burn, but hadn't.

She had left Benito a note telling him she had decided to elope with Torio. But that was all. No details. No clues. Except... if he found Torio's plans, he would still know everything.

She knew she should tell Torio... warn him. She knew Benito would come after her. She knew he would do whatever was necessary to prevent her marriage to Torio.

How stupid of her not to obey Torio's directive. How foolish she was to jeopardize everything because of sentiment. She knew better. And now she had to figure out a way to avert disaster.

Their journey had been heavenly. They had taken a bus to Manila, and during the trip, Torio had attended to her needs easily and graciously. They were able to hold hands and, when they could find a private place, kiss to their hearts' content. At first, shyly and gently, with all the fragile hesitancy of new lovers, and then with passion and commitment.

Manila had been as challenging as on her previous visit when she and Mario had passed through on their way to Tia Violeta's home in Makati. There were people crowding the streets, everyone with a place to go and unhesitatingly willing to push and pull and twist their way among the crowds to get there.

The smaller streets were narrow and dirty, overhung with decrepit houses leaning towards each other. Stalls of food and product hugged the walls of the storefronts, and hanging out of the second-story windows were clothes laid out to dry. Small street urchins boldly stopped people, demanding they buy whatever wares they needed to sell.

She had been happy to arrive at Nanay Nita's house. And then she had remembered that piece of paper, which she had unpinned from her blouse and had forgotten to pin onto her new blouse after her bath. She had been so preoccupied with packing and preparing for her departure with Torio. That piece of paper was still in the bath closet, on top of a shelf beside the soap and scrub brush. If Benito found it... she knew he would come looking for her.

By the time she was ready to go to bed, she realized there was only one thing she could do to foil Benito's intention to sabotage her marriage to Torio.

Not surprisingly, the standards for premarital sex were different for a male and female. Males were expected to accrue sexual experience before marriage. For a price, many young girls made a living by providing that experience for men.

Females, on the other hand, except for those young girls who were paid for their services, were expected to remain unblemished and pure for their wedding night. Marriage prospects diminished greatly for a woman who was no longer a virgin.

So Rissing decided to neutralize Benito's resistance by giving herself to Torio immediately... even before their marriage two days away.

Torio's resistance was only perfunctory. She had awakened him in Tio Ramon's office by kissing him.

When his eyes opened, she whispered, "Come sleep with me."

He'd been surprised, "Two days isn't such a long wait."

"We're already husband and wife in spirit."

"But..."

She kissed him again and laid on top of him. How could he say no after that. He followed her to her room.

Their lovemaking was an event of tumultuous passion, fed in tiny increments by many months of just touching fingers, or a gentle momentary touch of the hand. Yet the increments had built to such tension that the culminating fulfillment was a raging fire within them.

In the morning, satiated and more in love than ever, they discussed the final details of their wedding. Rissing still had about $34 of the $70 which her father's death had placed in her hands.

She had used some of the original money for the trip to Tia Violeta's home in Makati, and occasionally, she had accompanied one of the soldier's wives at Fort McKinley to the P.X., where her friend used her privileges to buy clothes for Rissing. She herself had no privileges at the P.X., but fortunately she'd become friends with several of the soldiers' wives.

She knew that she and Torio would need money to start their life together. It was her inheritance from Papa and she didn't want to waste it on trivialities. To her, a wedding dress was a triviality because a woman usually only wore it once after spending a lot of hard-earned money.

When Nanay Nita suggested they shop for a wedding dress, Rissing opened her suitcase and pulled out the dress which she had secretly crafted in the four weeks prior to her elopement.

Among the treasures she had taken with her after her father's death was a bolt of *pina* cloth, a fabric hand-loomed from pineapple leaf fibers. It was a beige-colored translucent fabric used in Filipino formal attire, usually the *barong Tagalog* for men, and very often formal *sayas* and even wedding dresses for women.

Rissing had taken this cloth and sewn herself a simple dress. There were no yards and yards of fabric billowing around her. There was no extravagant train.

It was a simple one-piece design with butterfly sleeves, the bodice form-fitting, and the skirt tucked at the waist and falling in loose pleats to the ground. The scoop of the neckline was enhanced with three pearls which had belonged to her mother. All she needed were shoes and a veil.

Torio was out running his own errands, and so Nanay Nita and Rissing spent the morning shopping for her shoes and veil. As it turned out, Nanay Nita paid for Rissing's purchased items, insisting it was her wedding present to Rissing.

Everything was moving along fluidly... no snags, no interruptions. Rissing began to hope that Benito had not found that incriminating piece of paper.

Just when she was feeling happy and excited about her marriage to take place the following morning, Benito finally showed up.

He was furious, barely able to contain his anger. His inherent courtesy required him to be civil to Nanay Nita and Tio Ramon, but he ignored Torio entirely. To Rissing, all he said was, "Pack your things. Let's go."

Torio stepped in front of him, "No, she's not going with you."

Even though Torio was taller and bigger than him, Benito challenged him, "It would take someone a lot stronger and bigger than you to stop me."

"Watch me stop you." Growling, Torio swung his arm back, ready to attack. Tio Ramon grabbed his arm and tried to pull him back. Nanay Nita grabbed his other arm.

Benito was shocked. He'd never seen a man change from calm to anger so quickly. Torio's eyes were red with rage, his face a fierce and savage grimace. The sheer energy of his attack mode pushed Benito a few steps backwards from him.

Rissing was immobilized. She was looking at a Torio she had never seen before. Never in all her daydreams about him could she imagine the sheer ferocity of this enraged creature before her.

On one level, it scared her beyond description. On another level, it thrilled her that she could inspire such passion from him.

Then she remembered who she was, who her brother was, and who Torio was. She remembered Torio's whispered endearments to her during their night of a different kind of passion.

Her fear dissipated and she stepped in front of Torio. "*Mahal ko, tumahimik ka na.*"

Torio looked into her eyes. Saw her love and commitment to him. He took a deep breath and struggled to find calm. Killing his future wife's brother was not a good way to begin a marriage.

Rissing walked to Benito, took his arm and pulled him away from the others. Softly and gently, she told him, "Benito, I know you think you're saving me from myself. I know it's only because you love me and want to protect me. I'm telling you that it's too late for that."

"It's not too late, Rissing. Papa made me promise to take care of you. That's all I'm doing."

"I've made up my mind, and I'm telling you, *Manong.* There's no turning back for me.

Now, even Papa wouldn't separate me from Torio. Do you understand?"

Benito let her words sink into his head. He knew she was telling him something important. Then realization hit as surely as a bullet pierces its target. He understood what Rissing was telling him. She had given herself to this man, and, indeed, for her, there was no turning back. No other self-respecting man would want to marry her now.

Yet, he had to ask, "Did he force you?"

She shook her head slowly, her eyes never wavering from his. *"Manong,* I love him." She watched his eyes change from anger to acceptance. His understanding and acquiescence touched her deeply. She knew the knowledge of what she had done was a great pain for him. But she also knew he would accept her decision now.

She hugged him fiercely, tears falling onto his shirt, "You've protected me better than Papa ever expected of you. But now it's Torio's job to protect me. Okay?"

Nodding, he kissed her cheek and turned to open the door. Before stepping outside, he said to Torio, "If you ever hurt Rissing and I find out about it, we'll find out who kills who." Benito was a trained boxer, quick and light on his feet, able to duck and swing away from punches and jabs that more muscular and bigger opponents tried to inflict on him.

Just as Torio had won awards in swimming, Benito had won awards as a lightweight boxer. He was confident he could prevail in a match with Torio.

He nodded politely to Nanay Nita and Tio Ramon.

Then he was gone.

* * * * *

For Rissing and Torio, that evening was a shocking revelation. They had discovered personality aspects in each other they had never seen before. Rissing now knew that Torio possessed an uncontrollable temper which flared from zero to a hundred in less than a second.

As for Torio, when Benito had walked away without protest after Rissing's quiet talk with him, he knew she had told her brother something which had defused not only his anger, but also his resolve to break them apart.

He wondered what she had told him.

After some introspective analysis, he thought he knew the answer.

Despite his spontaneous flare of rage against Benito for trying to prevent his marriage to Rissing, he respected the man for trying to protect his sister. So in thinking about it, he tried to imagine a scenario from inside Benito's shoes.

If one of Torio's sisters had run off with a guy who he felt would only hurt her, he'd go after them and try to prevent their marriage. So what could his sister say to Torio to make him realize that there was no stopping her.

What if she told him she intended to marry the guy no matter what he did or said. That still wouldn't be enough to stop him.

But... if she told him she'd already given herself to the guy, lost her virginity and any good chance of finding a decent man who'd marry her....

That might stop him. He now realized it had stopped Benito.

And Rissing had known it would. Which was why she had seduced Torio two days before their actual marriage... before Benito arrived to sabotage their plans.

She had known what she was doing. With brilliant clarity, Torio now saw that Rissing was indomitable in her resolve. Once she decided she wanted something, she wouldn't let anything stop her. Before falling asleep, Rissing's sweet body curved against his own, he wondered to himself: "God, what have I gotten myself into?"

* * * * *

Their wedding the next day was simple, short and sweet. Only Tio Ramon, Nanay Nita and the altar boys witnessed the event. However, Tio Ramon took out his camera and memorialized their wedding portrait.

In the portrait, Rissing's happy glow was so brilliant it was as if a nimbus of pure joyous light surrounded them. Torio – attired in his full dress uniform with all his medals in their appropriate positions on his jacket – stood proud and straight, as if he had won the greatest prize of his life.

"The greatest prize of his life..." He was to think this often in the years ahead, especially when he needed to pull himself up from the morass of pain, struggle and adversity which littered the terrain of their married life.

Torio used some of his precious money to pay for five days in a modestly priced hotel only a few blocks from Intramuros. Like any other honeymooning couple aglow with dreams of the future, they visited Dr. José Rizal's monument, Fort Santiago, San Agustin Church, and even attended mass at Manila Cathedral.

They browsed the open market – the *palengke* – and Torio bought Rissing slippers, a purse, and small tokens to commemorate their special time together.

They spent their last days in Manila back with Nanay Nita and Tio Ramon, taking long walks along Manila Bay, discussing their plans for a home of their own near Fort McKinley, and even planning the names for the children they would someday have.

Before they left Manila, Tio Ramon gave them 100 pesos as their wedding gift. On the bus trip back to Fort McKinley, they looked at their wedding portrait and believed that their future would be perfect and wonderful.

They made promises to each other on the bus in low voices, not meant to be heard by anyone else.

Rissing whispered to Torio, "We'll be happy together. I'll make our home cozy and comfortable. When we have children, I'll make them nice clothes and you'll be proud of your family."

Torio murmured back, "I'll always love you and take care of you, Rissing. If anything or anyone threatens, you, I'll defend you. I'll provide us a home, even if I have to build it with my own hands."

To himself, he silently vowed to restrict his drinking and gambling to once a month. Well... maybe once a week. After all, it was crucial to sustain a strong camaraderie with his military buddies. One day his life could depend on it.

Finally, they each swore silently to themselves that they would keep no secrets which would inevitably erode at their partnership.

In essence, they both had high hopes for a future filled with happiness, success and fulfillment. Rissing was young and a newlywed. Her name was Venturissa and that afforded her the luck to succeed in any venture she set her mind on. Torio was a celebrated hero. How could life deny him its rewards?

There was no way for them to know that Torio's heroic nature, coupled with Rissing's own fiercely independent spirit, would be the cause of many conflicts between them, as well as their only hope for salvation.

* * * * *

In her shopping foray with Nanay Nita, Rissing had purchased a simple gold band for Torio, using some of her precious money. When they returned to the base to begin their married life, they wore the tokens of marriage on their fingers, they had a wedding license, a beautiful 9 x 10 wedding portrait which Tio Ramon had given them, and a strong determination to work together to make their dreams come true.

In the dark warm intimacy of their bedroom, late into the night, they planned how their life would be. Torio liked being a soldier, and Rissing liked the benefits that came with being a soldier's wife. As a member of the Philippine Division of the U.S. Army, while Torio's monthly stipend was considerably less than what a U.S. soldier received at that time, he was nevertheless still entitled to free medical care for himself and his dependents, free housing, discounted prices at the P.X. (post exchange) and commissary, and the guaranteed stability of a long-term job.

Still, he knew that should he decide to leave the military, he could always become a full-time teacher. After all, he'd already been a principal in his early 20's in the barrio at Malinao.

Rissing thought there was more prestige attached to teaching than to soldiering, so in her usual manner, she had guided Torio to consider this possible change in career for him. But, for now, she was content with his military career.

Torio promised nothing, but he was determined to be open to all of his wife's suggestions. He discovered very early in their marriage that while she had achieved only 7th-grade level education, she possessed a keen and shrewd intelligence which balanced practicality with healthy ambition. She wasn't cynical, but she had a healthy caution when dealing with people, aware that success is more likely when one is wary and prepared. She instinctively understood that she could be taken advantage of if she wasn't careful. After all, she herself was quick to see advantage for herself in her dealings with others.

During the early years of their marriage, their life was a standard arena for give and take, for generosity and compromise, for the inevitable creation of something shaped and sculpted by each of them, and polished jointly by both to approximate the image of their shared dreams.

They came to know each other very well.

Rissing discovered that in addition to being a strong athlete, Torio was also an artist, a carpenter, an architect and a general handyman. He made tables to furnish their home, and drew pictures for her to hang on their empty walls. The promise of texture she had seen in him from the beginning expressed itself in his spiritual comprehension of the undercurrents of life.

Just as he understood and swam with the undercurrents of a river, he understood and swam with the undercurrents of his marriage. These two aspects of his life shared in common the subliminal interaction occurring beneath the surface, whether in people, events or the political exigencies of their daily lives.

Together, they were a team.

For instance, Torio knew he wanted a large family. Rissing agreed with that. She admired and respected the strong leadership her father had provided in raising her and her brothers. She herself looked forward to guiding the beliefs and principles of her own children. She would raise them according to the high standards she herself had been taught. Torio was looking forward to sharing his knowledge of the world with them. His background as a teacher had shown him the value of being educated and well informed about the ways of the world.

Despite their initial determination not to withhold secrets from each other, they quickly learned that it was often wiser to keep certain things to themselves. Torio never revealed to Rissing the chain of events which made it possible for him to acquire her engagement and wedding rings. It seemed to him she might feel diminished by the circumstances of his acquisitions.

As for Rissing, she never revealed to Torio that she had inadvertently left behind the plans he had written for her which had ultimately made it possible for Benito to find them. He never asked, and later she realized that Torio had just assumed Benito had dug up the information using the same resourceful determination he himself would have used under the same circumstances.

Her accounting lessons with her father had taught her the value of money, so habit and instinct influenced her choices on how to handle money. It was an aspect of her life that she kept to herself. She didn't tell Torio how she was carefully saving money from the allowance he gave her for food, nor that a maternal uncle had died, leaving her farmland property in the province of Aklan.

Through her friends – military wives she met at the P.X. or commissary – she found an attorney in Aklan who arranged to lease the farmland to a farmer who had lost his own property.

The farmer, Ignacio Fuentes, had sold his property to pay for medical bills for his cancer-stricken wife. After his wife died, he was left with no land and six children to support.

Her new attorney, Juan Delacruz, managed the details of the agreement. For providing use of her land to the Fuentes family, Rissing received 40% of the income the farmer generated. Given that the farmer had to provide his own seed crop, equipment and labor, Rissing felt this was more than a fair agreement. Friends had told her that some landowners often claimed 75% and 80% of the crop income from their lands, but she felt such a formula would foment resentment and revolution from her tenant, discouraging his initiative and loyalty.

She felt the same way about her marriage. She believed in "guiding" her husband and family to doing the right thing at the right time. Mario often teased Rissing that what she considered "guiding" was what others called "nagging."

If that was the case, then so be it. Since she herself had valued her father's "nagging," which inspired her to try harder and longer, she assumed Torio would appreciate her "guidance" in the same vein. Torio was not one to complain, so while Rissing felt his dissatisfaction during certain "discussions" between them, she assumed it was because he felt frustration with being unable to meet her expectations.

It wasn't an easy adjustment for either of them, but ultimately, Rissing and Torio learned to temper themselves according to each other's character flaws. Indeed, as Mario had suggested to his sister, Torio viewed Rissing's "guidance" as Rissing being an incorrigible nag. She was a woman of strong convictions and was quick to judge others if they didn't act according to her own moral and ethical values. She judged her friends and neighbors as quickly as she judged Torio himself. He learned to accept it was one of her primary personality traits.

On her part, Rissing learned quickly that Torio liked to gamble and drink with his buddies. To her, this was unacceptable behavior for a husband, especially when Torio gambled away his paycheck instead of turning it in to her for their household needs.

Torio felt strongly that he was entitled to his night out with the boys. To him, it was already a sacrifice to cut his night-out days from four times a week to one night a week. He was flexible about many things in their marriage, but this was one thing he refused to give up.

At first Torio tried to make peace with his angry wife by buying her gifts. As an example, after one particularly big gambling win one night, he bought her the latest-model Singer sewing machine on display at the P.X. She was happy to accept this gift, but it didn't diminish her anger the next time he took his night out with his poker friends. Since it wasn't alleviating the conflict, he stopped buying her peace offerings.

One night he came home smelling of beer. It was payday and he had gambled away his entire paycheck. Rissing was seven months pregnant with their first child.

When he walked in the door, she was waiting for him on the couch in their small living room.

"There's a crib at the P.X. I want to buy. It's small enough to fit in our bedroom."

"Huwag kang mag-abala."

Rissing stood up and confronted him. "What do you mean don't trouble myself."

"I'll make the crib." He was tired and depressed that he'd lost all his money. And he was certainly in no mood for a discussion about cribs or anything else.

He headed towards the *banyo*, his shirt already halfway off. He needed a long shower and then a good night's sleep.

"If Papa were alive, he would kick you out of my house. He would tell me that you're a man of low character with no prospect of success."

"I'll win back my money next time."

She scoffed, "Until you lose it again."

When Torio came out of the shower toweling himself, the door to the bedroom was closed. When he tried to turn the knob, it was locked.

He was furious. She had no right to lock him out of his own bedroom... in the house he was providing for her. He threw his body against the door. His shoulder hurt, but he was determined. He did it again. The bolt slid out of its housing and he was inside the room.

Rissing was standing by the window. She turned to face him, her eyes blazing with challenge. He took a step towards her, hand outstretched to hit her. She saw his raised hand but didn't move away, her eyes never blinking, never looking away from him.

The moonlight outside the window cast enough light on her face so that he saw the tracks of her tears.

Nothing could have moved him more than the nearly dry trail zigzagging down her cheeks. Suddenly he became aware of how much pain his behavior had caused her. How selfish and immature he was being.

Her hand lay gently over the mound of her belly, as if to calm the life snuggled inside her womb. He knew his flawed character disillusioned her and eroded her respect for him. He knew there were days when it was only sheer pride which kept her from running back to her brother Benito.

As suddenly as his anger had flared, it died. If she nagged him, she had good cause. Instead of hitting her, he reached over and caressed her cheek with his knuckles.

It was in moments like this that he realized what a treasure she was. Who else would have the fortitude to endure him when he was at his worst?

He left her standing by the window and closed the door behind him. He took out the *banig* from the hallway closet and made himself comfortable on the floor. That night, he only woke once... when Rissing came out of the bedroom to place a blanket over him. He pretended to be asleep as she stood above him and let out a deep sigh.

He knew his drinking and gambling were bad habits, but he couldn't help himself. Something would build inside him... a restlessness and boredom... and the only thing that could neutralize those feelings was gambling. It was as if his mind was a muscle that had gotten soft and flabby, and the only way to enervate it was to flex that muscle. To tempt the fates. To challenge the fickle inconstancy of the Gods.

After that incident, while she did close the door to the bedroom, Rissing never locked it again when he came home late from poker night with his buddies. When he saw it was closed, he simply took out his *banig* and made his bed on the floor.

Rissing nagged him about other things. About cleaning up after himself in the kitchen. About throwing out the trash. About repairing things around the house. About anything and everything.

Most of the time, Torio simply shut off his hearing when Rissing nagged at him. She usually had cause to complain, so he understood her frustration. And just as he couldn't give up his gambling, she couldn't give up her nagging. So in a way, they were even.

In this way, they slowly but surely built the foundation of their life together.

* * * * *

Their first child, Ramon Joseph Santos, was born a year after their marriage on June 1, 1933. Instead of inheriting the sturdy, muscular build of his father, Ramon was born with the small bones of his mother. He was a true Mestizo, a good-looking child with light brown skin and elegantly etched fine features. Torio was happy to be a father, and Rissing doted on her first child.

When Rissing became pregnant again in early 1934, she decided it was time for them to buy their own house. Torio had given Tio Ramon's wedding gift of $100 to Rissing for safekeeping. One of Rissing's friends, Imelda ("Meling") Tabayon – the very friend who had recommended her lawyer cousin in Aklan to Rissing – told her about a house across from hers which was for sale. It was in Makati, only a few miles from the base. The owners had to move to Mindanao immediately and were desperate to sell. Rissing and Torio met with them and they were able to make a deal. Rissing felt that it was her lucky streak which had made it possible.

By this time, Torio had achieved Sergeant status. Rissing's down payment and Torio's income was sufficient to buy them their first house. When Torio asked Rissing how she had acquired so much savings, she told him it was a combination of what her father had left her, as well as savings from what he gave her each month, and finally from the sales of the doilies, tablecloths and clothing she crocheted or sewed during her spare time which her friends and neighbors admired and bought from her.

He accepted her explanation and was proud that she was so resourceful and clever about money. He suspected that she wasn't telling him everything about her money, but he allowed her that independence, given how adept she was proving to be in handling their finances.

A few months after they bought their house, Torio had reason to trust Rissing with their finances. While Torio was normally a mellow and reasonable man, there were still certain buttons which set off his uncontrollable temper. Possibly it was a genetic predisposition, since an uncle and several of his cousins had the same character flaw. Challenges to his character were serious red buttons, setting off a frightening killing fury.

He was written up many times for his bad temper which had escalated into fist fights and brawls. In mid-1934, his company commander picked the wrong time to say the wrong thing to him, and Torio lost his temper and attacked him.

He was busted from Sergeant to Private, and if Rissing hadn't been pregnant with their second child, he was certain she would have left him for sure. In fact, Rissing was so upset by the news that she had indeed considered leaving him. She had immediately taken Ramon with her to visit her brother Benito, who was still living on base with his wife, Inez. They had married in 1933 and Inez was now pregnant herself.

Of course, once Rissing was face-to-face with Benito, she couldn't bring herself to complain about Torio. Instinctively, she knew it would be the wrong thing to do. How could she admit to her brother she had made a mistake in marrying Torio? Besides, Torio and Benito had learned to accept each other, and she didn't want to sabotage that tenuous friendship.

Instead, she and one-year-old Ramon went back to her new house, though she didn't speak to Torio for two days. On the third day, instead of going out for his night-out with his buddies, Torio stayed home and worked on fixing up the crib for the new baby. When he was finished, Rissing went up to him, took his hand and placed it on her rounded belly.

"It's another son. See how strong his kicks are."

That's how he knew he was forgiven and that things would work out after all. After a few months, he applied and was accepted for training as a Philippine Scout in the USAFFE (United States Army Forces in the Far East), and was assigned to the 31st Infantry Regiment.

Torio had decided that their first son would be named after Tio Ramon who, with

Nanay Nita, had been so generous with them at their wedding. It was Rissing's turn to choose the name for their second child. She loved St. Christopher, and she loved that "Christ" was part of the name, so they named their second son Christofero Joseph. It seemed sacrilegious to call him "Christ" so they called him JoJo. He was born on November 16th, 1934.

Her sister-in-law Inez gave birth to their first child at around the same time, and Benito named him "Julio" after their father.

When their new babies were baptized, Inez and Rissing became godmothers (*kumadres)* for each other's children. Meling had been Ramon's godmother, and she, Inez and Rissing became good friends, providing support for each other, sewing and crocheting together... and taking turns babysitting each other's children.

In fact, over the years Rissing had established a reputation for herself as a resourceful and quick-witted individual. Her neighbors had good reason to perceive these characteristics in her.

Her best friend was her *kumadre* Meling, the neighbor who had referred her lawyer cousin to Rissing. One day in 1938, Rissing was at Meling's home hanging up laundry on the outdoor clothesline when they heard shouts and screams. Meling grabbed her baby, 1-year-old Carmen, and they rushed outside.

Smoke was spiraling up from a wooded area half a block away, moving quickly towards a house adjacent to it. When they joined the crowds, a woman was sobbing uncontrollably, "My piano. My beautiful piano."

The wind was blowing the fire away from the first house; nevertheless, ground brush between the first and second houses had slowly ignited and the back of the second house was now on fire. A line of men and women were passing buckets of water but it was too little to do much good.

Rissing joined the wailing woman, "Is there anyone inside the house?"

"*Diyos Ko!* It's my piano. My beautiful piano. We just bought it last week."

Rissing looked around at the people around her. Wasn't anyone going to help this woman? Some strong and brave man ready to save the day?

She saw some likely candidates in the crowd, but they were staring at the fire with as much fear and perplexity as the women. As for the owner herself, she was apparently too distraught and helpless to do anything but wail and cry about her potential loss.

People who wailed and cried irritated Rissing. In their shoes, she would make some kind of decision and act to resolve the dilemma rather than just watching the loss of something important to her.

But still no one moved.

So it was up to her.

Rissing pushed her way to the front of the crowd and went so far as to climb up the porch and open the door. She saw the piano several yards away in the living room area.

Turning to the crowd, she pointed at a tall teenager, his muscular friend, and two other boys. "You, you and your friends. Come on."

They stared at her as if she were crazy. She grabbed the teenager's arm and pulled him to the door.

"It's not too late. We can save the piano. Come on."

The boy just stared at her in disbelief. Rissing slapped him. "Wake up. Come on." Rissing climbed up the porch and waited for the boy.

"*Aba!* What're you waiting for?" She went inside the house.

A man in the crowd ran after her, "Manang! Get out, get out."

Rissing was already at the piano, pushing it towards the door. It didn't look like she was going to pay attention to him, so he pulled the teenager into the house after him. His friends followed.

By now the house had caught fire and people were screaming at them to get out. In a few seconds, Rissing appeared at the door, shouting instructions to the men inside, "Don't try to carry it! Push. It has wheels."

The crowd fell silent, watching the drama before them. The flames were engulfing the roof and sides of the house now. The bucket brigade had given up and the fire truck bells were clanging up the street.

The piano appeared at the door, surrounded by five men. Rissing shouted at them, "On its side. Quickly!"

After a confusion of tangled arms and legs, the men managed to tilt the piano on its side, maneuvering the legs out of the door, followed by the body itself, and soon they had lifted it down the porch and onto the front yard. The crowd applauded and shouted encouragement as the piano saviors pushed the piano on the hard-packed dirt away from the burning house.

By now, the truck had arrived, and the crowd made way for the firemen to do their work.

The wailing woman fell into Rissing's arms, sobbing in gratitude and relief. "*Salamat*, manang."

The firemen were able to save a portion of the living room and the porch, and if Rissing hadn't initiated the rescue of the piano, that too would have been destroyed in the fire.

Rissing was not the type of person to sit back and let life happen. Yes, she believed that Luck resided in her being. She believed that her *kaluluwa's* love for her protected her from serious harm... even from distant Cebu where she knew he still lived in the forest. And definitely, she knew that God was willing to grant her whatever she prayed for. However, that didn't free her to sit back and relax. Not at all. She knew she had to set up circumstances so all those other forces could do their part smoothly.

This made her a controlling personality, and while some people resented it, others came to rely on her ability to get things done.

Her own children knew to obey her instantly and without question. She loved them and it showed in the way she healed their scratches and patched their clothing.

Ramon, first child and eldest son, certainly knew that his parents loved him. From the beginning, Rissing saw that he was not only intelligent. He was also sensitive... a trait which didn't always accompany intelligence.

She never had to explain the "why" of things to him. Somehow, he intuited it and understood. For instance, Rissing never had to explain to Ramon that when Papa was gone, he was in charge. Ramon intuited it by the way she asked for his help around the house.

For instance, she would ask him to throw the trash when Papa wasn't around. Before he could speak, he already sensed that the best way to avoid her nagging was to anticipate her needs and accomplish any task set before him quickly. Even if it was just going to bed and closing his eyes, pretending to be asleep until he actually was asleep.

JoJo was not as thoughtful or sensitive. He was an exuberant child lost in the wonder of his own being. Curious and filled with unending energy, his radar was focused more on what fascinating adventures he could accomplish that day, what excitement and fun he could generate for himself, that hour... that minute... that very moment. Like his father, he was fearless and athletic. By the time he was a year old, he was as big as Ramon, though they looked nothing alike.

Ramon was handsome with brown eyes, fine features and a slender physique. JoJo was good-looking in a more robust way, with mischievous black eyes and a strong jaw that hinted at a pugnacious spirit.

Rissing miscarried in 1936, but on August 12, 1939, she gave birth to a beautiful girl, Flora Maria. Torio had suggested the name. He hadn't told Rissing, but the name was in honor of Flora Guapo, the mother of Rodolfo, the young boy he'd rescued from the Belan River years ago. The baby was born with soft, pale skin and a pretty face. Future years would find her to be a graceful, shy child, with a sharp and cunning mind. She tended to be silent, but when she spoke, it was blunt and to the point.

One day in late 1939, when Torio was watching his sons at play, he noticed how JoJo's physical strength and coordination so often put Ramon and their cousin Julio at a disadvantage.

They were playing with sticks and wheels. One of Julio's wagons had lost a wheel, and it was Ramon's idea to take out the other three wheels, cut off the twigs from three long sticks and use the stick to guide the wheels to a finish line. The first wheel to cross the line won the game.

Ramon was six years old, and JoJo and Julio were five. Torio was repairing the wire enclosure around the vegetable garden, and he watched them surreptitiously.

It took Ramon the longest to find the stick he wanted to use, because he was concerned about balance and appearance, appropriate length and thickness. He broke off each twig with care and used a sharp rock to rub away the bark. Julio watched Ramon and tried to imitate his older cousin's work.

Not JoJo. He couldn't be bothered with the balance and appearance of a tool. He grabbed the nearest stick he could find, used his foot to break off the twigs and was ready to play, even though his stick was crooked and rough and even somewhat imbalanced.

But when it came time to play, JoJo won nearly every time. The other two boys simply couldn't match JoJo's quick eye/hand coordination and inherent muscular control.

Julio complained, "JoJo, that's not fair. Your stick is better than mine, and that's why you keep winning."

Shrugging, JoJo handed his stick to Julio, "Okay, little cousin, let's trade."

With Julio's better-shaped stick, JoJo won even more quickly than before. So he decided to give them an edge. Normally right-handed, he used his left hand to push the wheel to the finish line. He still won nearly every game.

To make the win more interesting for himself, JoJo created self-diversions. After pushing the wheel a few feet, he'd stop and pump his stick up in the air, point his little butt into the air, and shout, "*Utot! Utot!*" ("Fart! Fart!") A few times his rear end even managed to sound off the requisite "ppuuutpootoot!" Then, grinning happily, he'd resume his game.

Because of JoJo's self-distracting little ploy, Ramon won several times and even Julio managed to cross the line first a few times.

However, after 15 wins, JoJo got bored and decided to help his father with the fencing instead. Julio, disillusioned with his losses, joined him. Meanwhile, Ramon refused to give up until he had mastered the game. Again and again, he pushed and guided the small wagon wheel to the finish line.

After a while, JoJo lost interest in helping his father. He picked up his stick and challenged Ramon to a game, and this time, Ramon won.

And won the next game again. And won four more of the next seven games.

During dinner that night, Torio continued to study his sons. He saw that Ramon was quick to help his mother prepare food and set the table. JoJo had helped to prepare the rice for cooking that evening, so he felt his share of the work was done and he was out the door playing with the neighborhood children before the table was even cleared.

When little baby Flora woke up and demanded her mother's attention, Ramon cleared the table and set the dishes up for washing. Rissing insisted on washing the dishes herself. She complained that Torio and the boys left remnants on the utensils when they performed dishwashing services.

After dinner, Torio decided it was time to have a man-to-man with his oldest son. Filipinos were not only very nationalistic, they possessed strong family values. One revered one's elders, respected parents, aunts and uncles, and assumed responsibility for younger siblings. Rissing tried to instill strong moral values in her children, often demanding higher standards than Torio himself.

Her guidance tended to be dictatorial whereas Torio liked to explain things because he wanted his children to understand why certain behavior was necessary.

Rissing would tell Ramon it was his duty to take care of JoJo because he was older, and because she said so, that was that. Torio was not so abrupt about it. He took time to explain to Ramon that being older gave him more experience so he knew more. And because he knew more, he had to use his knowledge to make sure JoJo made the right choices in life.

And now he wanted to teach his son something else. Torio asked Ramon to help him finish the fencing for the vegetable garden. "JoJo's lucky to have an older brother like you."

Ramon threw the weeds in his hands aside and looked up at his father. "He's bigger and stronger than me. He doesn't need me to watch over him."

"Being strong is good. But there are times when it's better to be smart than strong."

To be honest, Ramon had moments when he was very jealous of his brother. He even resented that whenever JoJo got in trouble, Mama blamed him... not JoJo... just because he was older. So his emotions were often conflicted about JoJo. Ultimately, however, he was loyal and felt his responsibility keenly. Now, he rushed to defend his brother, "JoJo's not stupid."

"No, but you're smarter. You're more careful. You study a situation first before you act. There are times when that's the best thing to do."

Tears welled up in Ramon's eyes. "But when Totoy pushes me around, JoJo has to fight him for me. Because... because..."

"That's what brothers do. They help each other. You help him with his homework, don't you?"

"Yes."

"So you use your mind to help him and he uses his muscles. That's fair, *hindi ba*?"

"I guess so."

"Just remember. You have two things going for you. You're older so you have more experience about things. And you're smarter."

Torio could have elaborated. He could have pointed out that Ramon's inherent thoughtfulness and ability to concentrate were also advantages over JoJo's character. Because his radar was focused outward, he made friends more easily because he possessed a natural desire to make the people around him happy and comfortable. As an example, his cousin Julio admired and respected him, while often finding himself overwhelmed by JoJo's often obnoxious exuberance.

It was Torio's intention to guide his son and help him shape his beliefs, but he could not have known how deeply this talk influenced Ramon's character. Ramon's overall strong sense of responsibility for his little brother, and indeed, all his younger siblings, never left him all his life.

In September, 1939, Hitler invaded Poland, and the onset of World War II was triggered. England and her allies found themselves committed to supporting Poland, and over the months, more and more European nations found themselves inevitably pitted against Germany. The United States had not yet entered the fray, but Torio and his fellow soldiers spent many hours considering the possible embroilment of their own Philippines in the ever-expanding war.

Late in 1940, when Ramon was seven years old and JoJo nearly six, Torio decided it was time to teach the boys how to hold and shoot a gun. He had discussed it with Rissing, and she hadn't disagreed. She had friends herself who were scared that war might come to the Philippines. Her world centered around her family, so she didn't think too often about the outside world and its challenges, but she had a bad feeling about the whole thing.

Her sons were children, but she knew war didn't care about old/young, strong/weak, and bad/good. If war came, her children needed to face all its accompanying ugliness with eyes wide open. Torio was a practical man – a soldier – and she understood that he wanted to prepare their children for the harsh realities of war. So she didn't resist his intention to teach their sons the weapons of war.

Torio called his two sons to him. They were about the same height by now, but JoJo's muscular body made him look bigger than the slender Ramon, whose thin limbs possessed a tensile strength of their own, but not enough to suggest that he was, in fact, one-and-a-half years older than his younger brother.

Holding up his army-issued, Colt M1911, Caliber .45 handgun, Torio tried to keep his voice calm and casual, "You're both old enough to understand what I do. I'm a soldier, and that means that when my country needs me to fight, I have to use weapons – like this one – to protect myself. If I want to live, sometimes that means I have to kill my enemy."

He explained to them as simply as he could the basic principles of how a gun worked... how pulling the trigger moves the striker to shoot the bullet to its target.

In their back yard, surrounded by trees which provided them privacy, Torio showed them how to shoot the gun. He drew a red circle on a piece of large newspaper and nailed it to tree trunk. He stepped away several yards from the target, aimed his gun and pulled the trigger.

JoJo ran up to his father and held out his hand for the gun. "*Ako!* Let me, Papa."

Torio wasn't surprised at JoJo's eagerness. Somehow, though he was younger than Ramon, his hand-to-eye coordination was better developed.

"Ramon goes first. He's the oldest." Torio positioned the gun in Ramon's hand, placed Ramon's finger over the trigger, and holding it steady for his son, urged him to pull the trigger.

Ramon was shaking. His mind was still processing all the information his father had explained. It was stuck at the idea of killing someone... which translated to the fact that in his hand, he held the power to cause someone's death.

It was alien to his nature... to even conceive of the idea that one would even think of killing another person. But he wasn't stupid, he knew war meant people died. He loved and respected his father. Most of all, he wanted to uphold his role of protecting his family, should his father not be around to fulfill that responsibility. So he pulled the trigger.

If his father hadn't been supporting him, the recoil from the gun would have knocked him to the ground. As it was, he could feel the reverberations traveling along his arms and throughout his entire body.

They walked to the target and looked at the hole the gun had made.

Then his father put the gun in his hand, "This time by yourself."

It was heavy. He had to use all his body strength to hold it up so it was aimed at the target. His father's voice was a background noise as he focused on the newspaper nailed to the tree.

"Hold it as still as you can. Concentrate on your target. Don't move your eyes around. Now pull."

Ramon pulled and even though he tried to prepare for the recoil, he still got knocked to his feet. The bullet went flying away into the trees. He was a failure and he knew it. He tightened his lips together to strengthen his resolve. He refused to cry, even though he hated the gun because it killed people, and he almost hated his father for making him hold this gun and use it. His mother he couldn't hate, and when he thought about it, he knew he didn't hate his father either. They were only preparing him to be a man. As eldest son, that was his job and responsibility.

Five more times he fired the gun, and it wasn't until the last time that he was able to stay on his feet. Then it was empty, and he watched his father release the spent magazine and slap a new one onto the holster.

In routine instinctive form, when it was JoJo's turn, JoJo put one foot before the other, and imitating what his father had done, and avoiding the mistakes Ramon had made, he aimed for the target and pulled the trigger. Unlike Ramon, he didn't fall. Rather, he allowed the recoil to trigger his movement backwards several steps, where he crouched once again, lifted the gun and took two steps forward, balancing himself before pulling the trigger once more at the target.

When he pulled the trigger, he could picture the bullet shooting out of the barrel, and he could picture the bullet speeding towards the inner red circle nailed to the tree in front of him.

After using up all the bullets in the magazine, JoJo handed the gun to his father, barrel pointed up, holster first.

Torio had watched where the bullets had landed. While only one of Ramon's bullets had entered the red circled target, five of JoJo's bullets had been inside, with the last bullet nearly dead center.

Torio hid his pride and amazement at JoJo's natural instincts. They were different boys, with a different set of skills and natural ability. He was careful not to set one up above the other. He nodded his head at both his sons, meeting first Ramon's eyes, then JoJo's.

"Good. But you both can get better. We'll practice a few times a week. Ramon, remember that you control the gun, so you shouldn't be afraid of it. It's just a lump of metal without you to tell it what to do. JoJo, don't forget that this gun can kill. It isn't a toy. You only use it if you have no other choice. Both of you, remember to always keep the safety on unless you intend to use it."

JoJo saluted him, "Yes, sir, Papa." Then he went scampering off to play with his friends.

Walking beside his father, Ramon accepted that JoJo was more proficient with the gun than he was. But, like his father said, he had more intellectual awareness. And since that was the case, he was going to use that to his advantage.

"Papa, I want to see inside the gun. I want to see exactly how it works."

Torio studied his son. He could see that Ramon had already accepted JoJo's superior ability with the gun, but rather than allowing that fact to diminish his self-esteem, he was going to excel with the gun another way. He would understand it.

And so Torio showed Ramon the workings of the gun... how the receiver housed the lower components, and the slide the top components. He explained about the recoil assembly, the striker, the trigger, and the magazine holding the bullets. They collected the spent casings of the bullet, and Torio talked about how the gunpowder inside the shell was ignited to propel the bullet out the barrel, and then the spent shell was ejected out of the top of the gun.

At the end of the demonstration, Ramon was no longer afraid of the gun. He appreciated the ingenuity and knowledge which created the gun, and he understood what a brilliant and effective weapon it was. Finally, he reminded himself that a weapon was just a tool. Tools are made for the use of a person who has an intention for it. A gun was useless until a person held it in his hand and pulled the trigger.

By late 1941, when Rissing was pregnant again with their fourth child, thanks to Torio's carpentry skills, their house had expanded, with a large living room, two small bedrooms, a large kitchen, and master bedroom behind the kitchen.

The outhouse was properly distanced from the main house, surrounded by trees, and separated from the main house by a small garden of vegetables and fruit trees.

Torio and Rissing were well on their way to establishing their life according to plan. It had taken many adjustments, compromises, spoken and unspoken agreements to sustain the marriage thus far.

Like any other family, they established relationships with relatives near and far, participated in community events, bonded with neighbors, and generally lived life according to the customs and traditions of their country.

Then, on December 8, 1941, Japan attacked Clark Air Base in Pampanga, just ten hours after their aerial bombardment on Pearl Harbor, Hawaii.

World War II had arrived.

* * * * *

CHAPTER 5
PREPARING FOR WAR
Makati, Philippines, 1939 – 1942

The ingredients leading up to World War II were not thrown together overnight. In fact, the stew had been left simmering from as far back as the previous world war which ended in 1918. Despite treaties and agreements among the nations involved, post-war resentments festered both internally in each country and externally throughout the world.

In addition, civil wars plagued the major powers – Russia, China, Japan, Spain, Italy and Germany – and neighboring countries plagued each other. In fact, Japan had long conducted a campaign to take over territory in Manchuria to supplement their need for farmland and natural resources. By autumn of 1938, they controlled half of China, all its major cities and most of its railways.

In September 1939, Germany invaded Poland, triggering declarations of war from France and the British Empire. War was spreading throughout Europe, and the United States was reluctant to join the fray. With Japan's attack on Pearl Harbor on December 7, 1941, the United States was suddenly and immediately committed to the war.

Even if the Philippine Islands were not a commonwealth of the United States, when Japan attacked it, it was inevitably drawn into the war. While the Filipinos knew about the wars in Europe, most of its people had no immediate concerns about their personal involvement. The presence of the U.S. military in their country generated a bustle of construction throughout the islands and most people lived their daily lives secure in the belief that peace prevailed in their country.

Americans with their U.S. dollars enjoyed easy living in Manila, where things were purchased with pesos and the exchange rate (US-$1/2P) – as well as Filipino lower price index – afforded them luxuries they couldn't even dream about in the U.S. One week before Pearl Harbor, American soldiers were still flocking to posh spots, like the Polo Club in Manila, and dancing halls in every major city of the islands.

Everything changed when the Japanese attacked Clark Field 50 miles northwest of Manila.

From a relatively easygoing program of alerts and drills, maintenance of his bed and clothing, an occasional assignment of KP, a soldier's day was usually his own after 2:00 PM, and 10-day passes were easy to obtain.

With the arrival of the Japanese, the aura of easygoing peace disappeared and the very air became charged with an electric tension that simmered in the gut and intensified until a person wanted to scream. Everyone was on edge, and people were quick to anger and paranoid with fear. Panic changed the inherently friendly Filipinos into a roiling, desperate mob.

Fortunately, while Japan's squadron of Zero fighter planes attacked Clark Field from the air on December 8th, their main infantry attack was not to occur until December 22nd, several weeks later.

This gave General Douglas MacArthur, Commander of U.S. Army Forces in Far East, time to come up with his defense strategy, and it gave Fort McKinley time to organize itself for serious combat preparedness. A lot of soldiers had to be located and recalled from their off-duty passes. Reservists had to be notified and collected from all the islands of the archipelago.

* * * * *

Fortunately for Torio, it gave him time to help his family prepare for evacuation. Unlike many of his buddies, he'd had a gut feeling all along that war might happen. As soon as Hitler had invaded Poland several years before, he'd started digging an underground shelter beneath the kitchen. Its access was a camouflaged breadth of lumber which was used as a storage shelf underneath the cooking platform. Whenever he could, he took home pieces and scraps of lumber and sheet metal discarded as unfit for use by the base.

He and Felix, Meling's husband and his *kumpadre*, took turns at each other's homes, digging, moving dirt, and carving out a cellar, 12 foot deep, 8 feet wide, and 15 feet long. Torio, a talented carpenter, used the sub-standard rejects from Fort McKinley to buttress and support the cellars. The cellars were completed within a month of each other by early 1941. The men had done their share.

Next, Rissing and Meling stocked the built-in shelves with rice and other non-perishable food. It was their duty and responsibility to recycle the food in the cellars so that the stores remained reasonably fresh. Their children were warned not to tell others about the cellars... because whatever was down there was for their emergency use. It also held many of the valuables which thieves would steal if they knew about it.

Torio and Rissing made plans about what to do if and when war came to their homeland.

Rissing didn't want to leave their home, but Torio had seen the destruction bombs could generate. He knew that any effective attack against the Philippines would have to be aimed at Manila, and he didn't want his family there.

In their many get-togethers, Meling agreed with Rissing, but her sister-in-law, Inez, tended to agree with Benito. Rissing's influence over Inez was never as strong as her influence over Meling. When she asked Benito why Inez tended to disregard her opinions, Benito scowled at her, "Why should she pay attention to you when I'm her husband?"

Benito believed it highly unlikely that the European war would spread to the Philippines, and he reassured Inez again and again that his own sister was being paranoid and overcautious in planning for war. Besides, if war came to the Philippines, the aggressors would want to preserve Manila so they could occupy it in some relative comfort.

Inez believed him, and so when Rissing and Meling talked about what they would do if war came, Inez just sighed and ignored their discussions.

Unlike Torio, whose gut feelings were an instinctive amalgam of watching news reels, listening to officers discussing the progress of the European war, and gossip among his poker buddies and scout friends, Rissing's feelings of danger were more elusive and subtle.

After leaving Kal, her *kaluluwa,* in Cebu, Rissing often had dreams of him... sometimes just looking at her with sadness in his eyes, sometimes with fond yearning for her company. He never spoke in those dreams, but she could always sense what he was thinking and feeling. The night after Torio had told her of his decision to build a cellar, she'd dreamt of Kal, and he was smiling at her, nodding and pointing to the earth.

She'd taken that to mean that he approved of Torio's idea for the cellar underneath their home. She thought to herself that if Kal thought the cellar was a good idea, then it meant war was indeed coming to the Philippines.

Of course she tried to warn Benito, but he flatly refused to give her fears any credibility. And she wasn't about to tell him that her source for the intel was her very own *kaluluwa*. She was practical enough to know that Benito would only scoff at the idea of a *kaluluwa...* much less that she had befriended one.   And then that she was actually communicating with it still?

A month after the cellar was finished and ready, Rissing had a dream.

In the dream, she was a little girl again, running through the woods near her home in Cebu. Kal stepped out from behind an Aglaia tree, holding up both hands, pleading for her to stop.

In real life, Rissing had never touched Kal... although once, when she was placing *biku* into his hand, her fingers had lightly felt his skin, soft and moist. But that was all. It seemed such a sacrilegious thing... to touch him. But in her dream, she ran up to him and hugged him. His long white fingers stroked her long black hair. And then he stepped away from her, one finger lifted.

She understood that she was to pay attention. He stretched out a hand and a large rectangular piece of cloth appeared in his hand... a *patadyong*, normally wrapped around the lower body to form a skirt. She watched as he took two opposing corners of the cloth, tied it, and then slung it over his head so that it hung down his side with the folds creating a loose storage bundle. In his hand appeared a bag of rice, which he placed inside the cloth. Next he placed a large bolo knife beside it. Then he slid the bundled cloth off his shoulder and extended it to her.

As Rissing saw her dream-self accept the bundle, she saw that she was now an adult... and big with child. In the dream, she took the bundle from Kal and worked it over her head and onto her shoulder.

Then she had awakened. She didn't know what the dream meant... except maybe that she was going to be pregnant again, but that was a given, since she and Torio were planning for a big family. She went back to sleep, feeling confident that she and Torio had another child on the way.

Which, ultimately, proved to be true. And now, war had come to her country, and, as in the dream, she was pregnant. It occurred to her that Kal was telling her not to stay in Manila... but to leave it behind, and to use bundles to carry the goods she needed to take with her, primarily among them, rice and a bolo knife.

So when Torio came to tell her it was time to evacuate, she was already prepared. Most of the things they wanted to save were already in the cellar, and it was just a matter of last-minute packing and planning and she was ready.

She waited for Meling and Inez to arrive. Benito had finally agreed that Inez should accompany her *kumadres* with all the children to Aklan province, where Meling and Torio had relatives, though not in the same municipality. Meling's relatives were in Banga, and Torio's parents were, of course, in Malinao. The plan was that after accompanying Meling to Banga, Rissing and the children would move on to Malinao.

Meling had four children: Andrew (8); Felicita (6); Carmen (4) and Ricky (2). She was five months pregnant with her fifth child.

Inez had two children: Julio (7) and Cencia (3).

Ramon was now 8½ years old, JoJo was 7, and Flora was 2. Rissing was in her eighth month of pregnancy with her fourth child.

Remembering her dream about Kal, Rissing had planned for her travel outside of Manila carefully. She had created a belt with small pouches which she tied under her breasts, over her bulging stomach. In these pouches went her jewelry and money, ointments and balm in case the children got sick; a sewing kit with different sizes of needles and different colors of thread; a few crochet hooks; a spool of thick twine, a few sticks of candle; a tiny statue of Santo Nino, her beloved saint, and identification papers for herself and the children.

As per Kal's suggestion, she had shaped her bundles from her *patadyongs*. One bundle hung on her right side; another on her left side, and finally one on her back. If her stomach had been flatter, she would have carried a bundle on her front as well.

Inside these bundles were clothing for herself and the children, a few towels, and rags to be used for cleaning. Wherever they were on the road, if there was water and rags, they would look reasonably presentable. People would treat them better if they looked presentable.

Hidden inside the towels was a large *itak,* a bolo knife which Torio had used mostly to crack open coconuts. She trusted Kal, and if he wanted her to bring one, no questions asked, she'd bring one. It made sense. They might need to hack their way out of a wooded area. Or behead a chicken for supper.

The blade of the knife was 11 inches long, a quarter-inch thick at the spine, and an inch wide where it attached into the wooden handle. The blade curved out to two inches at its widest, and then curved back towards the spine into a sharp point at the tip.

As for Torio's spare gun, Rissing kept that inside the rice pot which Ramon carried in his side bundle.

Ramon was also responsible for carrying the bag of rice on his back. Rissing had sewn a cloth handle onto the rice sack so it could be lifted in and out easily as they traveled. JoJo's back bundle contained 2 cooking pots, a hammer, pliers, nails, a small knife and other utensils. Two *banigs* were secured to the back bundle as well in case they had to sleep on the ground. His side bundles contained food they could cook along the way – sweet potatoes, sugar cane lengths, and assorted vegetables – as well as some spices and flour.

Even little Flora carried a bundle of hardcakes around her neck. These hardcakes were not the delicious confections bakeries sold... they were small flat biscuits made out of flour and water with a touch of honey or sugar, whichever Rissing had handy in her pantry. The flour was either corn, cassava, wheat or rice flour. They were nearly tasteless, but they certainly quieted the growling of an empty stomach.

When Benito arrived in a borrowed jeep to deliver Inez with her two children to the house, Rissing stared at her sister-in-law in disbelief. She had four pieces of luggage with her, and she wore a pina cloth butterfly-sleeved blouse over a black *tapis* skirt embroidered with flowers. A pearl necklace fell delicately around her neck to her cleavage line.

Her children were in their Sunday best.

"*Sus naman!*"

"What's wrong?"

Rissing took Inez into her bedroom, "We're not going to mass, Inez. We're going to war."

Inez shook her head. "We're not soldiers, Rissing. They won't hurt us."

Taking her sister-in-law's hands into her own, Rissing squeezed gently, "We'll be riding and sleeping in an oxcart."

"But they won't hurt us! We're not the enemy."

"We're Filipinos. Yes, we're the enemy."

"Women? Children? No, I don't believe you."

"Four suitcases? What happens if we have to walk? You'll carry two and Julio and Cencia will carry the other two?"

"Can't we hire someone...?"

"What if we're stuck in the woods and it's just you, me and the children?"

Inez stared at Rissing, brown eyes wide in horror, mouth working. Then she collapsed on the bed and tears poured down her face. Julio, holding Cencia's hand, entered the room. Saw his mother in tears. Julio fought manfully not to cry, but soon he and Cencia were clutching their mother, crying along with her.

Rissing sighed and pulled Julio and Cencia away from their mother. "Go wait outside with Ramon. Go on." When they left, Rissing sat down beside her sister-in-law.

"Listen to me, *maré*. This is war. The Japanese are out there shooting and killing people. If we get in the way, they'll shoot and kill us too. We have to be smart. Keep our heads down. Be prepared to move fast. Be prepared for anything."

"I don't want to go. Why can't we stay here?"

"We're two miles from Fort McKinley. Any attack aimed at the base could hurt us too. If they take Manila, who knows what'll happen."

"Benito says..."

"Benito isn't always right."

Inez looked helplessly at Rissing. If she couldn't count on Benito to take care of her and their children, was it right to count on Rissing?

It wasn't that Inez lacked intelligence or that she was a coward. It was, perhaps, that she was spoiled. She was a menopause baby, born when her mother was 47 years old, and her father 56, both now dead. She had one older sister, Lucinda, who was 10 years older than she. Lucinda was a history professor at Santo Tomas University.

Throughout their life, Lucinda had been the one to guide her, teach her, and support her. Her parents (Pilar and Joseph Trinidad) were caught up in their business, a textile mill in Cebu, which they co-owned with Joseph's brother, George. When a storm capsized their ship on a trip from Cebu to Luzon, Lucinda was 19 years old and Inez had just turned 10. Lucinda and Inez sold their inherited portion of the business to their Uncle George, and Lucinda and Inez made a comfortable life for themselves in Manila, where Lucinda bought a house, focused on her education, and raised her younger sister by herself.

Lucinda wasn't inclined to deprive her younger sister of anything, so Inez had generally gotten whatever she wanted, whenever she wanted it. She dressed in the latest fashions and partied with her friends, whose parents were wealthy and privileged. While kind-hearted and sweet, she tended to be self-centered and more concerned with her appearance than in the practical necessities of life. By the time she was 18 years old herself, her share of the inheritance money was greatly diminished, and she decided to find a husband to support her rather than seeking further education to support herself.

She met Benito at a dance in the Manila Hotel, and Benito's heart had been captured. A popular man among the many women he knew, once Benito met Inez, he focused exclusively on her and they had married within three months of meeting. Because Benito was a man of strong character, guided by idealistic standards and beliefs his father had instilled in him, it was easy for him to take control of Inez.

As for Inez, raised by a strong-minded sister who guided all her important choices and decisions, Inez was already conditioned to obey and serve and submit to a stronger personality than her own.

Now, looking into Rissing's eyes, she knew she couldn't be the kind of person Rissing expected her to be. Walking in the woods? Facing the enemy? No, she couldn't do that.

Rissing was a good person... the type who always knew what to do no matter the situation. She was strong-minded and confident. Inez loved her and looked up to her even though her sister-in-law tended to be bossy and nagging.

But she wasn't prepared to entrust her children and herself totally under her care. So, in a rare moment of being decisive, she reached out and grabbed Rissing's hands, "No, I can't go... we can't go. I don't think I can handle it out there. Lucinda wants me and the children to stay with her. I think that's what we'll do."

"It could get bad, Inez. When the Japanese arrive to occupy Manila, you don't know what they'll do to military families. You'll need identification for yourself and the children. The only identification you have is tied in to Benito... and he's a soldier."

"I've already asked Benito and he wanted me to be with you, but I told him Lucing's all alone here and she won't leave."

"She can come with us."

"She won't leave the university."

Rissing tightened her hold on Inez's hands. Personally, she didn't think Inez would be that helpful on the road. She'd always considered her sister-in-law sweet and devoted, but somewhat fragile and helpless. Maybe it would be cruel to force her to endure a journey she wasn't prepared for.

"Please, Rissing."

Rissing put an arm around the trembling Inez. "I'll miss you."

Inez hugged Rissing fiercely. "I'm sorry, Rissing, that I can't go with you, but thanks... thank you... for understanding."

Felix and Meling arrived with their children and bundles as Rissing and the others watched the jeep drive away. Benito waved at her and she felt her heart tug. Inez, beside him, clutched Cencia in her arms, and Julio waved at them as he stood in the back with the suitcases. She couldn't define her feelings as she watched them go. Sadness. Regret. Maybe she'd never see them again.

Meling and her four children carried cloth bundles and wore sturdy clothing and shoes. They all went back inside and Rissing explained to Meling about the change in plans.

"I'm not surprised, *kumadre.* She wants to be with her sister. Lucing's a tough lady. She'll take care of them."

Rissing and Meling stood with their children inside the house. It was a practice run, everyone bundled up with the bundles they were responsible for if anything should happen and they had to walk.

Torio and Felix watched Rissing drill the group. Torio was proud at how Rissing took charge of her troop. It reminded him of that first day when he saw her drilling with the Junior Unit at Fort McKinley.

Bundles loaded on both sides and back, bulging stomach curving out like a prow of a ship before her, hands on her hips, she was a paragon of courage and leadership.

Torio felt something break inside of him... what a woman she was. Strong and unafraid. Facing the enemy with stalwart spirit and refusal to surrender.

Rissing didn't believe in sugar-coating the truth. She wanted her children to be aware of the ugliest possibilities ahead of them.

"We have to leave behind our homes because the enemy is coming. The Japanese want our country so we have to fight for it. But it means we could get hurt. Or even killed."

Rissing felt Meling's hand squeeze her arm. Rissing patted that hand.

"It means everyone has to do whatever I say. Obey me without question. We're like a little military army of our own. Just like your papas, we have to fight too. But we fight by staying alive so your papas will try harder to save our country for us? Okay?"

Because Ramon and JoJo knew their parents, and because their parents often lectured about the right and wrong of things to them, they understood and accepted her words without question.

Even little Flora's lips quivered. But she looked at her brothers. Saw how straight they stood, and she straightened up herself, adjusting her bundle of hardcakes against her chest.

Whatever was breaking inside Torio reached his eyes and he could feel a lump in his throat and tears filling his eyes. He couldn't stand it. He turned and walked out of the room. Felix was right behind him.

Outside, they pretended not to notice each other's tears and state of mind and busied themselves checking windows to make sure the wooden boards they had nailed were secure.

Inside, Rissing continued, "If I'm not there to tell you what to do, listen to my second-in-command here." Again she patted Meling's hand.

Andrew, Meling's eldest, was trying manfully not to cry. Felicita held Carmen and Ricky closely against her. The two younger children hid their faces in her skirt.

Rissing was determined to get her point across. She knelt and turned Carmen and Ricky to look at her. They were both sobbing.

Meling picked up two-year-old Ricky and pointed to Rissing, "Pay attention."

With everyone looking at her, Rissing continued, "Am I clear? All of you understand I'm the commander?"

Ramon and JoJo saluted her, "Yes, mahm." Flora did the same a moment later. Andrew and Cita looked at their mother and Meling nodded. "Yes, mahm," They echoed. Carmen, still holding Cita's hand with her right hand, used her left hand to salute and repeat, "Yes, mahm." Finally, Meling whispered to Ricky and helped him to raise his right hand in salute.

Rissing smiled, "Good. At ease."

With that, Ramon and JoJo ran outside. The Tabayon children did the same and Meling and Rissing were alone. Their eyes met.

"I don't know if I would have told them about the getting killed part."

With a look of censure, Rissing disagreed, "War, Meling? You don't think we'll see people being killed? It'll do things to their minds if they aren't prepared."

"It's doing things to their minds now if they're imagining it happening to them!"

"Maybe." She sighed. "Maybe. But so far they're innocent and they don't know that much about death, so hopefully, their imaginations are limited. But we have to toughen them up, Meling. And we have to toughen ourselves up."

"*Diyos ko.* Look at us. How tough can we be? At least I'm not as big as you... but, look at us. We're women carrying babies. Inside and out."

"That's the secret. We use our weakness and make it work for us!"

Renzo, Torio's 2nd cousin, arrived with his oxcart, pulled by a *carabao,* whom he called "Tonto." He was a plump man in his mid-40's, wearing a pirate's patch over his blind left eye and a bandanna around his head to catch sweat. He was missing several teeth but it didn't make him shy in the least. He hugged Torio enthusiastically and gave Rissing a big smile.

Torio and Felix carried a small barrel of water and placed it in the oxcart. Netting covered the top and sides of the cart to provide cover for the passengers. Woven rice baskets had been lashed to the roof, and hanging over the sides for additional shading. To onlookers, the oxcart would appear to be a supply wagon selling rice baskets.

Next, the men packed the clothing and supply bundles in the oxcart, and laid out the *banigs* on the bed of the cart.

Then it was time to say goodbye.

Torio looked at his wife, hugely pregnant, and his children huddled around her. Looking into her brave, determined face, once again, he realized what a treasure he'd married. God only knew what challenges awaited her, and she returned his look with steadfast confidence that she would prevail. He hugged and kissed each of his children. Whispered in Ramon's ear, "Take care of your mama, Ramon. I'll come when I can."

Into JoJo's ear, he whispered, "Pay attention, JoJo. Help Ramon as much as you can."

When he hugged Rissing tightly against him, he had to struggle not to cry. He was determined to survive the war because it was unthinkable that he would abandon his family. He kissed her, looked into her eyes, and whispered, "*Mag ingat ka.*"

She straightened her back and nodded, "You be careful too."

They didn't declare their love for each other because words seemed so trivial given all the feelings bursting in their hearts, but it was in their eyes as they finally separated.

Meling sat in the back with the 7 children, while Rissing sat up front with Renzo.

It was going to be a long and uncomfortable journey, but Rissing was prepared.

* * * * *

Thus it was that in the early morning of December 10th, 2 days after the Japanese attacked Clark Field, Rissing, Meling, and their seven children left behind their homes in Makati to begin their journey to safety.

Their plan was to travel to Balayan, a city in the province of Batangas near the southern tip of Luzon, where Meling had an uncle who owned a sugar cane farm. He would arrange a boat to take them to the Visayas islands, to the province of Aklan, where Meling's parents owned a farm.

Torio had assumed that his family would stay with Meling's family indefinitely. Since Rissing had never told him about the farm she had purchased in Aklan, she didn't tell him her true plan. Her true plan was to visit the farm she had inherited and which Ignacio Fuentes was now leasing from her. She also intended to meet with Meling's cousin, Juan Delacruz, the attorney who was keeping track of her share of the income from the farm.

Yes, indeed, she had plans. Rissing was not a woman who stepped into the unknown without plans. While the unknown didn't scare her, it was foolish to be unprepared for the future. Nevertheless, she had confidence that things would work out to her benefit. After all, she was Venturissa, and in all her life so far, Luck had never failed her.

* * * * *

CHAPTER 6
ADJUSTMENTS AND ADAPTATIONS
Manila, Philippines, 1941 - 1942

There was no question Lucinda Trinidad was happy that Inez and the children were staying with her in Manila. And yet she regretted the loss of unhampered freedom she enjoyed on her own. As much as she loved her younger sister, Inez tended to be needy and required a lot of her attention.

She knew it was selfish of her, but she couldn't help it. She had her passions, and she often resented anything or anyone which distracted her from what she loved.

Since Inez had married and gone off to be with Benito, Lucinda had finally found the time to focus on her pet project, a book she intended to write about José Rizal – his life and his loves. In fact, primarily, his loves. She wanted to investigate the women in his life and come up with a theory as to which one served as the inspiration for the heroine "Maria Clara" in his novel, *Noli Mi Tangere.*

Her work at the university kept her busy, but after Inez left, suddenly her time expanded to make painstaking research possible.

Of course she had Freddie, but he was gone most of the time, pursuing his own passions. Her boyfriend, Frederick Collier, was an American New York Times journalist assigned to the Philippines.

They understood each other and respected their separate priorities. As a result, not only were they enthusiastic lovers... they were also the best of friends.

Lucinda accepted that, according to Catholic tenets, she was a serious sinner and a fallen woman. She didn't care. She figured as long as she didn't confess to a priest about it, what she was doing was her own business and she'd deal with God when it was time.

As happened all over the world, a double standard existed in the Philippines. It was accepted that men experimented sexually before marriage and often had mistresses after marriage. Brothels were scattered aplenty in all the islands of the Philippines, and the women who provided services in such brothels were to be enjoyed and indulged in... but never wife-material.

However, if a decent woman wanted to be married, she had to be as innocent and pure as the Blessed Virgin Mary herself on her wedding day.

Lucinda felt nothing but scorn for such a double standard. What was good enough for men, was good enough for her. She was 38 years old, self-supporting and independent, thanks to her inheritance and her Associate Professor job at Santo Tomas University, which she loved.

When it was announced that the Japanese had attacked Pearl Harbor, after the first moments of shocked horror, her mind took over and she was thrilled. Her forté was history, and she was now living in the midst of major history in the making. She was an active witness to events which would be recorded in history books in the years to come.

Freddie understood perfectly, for he himself was thrilled to be where the action was happening. The stories and articles he would write as a result of this war would escalate his fame and fortune. His star was on the ascendant, and he was fueled and ready to tackle the challenge.

When Inez arrived with Julio and Cencia, Lucinda welcomed them with open arms, assigned the guest bedroom to them, fed them, and told stories about her job which made everyone laugh.

She and Inez cooked *pork adobo* and *pansit* that night. Lucing tried to make her words light, "We'd better eat well now while we can. Who knows what'll happen when the Japanese come to occupy Manila."

Inez disagreed, "We should be saving what food we can. Benito says if the Japanese occupy Manila, they'll probably be expecting the residents to cooperate with them and give them supplies and food."

Lucing scoffed. "*Hala!* More likely they'll be taking them without asking. Probably pillaging and raping as well."

Inez gasped and stopped stirring the *adobo* mix. "What do you mean?"

Lucing regretted her bluntness. "No, no. You're right. They'll need us alive. If they kill all of us, none of us can help them."

"You said Manila would be safe."

"Afterwards, yes. Our chances of survival are good here. But, historically, conquerors tend to pillage and rape. It's part of the blood-lust conqueror thing. It's how they prove to us they have power over us."

"You mean? We. You and I. We could be raped?"

"You're right, I'm probably exaggerating." But she didn't think so. Lucing was a practical realist. She'd studied enough history to know such things did happen and would probably happen. She and Freddie had already decided what they would do if captured. She hadn't told Freddie, but if she were captured and imprisoned, she'd survive by seducing some high-ranking Japanese soldier and using the man to accomplish her own agenda. She was already a sinner... why not a traitor as well. At least that's what some people would think. She didn't care.

There were different ways to serve her country, and she would do whatever she needed to do to survive, and if that meant fraternizing with the enemy, she'd do it. She'd also get information to help her people if at all possible.

Now, with Inez in the picture, she had to start preparing her sister to adjust to the new order of life.

Freddie had assured her that the likelihood was strong that Manila would soon be occupied. The Japanese had evidently been preparing long and hard for this invasion, and the Filipinos had spent the last few years feeling naïvely confident that the European war would never reach this far. The Filipinos just weren't sufficiently prepared enough to repel the enemy from Manila.

Above all else, Lucing trusted Freddie's sharp intellect and shrewd rationale. He was usually right about things, given his passion for facts... a passion which justified his job as journalist and which made it possible for him to see the overview map of a situation.

Now she was responsible, not only for herself, but for her sister, nephew and niece.

From the few times she'd interacted with Julio, she'd found him to be decidedly lacking in spunk and innovative thinking. He was a follower and not a leader. Cencia was more resourceful and less shy. Still, they were children.

So it was up to her.

She had always protected her sister by minimizing the negative and accentuating the positive. In retrospect, she realized that she might not have done Inez a favor. Because of how she'd always treated Inez, her sister was docile and timid to a fault. Lucinda felt as if all the bravado and confidence allotted to the Trinidad family had gone to her. Even her parents had been conservative and overly cautious.

While, on one level, she was glad to have her sister and the children with her, making it possible to keep an eye on them, still, she would have been content to see Inez and the children evacuate with Rissing and Meling. She suspected it would get ugly in Manila once the Japanese occupied it.

Well, she would try to shape a stronger backbone in her sister, if she could. Into a more mature evolution of her current self. What choice did she have?

Little choice indeed. What she didn't know was that the very ugly collateral damages of war she feared was ultimately the very thing that would propel her sister's true evolution.

* * * * *

Four hours on the road, the sun shed its relentless rays on them and while the rice basket roofing created shadowed protection for them, nothing could keep out the hot humidity. The roads were clogged with clusters of families trying to leave Manila.

Rissing noticed that, not far ahead on the road, there were blockades of jeeps and soldiers controlling the flow of people through. From her higher vantage point on the cart, she saw that cars and oxcarts were being pulled aside and emptied at the blockade. Families were standing away from the road beside their belongings while soldiers drove their carts and vehicles away.

"Ramon, run up ahead and see if you can find out what's happening with the oxcarts."

Without hesitation, Ramon made his way to the front of the cart and climbed down.

"Mama, can I go with him?"

Nodding, "Do whatever he says, JoJo. He's my Captain."

"Can I be Lieutenant?"

"You and Andrew are Lieutenants. That means that when Ramon isn't around, you're in charge. Andrew, since JoJo and Ramon are leaving for a while, you're in charge of the children, okay?" Andrew nodded, straightening his back. While Andrew sported a soldier's buzz cut, he tended to be fleshy and was not inclined to sports. His lashes were thick and long, shadowing soulful brown eyes.

He liked to play pranks on others, and Ramon tolerated him, while JoJo reciprocated in kind. His interest was in cooking, and he was a big help to Meling in that he often took over the cooking when she was tied up with other housekeeping chores.

While Ramon and JoJo made their way ahead, the rest of the children looked up at her so she continued, "Cita, you're House Sergeant. That means when the younger ones are hungry, it's your job to give them a biscuit. And you have to decide how much, because remember it might have to last us a long time."

Rissing considered Felicita a kindred spirit. Skinny and angular, not particularly pretty with eyebrows much too thick, she was bossy and a neat freak. Rissing was very much aware that this little one might enjoy her supervisory role too much. Rissing would have to keep an eye on that.

"Mama, what about me?" That was Flora speaking up. Only two years old, she had a quick mind and a no-nonsense approach to life. She had taken her responsibility seriously and refused to surrender the bundle of hardcakes to a safe place in the cart. She only gave out a hardcake after her mother approved the dispensation.

"You've been very good about taking care of the hardcakes, and you haven't complained once. So you're a Private First Class."

Turning to Carmen and Ricky, she continued, "Carmen and Ricky, you're Privates. Right now, that's the lowest rank... not because of age because I know Flora is younger than you, Carmen, but because you both have been complaining a little too much." Carmen was prettier than Felicita, and Rissing suspected their father tended to spoil her somewhat more than the other children. It made her more manipulative and needy.

To Carmen, "It's not your fault that you have to pee but you can ask your Mama or me to stop the cart in a quiet way. You don't have to start crying or complaining that we have to stop. Just ask quietly if we can stop. *Mas mabuti*, try to go when everyone else goes, instead of just waiting for when you're the only one who has to go."

"But what if I can't wait?"

"Then use the *orinola* in the back the way Flora and Ricky do. Okay?" Carmen tended to irritate Rissing. Not only did she whine and complain, but she cried much too often. Helpless and dependent, she didn't have a sweet or buoyant personality to offset her irritating traits. Fortunately, she did have big black expressive eyes which were quite arresting and dramatic.

Carmen nodded her head, trying not to cry. Meling bent down to whisper to her. Carmen saluted Rissing with her left hand and whispered, "Yes, mahm." Rissing saluted back.

Lastly, she turned to Ricky, "It's important that we all stay quiet and not make too much noise. So, you'll get a little promotion when you stop crying every time you want something."

Meling looked at Rissing as if to say, "He's just a baby." Then she bent closer to Ricky and assured him, "Sometimes if crying makes you feel better, that's okay. But Tia Rissing is right. When she puts her finger to her lips – like this – that means it's time to be quiet."

Ricky nodded, putting one little finger over his mouth.

Ramon and JoJo returned to an oxcart filled with very quiet people. Ramon made his report, "The army doesn't have enough trucks to carry their weapons and supplies. They're taking away the oxcarts."

One little oxcart wasn't going to make that big a difference and Rissing was in survivalist mode. She was not about to lose their ride to safety. She told Ramon and JoJo to sit up front with Renzo, and she herself got in the back.

"If anyone hears me groaning or anything like that, just please try to stay calm. I've been having pains and I think the baby's trying to come."

Meling gasped and moved beside Rissing. "How many minutes apart?"

"Enough." Rissing laid down and positioned herself in the traditional childbirth mode: knees bent high and apart, she motioned for Meling to kneel between her knees.

"You children turn your backs now. Everything will be all right. Just do what I say."

Of course Carmen started to cry, which meant Ricky was crying too. Flora had refused to leave her mother's side, her little hand brushing her mother's hair. But, as her mother had instructed, her back was turned away from what her mother was going through.

By the time they had reached the blockade, Rissing was groaning and Meling was trying to stay calm. All the children were scared, and only Ramon and JoJo were managing to hold back their tears.

A soldier was telling Renzo the oxcart needed to be emptied as quickly as possible.

Meling shouted out, "My friend's in labor right now. We can't leave the cart!"

The soldier looked inside, saw the mound of Rissing's belly, the blood dripping from Rissing's lip as she tried to bite back her screams. Rissing let out a desperate groan just then and the soldier withdrew quickly.

He returned a few minutes later to signal them on ahead.

Rissing's groans quieted. A mile later, she sat up. "False alarm. The pains have stopped so I don't think the baby's coming yet."

Meling met her eyes and Rissing winked.

Meling's mouth opened, "What?"

Rissing whispered, "That's what I meant about using our weakness to our benefit. Men usually don't want anything to do with childbirth."

Meling whispered back, "Except having their fun making babies."

Rissing giggled. Which she transformed to a cough when she noticed Ramon staring at her.

"Everyone pay attention now. Ricky, remember when your Mama told you sometimes it makes you feel better to cry?"

Ricky nodded and the others waited.

"I got a pain in my tummy and I thought the baby was going to come, so I was crying the pain away. But I'm all right now."

"You've been sitting up front for four hours now. Maybe you should rest, Rissing."

In fact, she was very tired. It was exhausting to know that you're the strongest person in a group and that it's up to you to keep things together and make decisions that would secure the safety of 10 people, seven of them children. Yes, it was good to be born lucky, but leadership was still a stressful and tiring thing.

What it amounted to was that she didn't trust Renzo or Meling to accept responsibility for the group. Call it conceit, but she knew she was the most resourceful of them all, the quickest thinker, and the best leader. And she did have some Army training prior to marrying Torio.

For now, however, trundling along in an oxcart pulled by a *carabao,* she figured it was safe enough for her to take a little nap.

* * * * *

CHAPTER 7
DEFEND AND ATTACK
Banga, Philippines, 1941 – 1942

The little lanterns Renzo had set on each side of the cart shed barely enough light to illuminate the road. Rissing decided everyone was too tired and it was best to stop somewhere for the night. Along the way, clusters of people were walking, dragging small wagons of precious belongings, carrying children and boxes and bags which they hugged closely against their chests.

She saw three children perched atop a little donkey led by a woman who looked to be about six months pregnant. An older boy and girl trudged beside her, heavily burdened with bundles and bags. She wanted to stop and offer them a ride on the oxcart, but she'd already learned it was dangerous to stop and talk to other refugees. Besides, it was too heartbreaking to choose which people to help out of the many who needed help, and her decision-making ability didn't extend to that level of ruthlessness.

As much as she hated herself for her cowardice and selfishness, it was easier to ignore them... to remind herself they had chosen their method of departure, and who was she to question their choice.

It was enough to assume leadership of 10 people... who was she to gather more under her wing... when they might ultimately turn against her and sabotage the security of her established little group.

As she sat beside Renzo, stoically sitting beside her, staring directly ahead, guiding his *carabao* through the throngs of people, she already regretted many things.

Three miles back, an older man had approached them, asking for a ride for him, his wife and three grandchildren.

Rissing had asked Renzo to stop. When the old man and his group approached, she apologized, explaining they didn't have much room themselves. When they asked for water, she willingly filled their cups from the cart's water barrel. The old man had then pulled a gun, pointing it at Rissing, demanding that everyone in the oxcart step out.

"How come the soldiers didn't take your cart? They confiscated ours... and we had to leave most of our things behind."

"I'm eight months pregnant, as you can see, and the soldiers decided we needed the cart more than they did."

"Good for you. Now we need the oxcart more than you. Step down or I'll shoot you."

Even for a practical realist like Rissing, this was an appalling act. The Japanese had attacked two days previously, and the situation was far from desperate. How could people have sunk so swiftly as to pull a gun on their own? And on a pregnant woman weeks away from delivery?

Before she could respond, a gun fired from within the oxcart, and the old man dropped his gun, grabbing his hand and howling in pain.

Ramon stuck his head out, the gun in his hand. He said nothing, met his mother's eyes, and waited for her reaction. Finally, Rissing nodded approvingly, not taking her eyes off Ramon. "Renzo, go!" She signaled for Ramon to put away the gun.

When she turned back to face the road, she lifted her chin, trying not to cry, her heart breaking at her son's defiant bravery.

Renzo prodded his *carabao* to move forward. Behind them, people were gathering and shouting and asking questions of the old man. Witnesses were shouting that the old man had pulled a gun on the pregnant woman in the oxcart. Others were saying how a little boy had shot at the old man.

It was drama and excitement counteracting the boredom and tedium of miles and miles of trudging along the dirt road.

A few people chased after them, but Renzo persuaded Tonto to hustle his skinny carabao to hustle as fast as possible.

"Good boy, Tonto. You'll get a nice swallow of beer tonight, old boy."

Renzo had confessed to Rissing that Tonto usually could hustle if he was promised beer at the end of the day.

So that incident was the first thing Rissing regretted. The second thing was that

Ramon, all 8-1/2 years of life under his belt, had been forced to act as protector of the group, aiming a gun at and shooting a man old enough to be his own grandfather. He had aimed for the old man's hand, thus avoiding killing him, but still... was this something that would give him nightmares for the rest of his life?

She surrendered to her thoughts as the oxcart bumped and jounced over the rough dirt road. In the heavily wooded area beside the road, lanterns flickered beside roughly made campsites, each site a short distance from the next, providing some privacy of sorts during this evacuation attempt by people all otherwise sharing the same experience.

A voice interrupted her thoughts. She quieted herself, trying to decide who was trying to talk to her. It wasn't Renzo. It wasn't anyone in the back of the cart. It was a voice inside her head, at once loving, protective and commanding. It said, "Take the path ahead... to the right."

Without hesitation, she gave the instructions to Renzo, and he guided Tonto to a little rutted path which led into the darkness of the woods.

They traveled for about 15 minutes, not knowing where the path led, or if anything was ahead. During these minutes, Rissing questioned the source of the voice, as well as the voice itself.

It had been impulse and instinct which had prompted her to guide Renzo onto this path. What was ahead? Why were they being led here?

Renzo glanced askance at her, "How did you know about this road? Have you been here before?"

Rissing shrugged her shoulders and shook her head. She didn't know. The voice had sounded like Kal's. But dreaming about the *kaluluwa* was one thing. To be awake and hear his voice telling her what to do was another. True, she had been sleepy... maybe she was in a trance-like state close enough to sleep that his thoughts could reach her.

Ahead, the path widened and they saw a big hut, made of roughly hewn timber, caulked with mud, and roofed with nipa palm leaves.

Renzo guided Tonto under the overhead roof which bridged the cabin's roof to that of a small barn beside it. In a strong, authoritative voice Rissing had never heard from him before, he said, "Stay here and keep everyone quiet."

She was impressed enough to do exactly as he said. When he came back a few minutes later, he nodded his head in assurance, "No one here. Looks like they left in a hurry. We can stay the night here."

Inside, the cabin was divided into three small rooms. Two bedrooms and a larger room which served as kitchen, dining and general family room. Rissing assigned Andrew and JoJo to make rice, and she asked Felicita and Ramon to look for anything in the pantry which would supplement their meager dinner. She and Meling found sheets to place on the beds, two in each room.

When Renzo returned from rewarding Tonto with his swallow of beer, he approached Rissing, "The outhouse is a little ways back. There's a path leading to it, but the older kids should keep the little ones company. Beside it is a shower area, using rainwater collected on the roof. The barrel is half full, and I'll refill our own water barrel first."

Rissing nodded gratefully to Renzo. "Torio said you might not be much help. That you like women okay but you hate kids. I disagree with him. From what I've seen so far, you've been a big help, Renzo."

Renzo gave her his brilliant gap-toothed smile. Rissing found herself warming to the plump and patch-eyed man. At times he appeared to be a simpleton, with little thought or care about the world. Now, she was seeing another aspect of him.

Renzo, one brown eye twinkling mischievously, replied, "I love Torio but he takes life too seriously sometimes. There's always a right and wrong to everything. It's not that way for me. I take care of myself. Period. If that means I have to twist the truth a little, or borrow something from you permanently, then I warn you now, I'll do it. And I have no use for kids because they can't take care of themselves. Now, I'm seeing that you and everyone with you don't need much taking care of. The children pay attention to you. And I'm seeing it might benefit me to work with you. So that's all I'm doing."

Rissing nodded and patted him gratefully on his arm.

Cita had found a vegetable garden in the back... most of the vegetables hurriedly harvested, but some tomatoes, not quite fully ripened, had been left on the vine, as well as some okra and squash. Ramon found a jar of *tuyo* hidden on the lowest shelf of the pantry. Andrew helped Rissing concoct a dish comprising all of these things with an appropriate dash of salt and pepper, which, when added to the steamed rice, summed up to a savory meal.

Halfway through, there was a timid knock at the cabin door. Renzo lifted one finger to his lips and, holding a cudgel in one hand, slowly made his way to it.

Rissing was right behind him when he opened the door.

It was the pregnant woman leading the donkey with the three small children. Her son and daughter flanked her.

"My name's Rosie. This is my boy, Oliver, and my daughter, Reyna. The little ones on the donkey are Pablo, Angie, and Vickie. We followed you because we thought you would find a safe place to camp tonight."

Without hesitation, Rissing opened the door wider, "Come in, Rosie. We were just having dinner. Everyone, please come in."

Renzo's eyes met Rissing's and she nodded her head. He shrugged and helped Oliver lift the young ones off the donkey. "I'll put the donkey to graze with Tonto."

"Just water, Renzo. Donkey doesn't need a reward tonight. Please."

Renzo laughed, and Rissing found herself smiling in response.

The three littlest ones were sleepy and Meling put them to bed, while Rissing assigned Cita to pick the rest of the tomatoes and okra. Andrew made a fresh pot of rice, and he made more *ulam* while Rissing showed Rosie the 2nd bedroom where she and her children could sleep that night.

After the meal, the women cleaned up and shared their stories. Rosie said that she, her husband and children had traveled on their oxcart from Tarlac to Manila. With a panicked populace clogging the roads, it had taken them all of yesterday afternoon and most of the night to reach Manila, where her husband Rudy, a Philippine Army reservist, joined the soldiers at the road block, taking the oxcart with him. He'd had no choice. Fortunately, they were able to keep the donkey, which had made it easier for the children to travel.

"We're trying to get to Binubusan in Batangas Province, where my parents live. Rudy thinks that when the Japanese infantry come, it'll be in Northern Luzon. He thinks we'll be safer in Southern Luzon."

"He's probably right." Personally, Rissing thought all of Luzon, north and south, would ultimately be a dangerous place. She herself planned to go to Aklan. If the Japanese decided to invade the smaller islands, it would be later rather than sooner, and that would give her time to make more solid plans for her family.

After the women put the little ones to sleep, Rissing, Meling and Rosie sat at the table in a corner of the kitchen, sipping on raspberry tea. Rissing assured Rosie that her store of wild raspberry tea was the best tea for pregnant women, strengthening the uterine walls, providing valuable nutrition for both mother and child, and ensuring an easier pregnancy.

"Meling gave me this tea, didn't you? I forgot who told you about it."

"Divina, remember her... she was born in Mindanao. She always liked to..." She glanced around the room.

Renzo was talking to Andrew, Ramon and JoJo in the corner of the room next to the cabin door entrance. Oliver wasn't eavesdropping on their conversation but hovered protectively behind his mother a short distance away. All the girls and little ones were already asleep in the bedrooms. "... talk about the noises her husband makes when they're... you know. Every time we saw her husband, all we could think about was the noises he made."

Meling and Rissing giggled quietly. Rosie found herself joining them.

Rissing felt sympathetic towards Rosie. Of course, she sensed immediately that Rosie was not happy with a leadership role, and would readily look to Rissing herself to make decisions. She knew she had no choice. She had to accept Rosie and her family into her group. How could she not include her after the woman had been guided to follow Rissing into the woods. Of course, that meant that her troop had instantly expanded from 10 people to 16.

Studying Rosie, she sensed the stolid loyalty of the woman. While she had a plump, kind face, with long dark hair tied in a bun behind her head, she was more petite in body than Rissing herself. In fact, she was a good deal smaller than Rissing, so much so that while she looked to be in her sixth month of pregnancy, she was actually in her seventh month. Yet, only 29 years old, she had borne six children already, starting when she was 17 years old. One of her children had died during childbirth... the one between Reyna, her 9-year-old daughter, and Pablo, her 4-year-old son.

Oliver joined them, and put a hand on his mother's shoulder. "Mama, you should rest now. We'll need to leave early tomorrow morning."

The women finished their tea.

Oliver continued, looking at his mother with a disapproving look, "The donkey was supposed to be for Mama." At 12, Oliver was small, lean and wiry, with a serious expression on his young face. He was a dark-skinned Filipino, a youth transforming into a young man, and acne was already making its appearance on his face. His facial expression, like his mother's, was inherently kind and gentle, though now anxiously concerned for his mother.

Rosie smiled in assurance at her son, and to Rissing, she demurred, "I feel strong enough to walk, but the little ones can't keep up with us. So…"

"Well, welcome to our group. We won't all fit in the oxcart, but the older ones can walk beside the cart, take turns on the donkey, and we women can ride with the little ones in the cart."

"Are you sure?"

"It's no accident you followed us here tonight, Rosie. When I saw you on the road, I wanted to offer you a ride with us, but I was worried all the other families might want lifts too. It's one thing to offer a ride to others, but it's another thing to give up the oxcart entirely and end up walking yourself."

"Thank you, Rissing." Rosie leaned in to embrace Rissing, which was fun, given their two bulging baby-mounds. They ended up giggling again.

Oliver's eyes were wet as he nodded his thanks to Rissing. Then he took his banig and joined Renzo and the other older boys in the corner beside the entrance.

Meling and Rissing, with their younger little ones, crowded in the 1st bedroom, which was slightly larger than the 2nd bedroom. Meling and little Ricky took one bed, Rissing and Flora, the 2nd bed. Felicita and Carmen slept on a banig on the floor. The women had padded it with blankets to soften the ground's hard wood surface.

Exhausted by the long day's travel, but surrounded by friends and loved ones, they all slept well. Their battle was for survival, and little challenges were already surfacing to test their mettle. But they were still in the early stages of war and couldn't guess yet what would be expected of them in the days, months and years ahead.

For now, sleep was good.

* * * * *

In the morning, it was still dark when Rissing awakened the older boys, who took turns at the outhouse. She also told them about the washing area in the back of the house.

Three water barrels rested on a bamboo platform above the ground. The area surrounding this platform had been enclosed with nipa palm leaves woven between bamboo stakes, giving it privacy.

Only a partial roof covered the area, leaving the portion above the barrels open so that water could be saved into the barrel whenever it rained.

Rissing was the first one to take a quick water bath, using a large cup to scoop water from one of the barrels onto herself. She encouraged everyone to wash themselves. The barrels had been full when they arrived, and she knew it rained often enough that they'd be filled quickly again no matter how much water they used.

Then, while the boys helped Renzo with the donkey and *carabao* and with packing all their bundles into the oxcart, Rissing and Rosie made fresh hardcakes, enough for breakfast for all of them, and enough to munch on throughout the day. Meling supervised the girls in cleaning up in the bedrooms. Then more showers and outhouse visits for the rest of the group, and finally, they were ready to continue on their journey.

The sun was just beginning its ascension when they took one last look at the cabin... and left it behind, cleaner than before their arrival, and richer with a half dozen pesos Rissing had attached to the back of a picture of Jesus hanging in the bedroom wall. It was her thank-you gift to the people who had unknowingly provided shelter for her group.

As they left the cabin behind, Rissing whispered a silent and loving *"maraming salamat"* ("thank you very much") to her beloved Kal. This incident had taught her, once and for all, that her *kaluluwa* was a spiritual guide on a par with Jesus, Santo Nino, and all of heaven's saints and angels.

While it was only about 65 miles from Manila to Batangas, as the crow flies, travel was slow along the roads passing through the small towns along the way. Often the road switched back and forth on the periphery of the mountains and rugged terrain.

Also, they were crowded. People were at the height of panic, their thinking caught in the other-side-of-the-fence syndrome. Wherever they lived, they wanted to move to another place, feeling that a different place would be safer than wherever they were already staying: Where their parents lived. Or cousins. Or children. Or friends from ten years ago.

This meant that at each town they passed through, travel slowed to one mile an hour. There were good things about it. It was slow enough that Rissing allowed the older boys to accompany the younger ones to convenient outhouses along the way. Or to spend a few precious *centavos* for *halo halo* from cart vendors taking advantage of the influx of travelers. More often than not, when they returned from their little trips, the oxcart had progressed only a few hundred yards.

By the end of the second day of travel, Rissing's group had accomplished only another 18 miles, for a total of 34. They still had 21 miles to go.

Fortunately, including Rosie in the group had added a levity and a sense of adventure that Meling and Rissing hadn't felt during the previous day's journey without her. For someone so little and timid, Rosie had a blunt and naughty sense of humor... which encouraged Meling and Rissing to loosen up and talk about their husbands in a faintly derogatory way. They were like schoolgirls unwrapping together the mysterious box of marriage... that box containing the often-imagined but never explored secrets of sex.

As for the children, unlike the fear and panic which loomed over them on their first day of travel, they themselves began to find adventure in sharing walks beside the oxcart, taking turns riding the donkey, and sharing jokes with each other.

Pudgy, would-be chef Andrew found resonance with 9-year-old Reyna, whose oval-shaped face rarely changed expression, but whose religious fervor for Mother Mary gave her eyes an innocent glow during prayer or while performing an act of tender kindness. She was thin and awkward, where Andrew was fleshy and moved with easy grace, but they understood each other's passions. She wanted to be a nun when she grew up, and he wanted to be a chef in a famous restaurant in Manila.

4-year-old Pablo with thick black hair, round, flat nose and riveting black eyes, found himself adoring 4-year-old Carmen. She had only to pout and he was attending to her, handing her a flower pulled up from the side of the road, or making faces to make her laugh.

Cita, who was self-consciously aware of her superior rank of House Sergeant, was loving her right to supervise over Privates Angie (3), Ricky (2), Flora (2) and the littlest one, Vickie (1-1/2). Flora sometimes rebelled, given that she wasn't just Private, but Private First Class. But Cita, being 6 years old and having a 4-year advantage in her grasp of language, was able to somehow maneuver Flora to subservience.

It was working out so well that by darkness, instead of driving on, they all decided to stop and camp for the night one more time, trying to prolong their time together.

When Rissing saw another small path breaking off into the woods, she suggested they turn into it, and this one led them 10 minutes later to a camp site, complete with a small waterfall feeding into a knee-deep stream trickling through the woods.

After a while, three other groups entered the camp site, and territorial prerogatives came into play. While the groups were superficially friendly, they each kept to themselves. War was too new in its power to draw people together in mutual desperation. People weren't seeing themselves in the same communal situation. Rather, each group still saw itself separate and insular from other groups, forming lines of defense and protecting its own supplies, food and members from other groups. It's only when war has absolutely ravaged its victims – when nothing is left, mentally, physically and emotionally – that it annihilates a person to lose all sense of self.

In Rissing's group, the women set up camp while Renzo showed the older boys how to tickle fish out of the pond. JoJo was the first to successfully catch a fish, of course, but some of the others soon learned the trick as well.

The other groups took their turn catching their own fish, and that night, the camp was filled with the scent of roasting fish. A singer from one of the groups took up his guitar and serenaded the evening with "*La Paloma*".

> *Cuando salí de la Habana*
> *¡Válgame Diyos!*
> *Nadie me ha visto salir*
> *Si no fuí yo.*
> *Y una linda Guachinanga*

S'allá voy yo,
Que se vino tras de mi,
Que sí señor.

Refrain:
Si a tu ventana llega Una Paloma,
Trátala con cariño, Que es mi persona.
Cuéntale tus amores, Bien de mi vida,
Corónala de flores, Que es cosa mía.
Ay, chinita que sí!
Ay, que dame tu amor!
Ay, que vente conmigo,
Chiquita, a donde vivo yo!

Stomachs full, the night sky reflecting its shining stars between the thick overhead foliage, soon even the children were joining in on the refrain. *"Ay, chinita que si!"*

At the end of it, they all shouted good night, group to group, and then withdrew to their own private gatherings.

Rissing wasn't happy with sleeping on the ground. Snakes crawled on the ground, and there were lethal snakes aplenty in the woods. She selected their camp a distance away from the others and guided Renzo and the older boys to dig shallow firepits in a circle around their camp.

They piled dried twigs and branches into the pits, set the twigs afire, and soon their camp was surrounded by a glowing circle of fire. Inside this circle, the three pregnant women and the little ones slept inside the oxcart, while the rest of the children slept around the oxcart on their *banigs*, which they had placed above dried brush to cushion the hardness of the ground.

Renzo kept watch for the first three hours. He awakened Oliver and JoJo to take the second watch, and Ramon and Andrew took the last. Rissing had arranged this, not wanting to be cynical, but realistically aware that just as an old man in his desperation would pull a gun on a pregnant woman, so would other people steal when someone else possessed something they wanted.

In the morning, all the other groups were still asleep when Rissing and her group left the campsite behind.

Rissing's group never questioned her instructions. The children might grumble and complain about her commands, but they knew better than to disobey her. Sometimes what Rissing told them to do didn't make sense or seemed bizarre, but by now they all saw that she had her reasons for doing things, even if she herself didn't quite fathom the rationale behind her decisions.

On the third day, the roads were clogged with people traveling towards Manila, as many as were traveling away from Manila.

They didn't stop this third day but continued into the middle of the night, when they finally reached Batangas.

* * * * *

After they delivered Rosie and her children safely to her family in Binubusan, Rissing and her troop arrived at Meling's

Uncle's sugar cane farm in Balayan. He had been expecting her for a few days now, unaware of the miserable roads filled with clusters of families trying to escape from or flee to Manila.

Renzo tried to brush away the 10 pesos Rissing gave him, but she stuck it into his pocket, "*Sige namam!* ("Go Ahead!") You took good care of us." Finally, he accepted the money. Rissing and Meling hugged him, and all the children surrounded him, shouting "Tahnk yu. Tahnk yu!" in their heavily accented English. They waved goodbye to him until the crowds on the road blocked their sight of him.

They rested a day at the sugar cane farm, and on December 14th, the fourth day after they left Manila, Rissing, Meling, and their children took a boat to Aklan, where Meling's parents lived.

* * * * *

Aklan, believed to have been established in the 12th century, was a province of the Philippines located in the island of Panay, one of a group comprising the Visayas islands.

It was in this province, in the municipality of Kalibo, where Torio had rescued Rodolfo, the mayor's son, 11 years previously.

Meling's parents lived, not in Malinao, but in Banga, a municipality adjacent to Malinao... in fact, only 7 miles from the very bridge where Torio had jumped heroically into the Belan River to rescue a swimmer captured by the powerful flow of its currents.

In Banga, Totoy and Salina Magsayan owned a 15-acre rice plantation. Totoy's real name was Bartolome, but since he'd been an only child, his parents never stopped calling him the generic name for "boy" and it had stuck.

While the Magsayans worked the 15 acres as one plantation, on paper, it had been subdivided into three parts: one part of five acres each to her two older brothers, who worked their acres and kept the profits for themselves. The third part was farmed by her parents and was intended to be Meling's apportionment of the property.

Totoy Magsayan was a descendant of Datu Magsayan, a chieftain of the region during the 15th century, who at that time owned three times the size of the current property. Time, inner family conflicts, and divisions among the descendants had attritioned Totoy's share to a mere 15 acres. Still, they were considered a prosperous family.

Nevertheless, while each of the brothers had their own homes on their properties, Totoy's and Salina's was the biggest and most comfortable, a wooden structure of two stories. Totoy had even installed an indoor toilet, a goal which Meling's two brothers aspired to. The pipes from the toilet drained to a cesspool pit a short distance away, but at least the family didn't have to run to an outhouse to do their business.

Every family had their own ideas of how the war would affect their lives. The Magsayans all believed that once Manila was occupied, the Japanese would encourage the farmers to continue their work in order to provide them with food supplies during the occupation.

As such, the Magsayans felt no guilt in choosing to remain farmers, rather than setting that work aside to become soldiers.

Meling's parents were as kind and warm-hearted as Meling herself, and Rissing found herself relaxing and allowing them to pamper and fuss over her as much as they did Meling. Meling reclaimed her bedroom, and Rissing was given her own room, to share with little Flora.

Christmas was coming, and Rissing accepted the Magsayan hospitality happily. She needed easement of soul, and it comforted her to look out over the land and see a serene view of nature's bounty still untouched by the war in Manila. A portion of the farm property fell on the slopes of a hill, the terraces a neat and beautiful pattern of green rice stalks hugging the curve of the land.

She worried about Torio and prayed every night. Like her, Mother Mary was about to give birth, and she felt rays of healing light and love from the Virgin Mary. She pictured Torio in good health and in a strong, positive state of mind. She prayed for her country, her relatives and her friends.

Meling wanted her to stay until after the baby was born, and Rissing considered it. But she still had so many things to do.

She wanted to meet with Ignacio Fuentes, the tenant of her farm two miles away and establish her identity with him. She wanted to talk to Juan Delacruz, the attorney Meling had recommended to her, who was keeping track of her share of the income from the farm. She wanted to get more emergency money into her pouch to prepare for the lean years ahead. Who knew how long this war would last.

In the end, she agreed to stay with Manang Salina and Manong Totoy until the first of the year.

* * * * *

On December 22nd, 1941, Lieutenant General Masaharu Homma and his 14th Army of 43,000 infantry troops waded ashore on the beaches of Lingayen Gulf, 120 miles north of Manila.

General Douglas MacArthur, Commander of U.S. Army Forces in Far East, actually could field three times that number, but 100,000 of them were raw Philippine reservists who were lightly trained and poorly equipped. MacArthur's pride were 12,000 Filipino Scouts, fiercely loyal to their country, and famous for their fearless military prowess in defending their homeland.

Once the Japanese landed, MacArthur knew his defense of Manila would be futile.

His forces were too raw. He had been committed to preparing the Filipino people for independence to occur in 1946, but as there was no sense of urgency, progress had been slow, so the Filipino Army simply weren't adequate enough to defend against the Japanese attack.

In addition, he didn't have enough equipment to conduct a strong campaign, and so he needed an edge. He decided to pull back his forces to Bataan, a 30-mile peninsula of wooded mountains, dense jungle and precipitous ravines. It separated Manila Bay from the South China Sea. Corregidor, located at the entrance of Manila Bay, would be his base of operations. He was quoted as saying, "Homma may have the bottle, but I have the cork."

There weren't enough transports to move his army to Bataan, so wooden oxcarts, jitney buses, and anything else that could move were conscripted for use. Several detachments of the army, many of them reservists, were cut off from the retreat, never made it to Bataan, dispersing into the hills and jungles to form guerilla bands. Many soldiers simply returned home to their families.

On Christmas Eve, MacArthur, his wife and son, and his son's nursemaid, Ah Cheu, gathered on the dock below the Manila Hotel for a 22-mile journey to Corregidor – "The Rock" – on an inter-island steamer, "Don Esteban". President Quezon had already agreed to meet MacArthur at the Rock, and before his departure, the President demanded *his people's unswerving allegiance to the Allied cause.*

As MacArthur made his voyage to Corregidor, in a Navy Yard in Cavite, south of Manila, his army torched a million barrels of oil to prevent the Japanese from using this precious fuel. On that night, the darkness of the night sky filled with explosive flickering flames from the destruction of the oil barrels.

* * * * *

CHAPTER 8
INEZ (IDEALIST) AND LUCINDA (REALIST)
Manila and Bataan, Philippines, 1942

On New Year's Eve, 1942, Freddie and Lucinda celebrated with a bottle of champagne, which they shared with Inez. Freddie told the two sisters that his intel were predicting that Manila would probably be fully occupied within the next few days.

Inez often wondered what would have happened if she had left the city with Rissing and Meling. Maybe she would have been safer with them.

She had taken care to maintain her appearance during the days after the landing of Homma's infantry at Lingayen Gulf. She thought to herself that maybe if the soldiers saw she was a lady, they would accord her the respect she deserved.

It was an idea she would never share with her sister's boyfriend, Freddie. She knew that whatever she had to say to him, she had better be prepared to defend her opinion. She wasn't a confrontational person and she hated the idea of defending her opinion. She felt something or she believed something... why did she have to know why?

In the times when she had actually opined her thoughts to him and she had actually explained why she thought what she thought, his eyes had glowed with curiosity and interest. He had become so enthusiastic about digging deeper into her opinion that her mind had gotten tired. It wasn't that he made her feel stupid or ignorant. It made her impatient.

Was it really necessary to always be thinking? To analyze? To understand? And then discuss and discuss whatever the outcome to death? Wasn't it enough to hold an ideal – the way things should be – and then act as if that was the standard of life?

Her sister Lucing loved Freddie's mind. She could keep up with him for as long as it took. It exhausted Inez just to listen to them.

Yet, despite Freddie's somewhat challenging character, Inez did like him, because he was, in fact, very likable. Of medium height, his dark brown bangs tended to fall over his brow, and he had a habit of tossing the hair away from his face with a quick movement of his head. His glasses framed hazel eyes which always looked like he was studying whatever he was looking at. When he looked at her, she felt like squirming under his microscopic gaze.

She liked the fact that he always wore white suits. No casual slacks or shorts for him. No casual shirts. It was always white suits made of cotton or linen. In one of the rare conversations when she and Lucing had talked about Lucing's relationship with Freddie,

Lucing told her it was because he wanted to maintain a professional appearance.

After all, potential interviews lurked everywhere and anywhere and popped up when a person least expected it. Freddie was not one to allow a journalistic opportunity to slip by.

He spoke fluent Tagalog, and he spoke it easily and quickly. His English was even faster. She could practically see his mind speeding like a racecar in his head.

Her thinking dulled by several glasses of champagne, Inez bade them good night and went to bed.

Watching Inez walk away, Lucing felt sorry for her sister. She knew that Inez missed Benito more than anything else. Without Benny, Inez was bored and frightened. She was one of those women who lose themselves in their husband's lives, reflecting her husband's likes and dislikes, and ultimately losing track of her own identity.

Freddie gently pretend-punched her, "Hey, she'll be all right."

Lucing poured herself the last remnants of the champagne and resumed her deep discussion with Freddie about whether it would be treasonous for the current government to cooperate with the Japanese, or whether it would be a practical move, enabling the cooperating leaders an opportunity to work from within to protect the Filipino people and soften the effects of war on them.

Lucing contended that cooperating with the enemy afforded one the potential of influencing the enemy for the benefit of the people.

Freddie, on the other hand, strongly believed that any act of cooperation with the enemy was tantamount to treason. It implied approval and support of their actions, including the arbitrary destruction of a country's populace.

Finally, as usually happened after an impassioned and prolonged deep discussion, Freddie and Lucing agreed to disagree on various matters. The one thing they did agree on was that the Filipino people deserved to be self-governing and independent of the authority of any other country.

They went to bed and made love, their disagreement in no way compromising their affectionate passion for each other.

They never discussed marriage.

By now, Lucing had accepted that she was an old maid. That didn't bother her in the least. She had no insecurities about her looks or intellect. She knew she was bright, and she knew she was attractive. Her features might be average, with shoulder-length brown hair which she hardly ever styled, but she had retained a slim figure filled out in the right places, her skin was clear, and the enthusiasms which lingered beneath her easygoing persona imbued her brown eyes with a youthful energy and glow which made men of all ages turn to take a second look at her.

She was hardly aware of that, because it didn't matter to her. She never wanted marriage for herself. She treasured her freedom too much... what kind of mother and wife would she be if all she wanted to do was read books and revel in the drama and excitement of the historical past.

The reason she and Freddie never discussed marriage was that he was already married. His wife lived in Colorado, USA, with their two children. They were in the throes of "discussing" a "permanent separation" of sorts, but meanwhile, since their discussions hadn't reached a decisive resolution and since it was so difficult to get a legal divorce, they were more or less enjoying an "open" marriage, where each partner was free to pursue other romantic interests.

As for Filipinos unhappy with their marriages, Philippines had no laws dealing with the concept of "divorce." A Filipinio married in the Philippines might go to America and get a divorce there, but once he returned to the Philippines, such a divorce wouldn't be considered legal. He'd still be legally bound to the wife he'd married in the Philippines.

All issues about marriage didn't concern Lucing in the least. She didn't want or need a permanent man in her life. What made her relationship with Freddie work was that they didn't answer to each other. If they saw each other, fine. If not, just as fine. If dates got cancelled, well, that was life. If he was in town and wanted to stay with her, he was free to stay as long as he wanted... or leave the next day.

Some of her friends pitied Lucing for not having any "anchors." Lucing just laughed at them. She had her sister, and her niece and nephew. They were what anchored her with their love.

Aside from that, there were too many avenues to explore... too many events to experience... too many things to discover.

She dated other men, but those men all understood and accepted her relationship with Freddie. There was a place for them in her life, if she chose, and if they didn't like that place, they were certainly free to leave. Ultimately, however, they all liked and enjoyed her too much to give her up simply because she wouldn't agree to be exclusive to them. The few who gave her ultimatums didn't last long in her circle of friends.

* * * * *

Freddie left Lucing's place before dawn the next morning. He left her a note that he and his photographer were off to get as close to the action as possible. He had been vague to her and Inez, but he was pretty confident that the Japanese would succeed in occupying Manila today.

The residents of Manila were in hiding. The streets were sparsely populated, and only those desperate enough to brave the dangers of the day were scuttling about. There was also the fact that MacArthur had conscripted nearly every vehicle in Manila to transport soldiers, equipment and supplies to Bataan.

His photographer, Perry Verdugo, an ambitious local Filipino anxious to make a name for himself, met him at their usual place, a pastry shop two blocks from the Manila Hotel.

Perry was 24 years old, a small Filipino with rough features, intense dark eyes and crooked teeth. He was quite a con artist. He'd ingratiated himself to Freddie by picking his pocket, and upon realizing that Freddie was a bona fide journalist working for the New York Tiimes in America, returning the stolen wallet to Freddie on the chance that the journalist would be grateful enough to use Perry's photos to accompany any articles sent to America.

How could Freddie refuse? It was such an absurd type of blackmail. He knew, without a doubt, such a resourceful man would be worth his weight in gold. And in so many ways, Perry had indeed proven his value.

Later that afternoon, Homma's columns of tanks rolled into Manila, making their occupation day official: January 2, 1942.

* * * * *

On the evening of January 2ⁿᵈ, 1942, a Japanese color guard assembled on the elegant lawn of the U. S. High Commissioner's residence. Acacia trees dotted the landscape and a breeze whispered reassurances to the Filipino people gathered to watch the proceedings.

A Japanese soldier hauled down the USA Stars and Stripes and dramatically ground it under his heel. The band struck up

"Kimigayo," the Japanese national anthem, while sunset guns boomed a salute as Japan's Rising Sun slowly ascended to replace the fallen Stars & Stripes.

All Americans and British were ordered to remain in their homes until they could be registered.

The next day, Homma's soldiers began rounding up British and American civilians for internment. On January 5, the Japanese published a warning in the manila newspapers. "Any one who inflicts, or attempts to inflict, an injury upon Japanese soldiers or individuals shall be shot to death." It was further made clear that if an assailant couldn't be found, the Japanese would hold ten influential persons as hostages.

The Japanese wasted no time in trying to win over the residents of Manila. The more cooperation from the people, the less soldiers would be needed to maintain the city, and the more soldiers could be deployed to win the battle in Bataan.

This meant they had to control would-be dissenters, and persuade influential people to their side. Radios aired non-stop programs featuring grandiose speeches linking the Filipinos to themselves as Asian people with a common enemy – the arrogant Americans encroaching upon their homelands. Posters were slapped onto buildings and billboards, decrying the white-skinned exploiters from across the ocean. It was a full frontal assault. The Filipinos had no alternative but to listen.

* * * * *

Freddie evaded the Japanese soldiers for several days, but upon arrival at his apartment on the second night, they were waiting for him. He was taken to Manila's Fort Santiago, a maze of dungeons and torture chambers built for the Spanish Inquisition during the 16th Century.

The cells were 10 x 10, and prisoners were packed like sardines, body to body. There was no room to sit or lie down. The prisoners had to devise means to sleep by leaning on each other for support.

In addition, certain prisoners were selected for special attention. For some reason, Freddie wasn't selected for that attention until several weeks after capture.

* * * * *

When Freddie was taken prisoner and interned at Fort Santiago, Perry managed to make his way to Lucing's house without being stopped by Japanese patrols.

His knock was controlled and revealed none of his inner panic.

But his face, when Lucing opened the door, reflected all the fear in his heart.

He entered at her behest, unable to say the words.

Finally, Lucing said it for him, "He's been taken?"

Perry nodded.

"Where?"

"Fort Santiago."

Lucing had to brace herself against the wall.

Inez came running out of her bedroom, followed by Julio and Cencia. She saw Lucing's face, quickly led her to a chair in the living room.

Perry followed them, not knowing what Lucing wanted him to do.

Finally, Lucing met Perry's eyes. "Will they kill him?"

"Maybe. I don't know. Maybe. Unless he cooperates. Agrees to write propaganda material for them."

Lucing shook her head and laughed bitterly. "Freddie won't do that."

Perry shrugged. "Then. Probably."

"One of the professors down the road was taken yesterday."

"Santo Tomas University is being converted as another internment camp. The Japanese are already collecting American and British citizens... herding them into the campus like sheep to the slaughter. If they can get the teachers at the University to cooperate with them..."

"You think they'll come for me?"

Again, Perry shrugged.

Lucing stood up and turned to meet Inez' eyes. She smiled at Julio and Cencia who flanked Inez.

Then she turned to Perry, "And you? Your family is all right?"

"What family? I live with three guys. Two of them Jitney drivers waiting to get their jeeps back from the army. The third guy's a man of all trades. Like I used to be before Freddie took me on as his photographer."

Lucing nodded.

"Would it be a hardship to move in here with us?"

Perry, taken aback, looked around.

Lucing's place was a scholarly mess, books piled on tables and chairs. But it had an air of warmth and comfort... a place loved by its owner.

"There's a mattress on the floor in the den. You're welcome to stay here with us."

"You trust me? I mean...."

"Freddie trusted you. That's good enough for me."

"I'll get my things. See you in a few hours." He was at the door and out before she could say anything else.

Lucing turned to Inez, "The Japanese are trying hard to prove to us that the Americans are the enemy and not them. If you stay out of their way, you and the children should be okay. Don't leave the house. Don't let the children out. Perry's a resourceful guy. I think we can trust him. He can buy groceries for you. Run errands."

She went into her room, opened her closet and took down an overnight case. Inez and the children followed, watching her as she filled the case with clothing, underwear, and overnight necessities.

"Luce?"

"If I go to them, they won't come here."

"What are you going to do?"

"I know the grounds of Santo Tomas like the back of my hand. I'm going to offer them my help."

She picked up a sheet of paper and wrote quickly. "Give this to Perry."

As Inez reached out for it, Lucing held it back, "Don't read it. If you read it, and you're caught, and they make you confess..."

Inez gasped, covering her mouth to cover the gasp. Her eyes misted over, "Lucing?"

"I promise I'll be fine." She handed the note to Inez, who took it and tucked it into her bra.

"I'll show you where the safe is. There's money in there. Memorize the lock numbers, but don't..."

"Don't?"

"Don't let Perry know about it. I trust him, but..." Lucing smiled at her sister. "... but I ain't no fool."

* * * * *

The university of Santo Tomas was originally located within the walled city of Intramuros in Manila. The Spanish Archbishop of Manila opened the university in the early 17th century as a seminary for aspiring young priests, taking its name and inspiration from Saint Thomas Aquinas, a Dominican theologian.

In 1927, the student population had grown to necessitate expansion of the campus, and the Dominicans purchased land at the

Sulucan Hills, in Sampaloc, Manila, and built its new campus on 215,000 square meters (approximately 53 acres) of land.

The new campus began accepting female enrollees, earning a reputation as a bona-fide institution of higher learning, conferring degrees in law, medicine and other academic pursuits. National heroes, presidents and even canonized saints had attended and graduated from this university.

As a full-time faculty member of Santo Tomas, Lucing's role as Associate Professor included undergraduate and graduate teaching, mentoring, researching and administrative services. She had been teaching at this university now for 10 years. Prior to that, she was an assistant professor for five years, and prior to that, she was a student at Santo Tomas, earning a doctorate with special expertise in Philippine History.

Yes, Lucing admitted... she was afraid. But she forced herself to take that fear and shape it into a confidence which she hoped would intimidate the soldiers enough to allow her entrance into the campus, and ultimately into the presence of the camp Commandant himself.

She would have to handle this situation very carefully. She was about to approach an enemy oppressor, and Freddie had warned her that the Japanese could be cruel to their enemies. In addition, she was a woman, and the Japanese did not view their women as equals. Rather, the women were traditionally viewed primarily as valuable bearers of children and as keepers of the home.

That meant she would have to be confident, but humble; intelligent, but in a non-threatening way; eager to help, but still loyal to her own country.

It would be a tricky balance. She approached the first patrol soldier she saw walking along the high iron picket fence surrounding the campus. She bowed her head respectfully at him, and extended her identification papers. She decided to use an exaggerated humility in talking to the soldier. She was a woman and an enemy civilian. Better to be obsequious than to be beaten.

"Please. This humble woman wishes to offer her help to the Commandant." She lifted her head but kept her eyes lowered.

A stocky young man who had probably not yet seen 20 years, the soldier stepped away from her, took the papers and compared the picture on the paperwork with her face.

He gestured for Lucing to follow him, and he led her into the gates, past the Arch of the Centuries, along the pathway through the plaza.

It was chaos inside the gates, thousands of internees milling around not knowing what to do. There were British, Americans, and other non-Filipiino families in clusters, talking and whispering among themselves. She didn't recognize anyone but she kept her head down to make sure no one recognized her either.

Lucing stayed close to the soldier leading her, until they reached a slender soldier with thick black hair. The first soldier handed over Lucing's identification papers to the officer with black hair along with a brief explanation. The superior officer barked a few words of Japanese at her, which she didn't understand. Lucing bowed her head respectfully, repeated her request, "Please. This woman wishes to offer her help to the Commandant."

After a short burst of Japanese to the first soldier, the first soldier put a hand on her neck and pushed her head down, until she was bent forward from the waist.

Lucing allowed herself to be guided by the soldier's hand, but as soon as the soldier released his hand, she straightened slowly and without looking into the officer's eyes, repeated her request in a soft, respectful voice, "This woman is an Associate Professor of this Santo Thomas University. She wishes to offer her help to the Commandant."

"Commandant. *Hai.*" He handed the paperwork back to the first soldier, and gestured them away, accompanying his gesture with a short sentence.

The first soldier led her further along the path until they reached the Main Building. At the entrance to this building, another superior officer sat behind a desk, sorting through papers on the desk.

As the first soldier handed the desk officer her paperwork, Lucing bowed from the waist and repeated her request. When she straightened slowly, even with her eyes lowered, she could see the officer's eyes glittering with shrewd intelligence and suspicion as he studied her. Finally, he answered in English.

"How do you intend to help Captain Nokorazu?"

Aha. So that was the Commandant's name. "This woman has studied and worked at this University for ten years. She wishes to offer her services in the adjustment process of the new conditions here at the University."

"You wish to help us?"

"This woman wishes to help in the adjustment process." The officer studied her for some moments, and she made a point to remain as still as possible, with dignity, but without looking into his eyes.

He actually smirked. Probably decided she was nothing but a prostitute.

"*So desu.* Follow me."

After assigning another officer to cover the entrance post for him, he led Lucing out of the Main Building and along the sidewalk, past the botanical garden flanking the Main Building's right side, and to the Santisimo Rosario Parish Church beyond that, which they entered. Rubble had been swept away from the entryway of the hall, but it looked otherwise intact. The doorway to the church area itself was boarded over top to bottom.

Eyes looking down the entire way, she followed him up the stairs to the third floor and along the corridor to the end of the hallway. They passed guards posted at intervals along the hall who saluted her guide. He stopped when they reached the last corner room.

Stationed outside the door was a very serious soldier, mid-twenties, probably. A scar, still red in recent rawness, curved from his right eyebrow to his right earlobe. He saluted her guide who offered a sentence in authoritative Japanese. The youth disappeared into the room for a short moment, closing the door behind him. He reappeared a few moments later, gesturing for them to enter.

To the right of the entrance was a desk on which were papers and maps in neat piles. Some of the piles were held down by mugs and assorted paperweights, one of which was a small statue of José Rizal.

To the left of the entrance were chairs facing a second bigger desk. Tall, narrow windows allowed the morning light to shed its rays onto the desk and onto the man standing beside them.

Her guide approached the man by the window, bowed respectfully, handed him Lucing's papers, and explained the situation in a few brief bursts of Japanese. The man nodded once, and Lucing's guide bowed again to the man before disappearing, closing the door gently behind him.

Lucing stood patiently before the desk, her eyes lowered.

"So you think you can help me."

Relieved that he spoke English, Lucing bowed from the waist, straightening slowly without meeting his eyes. "Yes, Captain-san. This woman attended college at this university and has been an Associate Professor for the past ten years on this campus."

The Captain turned away from the window and faced Lucing, "When we're alone, you may look me in the eyes, Professor Trinidad. I graduated from UCLA in California. I almost married a girl from Texas, and I'm not intimidated when a woman presumes to be my equal."

Lucing looked up and met his eyes. He was a trim man of average height, about 5'9. His uniform was filled out in a way which suggested he was muscular and probably in very good shape. He had deep dark eyes, a cleft chin, and his dark hair was in a neat crew cut. He was good-looking in a rugged kind of way.

"I've never been to America. When did you graduate?"

"1933. A Masters degree in Political Science."

The expression on his face told her a lot. She could see that he was a conflicted man. Almost married a Texas girl? Probably the antithesis of the ideal Japanese wife. Political Science? He understood the undercurrents of government and the people who ran it. He knew what elements shaped a country and pumped blood into its life. She felt sorry for him.

"Why didn't you marry your Texas girl?"

For some moments he simply met her eyes unblinkingly, and she worried that she might have presumed too much. This man was her enemy, and one who could order her killed without concern for the consequences.

Finally, he answered, a grim smile appearing just before the words came out, "It was... shall we say, politically incorrect."

"Your country's politics? Or your own?"

"My family's."

Lucing understood it all at once, perfectly laid out before her. His family had required him to marry someone of Japanese heritage, whose lineage and background, when combined with his, upgraded the status of both families involved. His sense of honor had necessitated his surrender of personal identity to the greater identity of family.

She thought that he had probably enjoyed his time in California. Maybe even learned to appreciate and love certain friends, certain American habits, certain cultural viewpoints.

He probably hated being enmeshed in a war which perceived a country he respected and loved as the enemy. But as he had sacrificed personal identity for family identity, he now had to surrender even more deeply to honor his national identity.

"And how many children do you have?"

"Two very young ones. A daughter, two years old. A son, four years old."

"Fortunately, too young to fight."

"And you? How free are you to... help me." He painted the word "help" with a strong smear of irony. She knew he knew that it wasn't about helping him, but about helping herself and those she loved... perhaps even helping her homeland. Still, the irony wasn't cruel or insulting. More... matter of fact.

"No husband. No children. My studies and work haven't left me enough time for such things."

"Then it won't be difficult for you to move into one of the rooms nearby. I'll need you here full-time. I'm sorry but if I accept your assistance, you must understand that your time is totally mine to use. Disabuse yourself of any possibility of attending to your personal studies and work. You'll be here to help me and nothing else. You will not be able to stay in contact with friends or relatives outside the gates."

Lucing nodded. She was virtually a prisoner here. Did she have any other choice?

"I'm sure Corporal Asahi will appreciate your being here, Doctor. If you hadn't arrived, he would be the one organizing that pile of papers on your desk."

One side of his mouth lifted... a half-grin as he pointed to the smaller desk on the other side of the room.

He opened the office door and spoke some sentences in Japanese to the young scarred soldier outside his door.

Back inside, that half-grin was back on his face, "Corporal Asahi's secretarial skills are... somewhat undeveloped, Doctor, and while this position is certainly beneath your status, I'm confident you'll be much better at it than he could ever be."

"He was properly thankful, I'm sure?"

"He's tasked with guarding you, so I think he'll do his best to keep you safe so you can do your job."

This banter relaxed her more than she could have imagined.

She was struck at how like a normal interview-for-a-job this felt. Then she realized it was because he was a civilized human being.

A human being.

A person.

Then, she realized how difficult it was going to be to remember he was supposed to be none of those things.

He was the enemy, and she had to remember that at all times.

* * * * *

On New Year's Day, 1942, buying time for all of MacArthur's army to cross the Pampanga River towards Bataan, General Wainwright and Major General Albert Jones desperately resorted to a number of delaying tactics against Homma's infantry, sometimes dynamiting bridges a mere few hours ahead of the Japanese forces.

During the weeks after MacArthur's departure, when 15,000 American and 65,000 Filipino troops entrenched themselves in Bataan, the impenetrable terrain, insufficient supplies, and other challenging conditions took their toll. There were only enough rations for 100,000 people for a month. Yet Bataan held 80,000 troops and 26,000 civilian refugees. In addition, ammunitions were insufficient and medicines in short supply – especially quinine, the only remedy for malaria at that time. Bataan had steaming jungles and mosquitos galore, and thousands of soldiers had already fallen ill with chills and fevers.

* * * * *

While Torio possessed a strong and athletic body, like so many of the other soldiers, malnutrition had made him susceptible to illness. He'd succumbed to malaria and was weakened by dysentery. In the few weeks since the Philippines had joined the war, he'd lost 10 pounds. Some of his buddies had lost more. But such was a soldier's life. It was part of the package.

Hungry, chilled and feverish, they did their job, entrenching themselves along a 20-mile line across the upper neck of the peninsula. They ate their meager rations of rice and canned meat, suffered through the chills and fevers, rousted themselves to build long stretches of barbed wire to mark their defense line, and tried to survive one more day.

Torio's corps, under the command of General Wainwright held the thick-wooded and precipitous western coast. Mount Natib, 4,200 feet high, with steep wooded slopes and snarled gullies, separated them from a second corps on the swampy eastern shore, commanded by General Parker.

On January 9, the Japanese offensive began. Concentrated artillery barrage pounded MacArthur's line of defense. Torio watched as soldiers around him fell, either dead or seriously wounded.

He didn't have time to worry about them. He was too busy trying to survive.

He was a practical man. Sticking your head out of a trench was not practical when enemy soldiers were firing indiscriminately in his direction. He was careful to time his gunfire right after a concentrated volley... careful not to make his head an apparent target.

When darkness came and cease-fire commenced, Torio, weak from the ills of his body, exhausted and riddled with minor injuries himself, helped gather the dead and wounded with the rest of his surviving troops.

People he had joked with the night before now sprawled on the ground in death postures, blood oozing out of eyeless sockets, torn limbs and bleeding chest wounds. He couldn't bear to look at the familiar faces. Instead, he focused on the work itself. Lifting and dragging the corpses into an organized row where someone would later identify them.

The smell was horrible. When he saw his fellow soldiers on the ground, vomiting from the stink of decaying bodies and putrefying wounds, he steeled himself to adjust to the smell and forced his body to do its work.

He marveled that he was still alive. He didn't know if he would be the next day.

Homma, confident of an easy win at Bataan, had sent his best division, the 48th, to a planned invasion of Java. For the offensive in Bataan, Homma sent his 65th Brigade, comprised of new, under-trained recruits to attack Wainwright's western corps.

On the evening of January 11th, Torio saw these under-trained recruits inching closer to his own position on the line of defense.

Filled more with adrenaline surge rather than experienced strategy, the 65th Brigade recruits yelled, "Banzai" with passionate fervor and surged towards the defense line. Their yell warned Torio and his fellow soldiers of their approach, and dozens of them fell from a volley of bullets before reaching the barbed wire protecting the Americans and Filipinos in their trenches.

As their comrades fell, the Japanese kept coming, yelling at the top of their lungs, stepping over their comrades in their frenzy to reach the enemy.

In front of Torio, Japanese soldiers fell against the barbed wire itself, forming a bridge over the barbed wire which the second wave clambered over to scale the Filipino-American defense line.

Torio had done his share of the killing. There were so many Japanese soldiers massed together it was hard to miss. Heart pumping, mouth clenched in determined focus, his rifle spewed out gunfire with indiscriminate and relentless focus.

Just as the Japanese retreat sounded, one soldier landed in front of Torio, two feet away. Their eyes met. They lifted and pointed their bayoneted rifles at each other.

Torio looked into the whites of the Japanese soldier's eyes. Suddenly he wasn't looking at a faceless enemy soldier. He was looking at a person, frightened, bolstered by a fierce patriotism, but... just a person. Like Torio, he too might have a wife and children. He too might want to live another day.

With a grunt, the Japanese soldier clambered back up the barbed wire fence, across the bridge created by the bodies of his dead fellow soldiers, and obeyed the call of retreat from his superior officers.

Torio stood frozen in position. He had been prepared to kill the enemy, but he had not been prepared to see the whites of an enemy's eyes, reminding him that, like him, this man was only obeying the call to defend his homeland. Many of the enemies were decent men, as he considered himself to be. Many, like some of the soldiers in his own corps, relished the violence.

He himself did not. He understood and believed in the necessity of defending his homeland, but he couldn't see the glory in destroying life to accomplish it.

He'd been fighting for only a month, now, and all he could see was the terrible tragedy of grandfathers, fathers, sons, husbands and brothers dying. Not just on one side of the defense line, but on both sides. It was such a waste of human life.

* * * * *

CHAPTER 9
THE OCCUPATION OF MANILA
Manila and Banga, Philippines, 1942

After Lucing left for her errand, Inez decided to move all of Lucing's books into her bedroom. Her sister wasn't the neatest person in the world, as evidenced by clothes hanging over chairs and thrown over the top of the closet door.   But the wall underneath the bedroom windows was clear, so she and the children moved the books from the den and created neat piles all along the empty wall.

When Perry arrived later in the afternoon, suitcase in hand and his photographic equipment piled in several boxes, Lucing still hadn't returned from her errands.

Inez helped Perry settle into the den, made fried chicken for dinner, and waited for Lucing to return.   Perry wanted to know if there was a basement in the house, and Inez took him down the stairs leading from the kitchen and showed him the small space underneath the house.   It was packed with boxes filled with books and broken furniture.

"You think your sister would mind if I cleaned up this space? I need a darkroom."

Inez shrugged. "She'll tell you herself when she comes back."

Except Lucing didn't come back that night. Nor the next night. Inez tried to hide her anxiety from Julio and Cencia, but a few times they walked into the bedroom and saw her before she could wipe away her tears.

"Is Tia Lucing okay, Ma?" Julio's thin face was drawn. She knew he was anxious when she was anxious, so the trick was not to show him her anxiety.

Inez managed a trembling smile, "Yes, she's working now, but she'll be home when she can."

On the third day after Lucing's disappearance, Perry gave her a note.

"January 6, 1942

"Dear Inez:

"I am fine, and I am safe. Please don't worry about me. I'm working for the Commandant at Santo Tomas, helping him organize the campus to make room for all the people they're bringing here.

"I've been provided a room next to his, and unfortunately, I have to make myself available whenever he calls for me, so I need to remain on campus.

"If you have a message for me, give it to Perry and he'll see that I get it.

"Perry has promised to take care of you and the children. Give him five pesos a week for groceries and two to keep for himself.

"Be careful. Speak Tagalog at all times. Stay inside. Do what Perry says.

"Love, Lucing"

She thanked Perry, clutched the note to her chest, closed the bedroom door behind her, and tried to silence the panic beating in her heart like a trapped bird. How could Lucing do this to her? Lucing was the one who had encouraged her to stay in Manila. And now she wasn't even here to help her with the children?

And Perry?

She hardly knew the man. What if she gave him grocery money and he disappeared? She knew the story of how Freddie had first met him... how Perry had stolen his wallet, only to return it because he wanted a job as Freddie's photographer.

How trustworthy would such a man be? Freddie might laugh and think the story was a good joke, but Inez herself was horrified that Freddie would overlook the theft and then hire the guy.

Lucing wasn't much better. Asking Perry to move in with them? No, not with them – because Lucing wasn't going to be here – but with her and the children. Alone with her and the children.

She was scared, unsure of what to do next, and she had two children to worry about. What good would Perry be to her?

A soft knock on the door, "Mama?"

It was Julio. She had to put up a brave front for her children. If nothing else, she couldn't show them her fear and confusion. They were depending on her.

She opened the door and tried to be decisive.

"Perry, how'd you get this note."

"I can't tell you. Lucing could get in trouble."

Her voice rose indignantly, "You think I'd tell them?"

Perry looked at Julio who stood manfully beside her, and then at Cencia, who was clutching her dress.

Inez turned to Julio, "Can you and Cencia run next door to Mrs. Mansillas? Ask her if she has any ripe bananas we can borrow. Maybe we can make banana fritters."

She gently pushed Cencia to go with Julio and watched them exit out the back door and into the back yard which connected to the Mansillas back yard.

She rounded on Perry. "How dare you! I'd never tell the Japanese anything that would hurt Lucing."

Perry sighed and shook his head. He took Inez's hand and led her to an armchair in the living room. He sat down opposite her.

"They do things to make a person talk."

"Torture? They're granting amnesty to Filipino soldiers and they'd torture me? A full-blooded citizen who's never done them any harm?"

"Listen, Inez. Your sister is assisting the Captain at Santo Tomas. They're watching her like a hen about to lay eggs in a chicken coop. The first thing is they'll assume she's a spy. You don't think they'd kill her if they thought so?"

And now Inez's heart was no longer a bird trapped in its cage... it was a lion trying to escape a trap. She couldn't talk. She could only stare in horror at Perry.

"But don't worry about her. She can take care of herself. I know she told you to do what I say, so you'll have to trust me."

"You read my letter?"

"How else am I gonna know what she wants us to do?" When Inez shook her head in disapproval, Perry patted her hand, "Don't worry. We'll be okay."

He got up and went into the den, moving equipment around. Inez placed a hand on her heart, commanding it to calm down. She went into the den and watched Perry pick up his camera.

"I'll be back. I have errands to run."

"Where are you going?"

"Don't worry, Inez. I promise I'll be back." He patted her cheek and winked. Then he was out the door.

She wanted to slap him for his impudence. For his easy assumption that she and the children would be fine without him.

Well, she'd show him she was as tough as he assumed. Why wouldn't she be? She was a soldier's wife. She had gone to meetings hosted by other military wives who talked about being prepared for risks their husbands might take in the performance of their jobs. About the possibility of difficult times while their husbands were away. About the possibility that their husbands might die.

She had listened during those meetings. But she hadn't really believed any of those things might happen. My God, if Benito were to die...

With one hand to quiet her heart, she steeled herself not to cry again. The children were at the door and she didn't want to upset them.

They ran in, giggling. Julio carried three bananas in his hands. "They only had three. But they said if there's any extra, please make them some too."

"They gave us the bananas. Of course we'll save some for them." She looked at her children, so scrawny and thin. They'd already lost weight since they'd arrived at Lucing's. When she couldn't eat, they couldn't eat.

She had to put on a braver face to them. She was relieved that they could still laugh. And she wanted them to be happy as long as possible.

Gathering the bananas, she smiled at her children, "C'mon. Let's make some fritters."

* * * * *

Perry wasn't worried about Lucing. She was a Philippine citizen cooperating with the Japanese, and she was smart enough to survive her ordeal. In the letter she had written to him, which was considerably longer than the letter to Inez, she'd assured him she had her situation in control... had even initiated a "mutually cooperative relationship" with the Commandant of Santo Tomas internment camp, whatever that meant.

Her attitude was positive, and sounded in good spirits... even excited. And she had included the full details of what the Captain intended to do at the camp. So far, conditions were not good.

Apparently, Tokyo wasn't assuming responsibility for the care and welfare of its prisoners. Japanese soldiers were collecting American and British civilians for internment, but from what Lucing had been able to deduce, once the prisoners were in the camps, the Japanese weren't providing food or other necessities to its prisoners.

The prisoners were virtually on their own.

His errands today included passing this information on to Rinaldo Sulat, a lawyer who had taken it upon himself to create a central base of operations for information gathering. Lucing said that her Captain had agreed to let families and friends bring food twice a day to prisoners inside Santo Tomas at selected areas along the iron fence surrounding Santo Tomas.

Whatever food was brought had to fit between the bars, and guards overseeing the process were known to keep some of the food themselves.

Apparently, however, not all guards were cruel and oppressive. Some even allowed medicine and clothing to be passed through the bars. However, radios were not allowed and those trying to pass radios were in danger of punishment. Even utensils were often confiscated by some guards.

Through Rinaldo, Perry had learned of the horrible conditions at Fort Santiago, where Freddie was interred. If he was concerned, it was more because of Freddie than because of Lucing.

First of all Freddie was American, and that in itself invited repercussions from the Japanese. Secondly, Freddie was proud... too proud for his own good. The man would say no if the Japanese asked for his cooperation, and he wouldn't just say it, he would throw it contemptuously in their faces.

* * * * *

Freddie hated his situation, and he wasn't alone. In fact, there were 11 other men sharing his 10 x 10 cell with him, and dozens of flying cockroaches which landed on them or buzzed at their faces.

It was so crowded that there was no room to lie down and sleep. The best that could be managed was for two men to sit, knees drawn up, lean back to back against each other, and get as much rest that way as they could.

After a few days, an aggressive American whose job had been to organize and manage the dances held at the Manila Hotel, suggested a schedule where men would team up and rest in this manner.

Freddie suggested that it was a good idea to keep moving so their muscles wouldn't atrophy, so included in the schedule was half an hour of walking around the cell in two circles, an inner and an outer circle. To make it interesting, they changed directions, and they moved from inner to outer circles.

They were only getting a bowl of rice each day, with some *tuyo* thrown into the bowl occasionally, so they all began to lose weight immediately.

After the first week, exhausted and weak from lack of food, they cut down their circle exercise to 15 minutes. After the second week, they cut their walking exercise even further to 10 minutes.

Also after the second week, Freddie was summoned by the Commandant overseeing the prisoners at Fort Santiago.

* * * * *

Captain Nannara was a short, wiry, older man – Freddie guessed him to be in his early 50's – with salt and pepper hair and small black eyes which emitted the iciest stare Freddie had ever seen. In fact, the entire man emanated cold... a human icicle.

His office was small, but still larger than Freddie's own 10 x 10 cell. The Captain sat behind a desk devoid of paper. Behind him and to his right, his country's flag draped from a pole stand. A picture of Emperor Hirohito of Japan, Son of Heaven, hung on the wall behind him.

The guard deposited him in front of the desk, and he stood before the Captain.

Freddie knew about the obligatory bow expected from prisoners, so he bent from the waist, and slowly straightened up. This process allowed him to create his strategy in dealing with the Captain. From his quick appraisal, he knew he was dealing with an inflexible, straight-by-the-rules, ruthless leader. So... he had to be humble enough to let the man know he understood his position, but strong and zealously patriotic to America... or this man would have such contempt for him, he might as well be dead right this minute.

His English was grammatically correct, but stilted, "Welcome to Fort Santiago, Mr. Collier."

By the time Freddie had straightened, he understood how to play this game. He stood ramrod straight, his eyes meeting Captain Nannara's stare with proud resolution.

"Thank you for your welcome, Captain. However, may I humbly bring to your attention that Fort Santiago's hospitality falls extremely short of standards established by the 1929 Third Geneva Convention relative to treatment of Prisoners of War."

A light switched on behind Captain Nannara's ice-cold eyes. Freddie knew he had the man's attention now.

Some moments passed before the Commandant responded to his statement, "You are a civilian, Mr. Collier, and not a soldier. Therefore, you are not a prisoner of war according to the letter of the law. You are a civilian internee."

"Which implies, Captain Nannara-San..." – Freddie thought adding that honorific, "San", wouldn't hurt under the circumstances – "... that, if anything, we civilian internees, who are innocent until proven guilty, should be treated with even higher standards than prisoners-of-war."

There was a curl to his lips when the Captain responded, "And what makes you think your conditions do not uphold the Convention standards?"

"Somehow, I can't believe, Captain Nannara-San, that your own soldiers are crowded together 12 to a room half the size of this office. Article 10 requires that prisoners be lodged in adequately heated and lighted buildings where conditions are the same as your own troops."

"And you have visited my troops' quarters so you know for a fact they live in luxurious comfort compared to you?"

"I certainly can't imagine their quarters are on the same standards as..."

Interrupting, "Mr. Collier, yes, you are a prisoner, and soon I will prove it to you by action rather than flimsy words. You are not here to 'imagine' anything. You are here to follow my rules and abide by my decisions or suffer the consequences."

"Nevertheless, I'm sure when authorized representatives of a neutral power arrive to inspect these camps..."

Again interrupting, "Ah, Mr. Collier. It remains to be seen which power remains neutral in this war, does it not?"

Freddie had no retort to a statement so eminently true. He dipped his head once in acknowledgement... a small surrender to the Captain.

"But let us speak of more civilized things."

The Captain stood and began to pace behind the desk.

"You are a journalist for a big magazine in America. It would please me very much if you agreed to cooperate with me by writing articles about the state of affairs here in the Philippines."

"For example, writing about the luxurious and comfortable living conditions of internees at Fort Santiago?"

The Captain stopped pacing. Moved around the desk until his face was six inches from Freddie's. They were of an even height, so it was eye-to-eye. "That would be an excellent start."

They stared at each other. Freddie considered attacking the man and escaping. But who was he kidding? Outside this office were dozens of guards, and outside this building, hundreds more. His white skin would stand out in a crowd of Asians so he'd be dead before he got two feet from this room. In fact, this guy, older than he, was in better shape and would probably kill Freddie before he could even lift an exhausted hand to try to strike at the guy. And 'try' was the operative word.

He had no illusions about his martial arts skills. They were non-existent.

"I humbly thank you for considering that I could be service to you, Captain Nannara-San, but I must decline on grounds that it would be an act of treason against my country to cooperate with you."

There was no discernible expression on the Captain's face. Freddie didn't know if he'd inspired contempt or respect from the man. It didn't matter. It was a matter of self-respect and national pride.

"Is that your final decision, Mr. Collier?"

"Yes, Captain Nannara-San."

The Captain gave a quick nod. Walked to the door and opened it. After a short burst of Japanese, two guards came in and shoved Freddie out of the room.

They led him through the narrow hall, past cell blocks and into another 10 x 10 cell. This cell wasn't empty.

Two large metal eye bolts protruded from the ceiling, with steel chains looped through each, and shackles appended to the end of each hanging chain.

They shackled his wrists and adjusted the chains so that his toes almost, but not quite, reached the floor. Then the torture began.

At first, he wanted to prove to these soldiers that what he lacked in physical strength, he more than compensated for in mental strength. He looked in their eyes as they took turns using him as a punching bag.

They took turns kicking him... all parts of him, applying martial arts moves to target his face, his shoulders, his chest, his torso, his kidneys, his stomach, and his knees. Filled with shame and self-contempt at his own weakness, it took only five minutes before he could no longer hold back his grunts and moans... much less hold his head up enough to look them in the eyes.

He didn't beg for them to stop. That would have been a waste of breath. He tried to fill his mind with nice thoughts, an image of his sweet children's faces, or the beautiful mountains of Colorado and sweet fresh air after a rain or crisp clean coldness after the end of a heavy snowfall.

But he could only ignore the pain for so long. His whole body hurt. Tears leaked from his eyes, and still he didn't beg. He prayed for unconsciousness and after half an hour of being kicked and beaten, he achieved this goal.

When he awakened, he didn't know how much time had passed, but his body was one whole scream of pain. He was still hanging by his wrists, and he was covered in blood. He had soiled his pants, and he was in a disgusting state.

For some time longer, he was in and out of consciousness. Finally, a splash of cold water on his face woke him up.

Two different guards unshackled him and stretched him out on the floor. One guard lifted his head up and poured water into his mouth. He swallowed the water greedily.

Turned his head aside when he was done. Except the guard continued to pour water down his throat. He choked and tried to turn his head. The second guard knelt down to hold his head steady, while the first guard continued to pour water into his mouth, stopping only when Freddie needed to take a breath.

Breathing hard, Freddie felt his stomach near to bursting with the water, and still they poured water down his throat.

Finally, they stopped, and Freddie could feel his heart pumping in panic, his stomach extended to its maximum capacity.

He lay on the floor, spread-eagled, wondering how much more he could endure.

Eyes closed, he tried to assess the condition of his body. Before his mind could start working, one of the guards jumped on his stomach, and he gasped as water and vomit was forced upwards and out of his mouth. His bladder emptied all around his legs, and still he felt bloated from the water in his stomach.

The guards splayed him out again, and he struggled to get away from them, but two against one... and one in his condition... made him the automatic loser. Spent, he surrendered to the inevitable. He had no doubt that if the guards continued this particular form of torture, his stomach and other internal organs would soon burst and he'd ultimately die.

As the second guard prepared his jump, a third guard entered and delivered a strong command. The first two looked up at him, then at each other, and finally, with the third guard still watching, they shackled him again and left him hanging in the room, trying to catch his breath, trying to gauge how badly he was hurt, trying to stay alive.

He wasn't sure he would survive this, but he was going to fight with all his strength and determination to do so. He wanted to be alive when this war finally came to an end. However many weeks, months or years it took, he wanted to see with his own eyes the day when his country vanquished this enemy. He knew America would prevail. How could it not? It was the land of the free, and freedom ultimately prevailed over tyranny.

After some time, Freddie lost consciousness, his clothes smeared with his own vomit, and feces and urine trickling along his legs. And pain. Unending pain throughout his entire body.

He didn't know how much time had passed when the cell door opened and a new set of guards came in. They splashed his face with water, bringing him to semi-alert consciousness. He tried to hold back his groans and to control his raspy breathing.

He tried to prepare himself for more torture.

It didn't happen.

Instead, they stripped him naked and washed away the vomit and waste surrounding him. The filthy water washed down the drain at one end of the sloping cell. They turned him over and threw more buckets on him, using his filth-ridden clothes to wipe away the dried vomit and feces.

Then they left him again to dry out on the cell floor.

Half an hour later, Captain Nannara himself entered the chamber, fresh clothes in his hand. He threw them at Freddie. Freddie's eyes were swollen nearly shut, but he could see that the clothes weren't really that "fresh." They looked like the unwashed clothes of another prisoner... in much better condition than his own had been, but still covered in dirt and torn in several places.

"You are not without courage, so your life has been spared. Please put on these clothes and we will return you to your cell. You will have time to deliberate your response to our next talk."

A few of Freddie's fingers had been broken when he had used his hands to try to protect himself, so he had a hard time pulling on his pants. The Captain watched in silence, ice-cold eyes without expression. When he tried to lift the shirt over his head, he couldn't raise his arms high enough, so he tied the sleeves around his neck.

They had to carry him to his cell, and once there, he couldn't stand or sit. He could only collapse to the ground.

He wanted to close his eyes and just sleep and never wake up until there was no more pain.

His eyes barely open, he could still see a white-haired, white-bearded and wrinkled white face bend closer to him, "Don't move. I'm Doctor Rob. I'll help you as much as I can, but it'll hurt."

He opened his mouth to tell the doctor that his hurt couldn't get any worse, but then he felt hands on his shoulders to hold him down and then a horrible pain, as the doctor shifted bones into place.

He didn't even have enough strength to scream properly before he fell into sweet darkness.

* * * * *

Despite the pampered comfort of her stay with Manong Totoy and Manang Salina, Rissing slept fitfully, unable to control her anxieties and concerns about Torio. She knew MacArthur's forces had been deployed to defend Bataan, and she knew there were numerous battles being waged.

Would Torio survive? Would his body be so injured he would never be a whole man again?

On January 3rd, 1942, Rissing washed her long, waist-length black hair, rolled it into a bun at the nape of her neck, and dressed herself in one of her ankle-length maternity skirts and a short-sleeved *pina*-cloth blouse.

Meling arranged for one of the plantation workers to drive Rissing to the city in the family *calesa.*

Early in the morning, as the horse-drawn *calesa* trundled away from the house, Rissing turned to see a little figure running after the carriage. She told Paolo, the driver, to stop until Ramon, breathing hard, stood at attention in front of the *calesa*.

"Ramon, what's wrong, *iho.*"

"Mama, you need an escort. Let me come with you."

Rissing stared at her son. He had put on clean shorts and shirt, his handsome face was wiped clean and his hair had been brushed back with a wet comb.

Her young eight-and-a-half year old protector. Her throat tightened and her eyes misted.

She smiled at him tenderly, "Get in."

Ramon used his hands to lift himself up to the first step of the *calesa* and seated himself between his mother and Paolo.

Juan Delacruz's office was in the center of town, about three miles away from the Magsayan plantation. Unlike her journey from Manila to Balayan, the dirt road to town was relatively clear of other vehicles. Occasionaly, they passed an oxcart plodding slowly with wares piled neatly in its wagon bed.

Nevertheless, they took their time, and with her son beside her, Rissing enjoyed the journey. Banga was famous for being a beautiful town and she could see why.

It was a third-class municipality with a population of over 20,000 people. Once they entered the urban area, she noted the clothing stores, the business buildings, the restaurants and little sari-sari finger-food shops interspersed here and there, colorful signs hanging above the various businesses to announce their trade.

At one sari-sari store, Rissing asked Paolo to stop and buy them some fried bananas to munch on as they traversed the streets of the city.

It was late morning when Paolo finally stopped in front of a two-story brick building, where the name "Delacruz and Delacruz" was tastefully displayed on a bronze bar above the entrance. He got out and helped Rissing onto the street.

It was a prosperous looking building. Rissing was immediately reassured to note this. She thanked Meling silently for recommending this law firm to her.

Ramon took his mother's hand and they entered the building together.

The receptionist was a round-faced young girl barely out of her teens, with black hair and shiny white teeth. Her bangs reached past her eyebrows and nearly covered her pretty brown eyes. She smiled in welcome at them.

"I'm Venturissa Santos and I have an appointment with Mr. Juan Delacruz, please. I'm a few minutes early." Actually, she was half an hour early, but better to be early than late.

"Yes, he's expecting you. Please have a seat and I'll be right back."

Rissing and Ramon sat down on the rattan couch positioned to one side of the receptionist's desk. A coffee table with magazines neatly fanned out on one side separated them from the desk. The couch, table and desk were all of beautifully crafted rattan. The couch cushions on which Rissing sat were thick and soft.

Stairs behind the receptionist's desk led up to the second story, but the receptionist headed for the first door directly to the left of the entrance.

She came out a minute later, her smile displaying her beautiful white teeth. She motioned and Rissing and Ramon, hand in hand, walked toward her. Ramon tugged at her hand and she looked at him.

He whispered,"Mama, I have to use the toilet."

When they neared the receptionist, Rissing whispered to her, "Ramon would like to visit your restroom?"

"Of course, Mrs. Santos. I'll take him there and afterwards he can stay with me while you meet with Mr. Delacruz." To Ramon, she said, "I'll bet you'd like a bottle of coca cola, huh?"

Rissing thanked her and went into her lawyer's office. The outer office, also furnished in beautifully handcrafted rattan, was small and neat. The woman behind the desk in this outer cubicle was older... maybe in her mid-30's, and rather plain with curly-kinked brown hair. She wore glasses which hovered on the tip of her nose, "Hello, Mrs. Santos. I'm Anna." Rissing shook her hand and murmured some polite words.

Anna opened the door located at the front left area of her desk and stepped back to let Rissing in.

Rissing entered and watched the door close behind her. She turned her attention to the man standing behind his desk, and met his eyes.

And, meeting his eyes, she found herself frozen. His eyes were... extraordinary. A normal brown color, but expressive of a cultured sensitivity and intelligence which saw worlds within worlds.

Instinctively, she knew she had finally met a man her father would have approved of, because this man was most definitely high class.

She watched him walk around his desk – an elegant walk which matched his slender body and handsomely refined face – as he took one step, and then another, until he was standing right before her, his dark eyes warm, patient and wise.

She thought to herself, "Oh, Papa, this is the man you wanted for me. This is the man who should have been my husband, but it's too late. Much too late now."

She was suddenly self-conscious about her bulging stomach, and she put a protective hand over her baby due to be delivered within the next few weeks.

When he spoke, she released her held breath, recognizing his confident, soft voice. While not as deep, the tones of his cultured voice were so similar to that of her father's, she wanted to cry. She realized at once how much she missed her father. Tears misted over her eyes.

"Come," he murmured, "you must be tired from your long ride in the sun."

* * * * *

Juan couldn't explain to himself why he was so taken with her. When she had turned to face him, he thought to himself that she was the most beautiful woman he had ever seen. Pure, creamy complexion gently browned by the inescapable Philippine sun; black hair smoothly drawn back in a bun at the nape of her neck; slender limbs gracefully extending from the sleeves of her blouse. And, my God, she was in the last trimester of her pregnancy.

He was drawn to her as if a string connected them, heart to heart, and the beating of his heart pulled him closer and closer to her, and to stop moving was to stop the beating of his own heart.

When he stopped before her, he saw something emotional playing out in her eyes... misting her eyes, and he wanted nothing more than to ask her... *"What? What moves you so, dear one?"*

Instead, he suggested, "Come. You must be tired from your long ride in the sun."

He took her elbow and a tingle, like an electric current, ran up his hand. He let go. Instead, he gestured to the armchair and she walked to the well-cushioned bamboo armchair facing his desk. She sat and he went to his own chair and smiled at her.

To herself, Rissing thought that it wasn't only that he was a physically beautiful man... he was a beautiful cultured being. In one look, she had recognized all the elegance and refinement in him which would have justified her father's choice of him as her husband.

Except... if she hadn't married Torio... if she hadn't befriended Meling because of being a soldier's wife, if the war hadn't come, if, if and if... she would never have met this man.

So... she could only conclude it was not meant to be.

She took a deep breath and forced herself to leave behind that illusive state of dreamy idealization.

In the part of her mind that was practical, she reminded herself that she was Torio's wife and mother of his children, and the reality was this man was ultimately not destined for her. She glanced at the family pictures on the wall behind him and saw him posed with a lovely woman and three children in several of them. Yes, he already belonged to someone else.

It wasn't so much her features which made her beautiful, Juan decided as he watched her, it was an inner glow which shouted to him that she was a woman of extraordinary inner brilliance... possessed of a quick mind and extraordinary perceptions of the world. How could he help but stare at her in wonder.

"Thank you for your concern. The ride wasn't that long. Not compared to the trip

Meling and I took in an oxcart from Manila to Balayan, and then by boat here to Aklan."

"An uncomfortable trip, I'm sure."

"*Talaga*." She laughed, patting her stomach. "Considering my condition. And Meling is expecting also. At least we had an oxcart."

The smile lingered on her face and he tried to imagine what circumstances on that uncomfortable trip would make her smile in such a way.

"Your husband?"

"A Scout in MacArthur's army." She didn't need to explain beyond that.

Rissing settled back against the chair, "Thank you, Mr. Delacruz, for taking me on as your client. I realize now I'm probably less... that I don't bring in the kind of income you're used to."

"For Meling, I'm happy to be of service. Totoy's family has always retained my family. My father died several years ago, but my brother and I continue the business. And please, you've been my client now for almost ten years, so call me Juan."

"And my friends call me Rissing."

They smiled at each other.

"Can you please tell me how my farm's doing?"

Juan had reviewed her file earlier that morning, so he was up to date on the information she wanted. He decided not to go into too much detail... that one year, Ignacio's sweet potato crops had been destroyed by worms invading the tubers, and Juan had decided on his own to advance Ignacio from Rissing's share to finance his next year's crops. It had taken Juan only three years to repay the loan, and then increase his yield to increase Rissing's profits as well.

When he started to tell her the balance on her account, he decided that the relatively small percentage he was supposed to retain as his fee didn't amount to much when compared to his other clients', so he added his fee to the total he gave to Rissing. Her eyes and face glowed in surprised satisfaction and he couldn't help but feel happy about his decision.

"I'll just need about 1200 pesos of that for now, Juan. I don't know when I'll pass this way again." This was about $2/3^{rd}$ of the balance in her account, and it was a lot of money to carry around, but Rissing didn't trust the solvency of banks during wartime. She'd put half of it in a metal box and bury the box somewhere at the farm.

Of course Juan, who probably made in a month what she made in a year, nodded easily, "I'll walk you to the bank myself."

Rissing scooted forward to stand up, and Juan hurried around his desk to help her out of the armchair.

For some moments their faces were very close as he looked down at her, and he felt a strong protective wave overcome him. He found himself overwhelmed with an unexpected tenderness towards her that he rarely felt for his own wife.

His wife, Emiliana, came from a family who owned a rice mill and did a fairly prosperous business. He'd known her almost their entire lives, and their marriage was something both families expected as a matter of natural course. She was a good person, but rather spoiled by an easy life. He couldn't imagine her riding in an oxcart from Manila to Balayan and then a boat to Aklan and smiling at the end of it. More likely, she'd complain all the way.

Rissing headed for the door and he followed her, opening it just as she reached it. "After the bank, can you join me for lunch? It's just about that time." As he spoke the words, his heart lurched. He already had lunch plans, although that could always be changed.

Still, he was alarmed at his own spontaneous invitation. It simply wasn't appropriate to prolong his time with this woman for no practical reason. Except, he thought, it was actually good business to get to know his client better.

Anna looked up from her desk and raised her eyebrows. As Rissing headed for the outer door, he turned to Anna and signaled for her to change his lunch appointment.

In the hallway, Ramon hurried to join her. She put her hand around his thin shoulders and looked up at Juan, "This is my son, Ramon, who escorted me on my trip here." To Ramon, she said, "This is Mr. Juan Delacruz, our lawyer. He wants to take us to lunch. Shall we go?"

Ramon looked up at his mother, who smiled and nodded her head, and Ramon extended his hand, "Yes, thank you, Mr. Delacruz."

As Juan led the way to the entrance of the building, he chided Ramon, "Your mother has known me for ten years, Ramon, so you must call me Juan."

"Manong Juan," Rissing corrected.

Ramon was thrilled to be treated so kindly. He nodded, "Okay. Manong Juan."

* * * * *

After Rissing withdrew her money from her account, they went to lunch at a nearby restaurant – "The Nipa Hut" – not too fancy, but much nicer than Rissing or Ramon had ever patronized before.

Ramon couldn't help himself. He looked around and studied everything in the restaurant – the pretty girls in pretty pink dresses with white aprons who stopped by their table and brought them drinks and food. The *adobo* was good but not as good as his mother's. Unlike the simple fare at home where their rice was eaten with one *ulam*, there were other dishes on the table. There was also *lechon baboy*, and *halo-halo* for dessert – so much food he didn't know how they could eat it all.

His mother looked very happy and so he felt happy.

He knew when his mother was happy because she glowed. Her eyes became filled with light, like the stars on a dark night, and her skin glowed and she looked so beautiful.

She laughed and smiled at Manong Juan, and he guessed it was because she hadn't seen him in a long time even though she'd known him ten years now.

He wondered how they had become friends. He'd known his mother all his life and had never seen her leave Manila long enough to come to Aklan and become friends with Manong Juan. But maybe Manong Juan had come to Manila and that's how they'd become friends. It was a puzzle, all right. Maybe Papa would know.

Manong Juan turned to him and asked, "Ramon, did you enjoy your trip from Manila?"

"Mostly. But I got really scared twice."

"Twice?"

"Once when I thought Mama was going to have her baby. They were going to take the oxcart away from us, but she was in the back with stomach pains so they let us keep it."

Rissing could have died with mortification when she heard this. She wasn't sure she wanted Juan to know about her skills in misdirection, and now her son was innocently talking about it to the man.

"And the second time when this old grandpapa pointed a gun at my Mama and I had to..." Ramon's face became serious and he looked like he was about to cry. "I had to shoot the gun out of his hand so he wouldn't kill my Mama."

He turned his face into Rissing's shoulder and she leaned against him and stroked his head, "You saved my life, *iho*. Your father will be so proud of you."

Her own eyes had teared up and she looked at Juan and shook her head. Ramon extricated himself from his mother's embrace and straightened his back, holding back his tears.

"But then we met Andrew and his sisters and we had fun."

Juan watched this scene play before him, and his imagination took flight. My God, labor pains in an oxcart on a godforsaken dirt road surrounded by people fleeing from war, and a gun pointed at her head. He could only stare in wonder at Rissing's bravery as she shook her head at him.

"Yes, we did. And now we're here having a nice lunch with Manong Juan."

He wondered what he would have done if someone had pointed a gun to his head.

"What did you do when the old man pointed a gun to your head."

Ramon answered before his Mama could, "Mama tried to talk him out of shooting her. But I could see it wasn't working." To Rissing, "Ma, I can't finish all this food."

"Then don't force yourself. We can save it for Paolo."

Juan took the hint and asked for leftover bags.

When they exited the restaurant, Rissing waved to the driver of a *calesa*, and the driver guided the horse to where they stood.

Rissing turned to him, "Juan, Ramon and I thank you for a delicious lunch."

"It was my pleasure." Juan took her hand and kissed it. Then he wondered if that was too much. He looked into her eyes and she was smiling warmly at him, eyes bright and shiny. No, it was just the right thing to do.

Before Paolo could step down from the *calesa,* Juan lifted Ramon into the carriage beside Paolo, and then turned to Rissing. Her eyes became distant and sad. He wondered what she was thinking. Then she smiled a beautifully warm smile at him, stood on tiptoe and kissed him on the cheek, surprising him so thoroughly that he barely recovered quickly enough to help her up the steps and into the carriage.

A smile lingered on her lips as Juan stood there, watching them drive away. He returned Ramon's vigorous waving with a more subtle wave and didn't move until they turned out of his street and out of his life. He was very aware that he had just spent nearly two hours with an extraordinary woman he might never see again. He felt his heart breaking... or maybe it was just the sensation of a tiny space opening up... just wide enough for Rissing to emplace her irrevocable presence in his heart.

How could he forget her? In their short time together, his life felt so diminished when compared to hers. Her experiences encompassed a magnanimous territory of labor pains in an oxcart and a gun pointed at her head. What adventures could he himself boast of?

He stood there, watching the street long after the *calesa* was out of sight.

Her beautiful face lingered in his mind's eye as bright and fresh as if she was still standing there, returning his gaze. He felt as if he'd known her forever. He imagined how brave and strong she'd been when facing the old man with the gun. How her courage and grace would forever reduce any other woman in his life as mediocre.

In his memory, he replayed the tender, gentle movement of her head as she bent to touch her brow to her son's forehead. The way her hand reached up to comfort her boy.

And how, when her eyes looked into his own, they shone with such a powerful emotional light.

Someone bumped into him, apologized, and moved on.

He barely felt it.

She was gone now. They'd spent several hours together, but it hadn't been long enough. If they had spent several days together, even that wouldn't be long enough. He already missed her presence. He wondered if he would ever see her again.

In that instant, he understood that he'd been touched by someone... something so far beyond his humdrum existence he knew that he would never be the same again.

* * * * *

CHAPTER 10
SURVIVAL ISSUES
Bataan, Philippines, 1942

After Homma's forces were launched against the Bataan defense in early January of 1942, two weeks of hard fighting ensued. Tanks and artilleries were employed by both sides. Because Philippines had been unprepared for the initial air assault at Clark Field on December 8th, half of MacArthur's air force was destroyed during the first hours of the attack. That meant the Japanese had complete control of the air.

Homma's regiments along the slopes of Mount Natib had maneuvered Wainwright's and Parker's corps into a situation of no retreat, so MacArthur ordered a withdrawal to a new line of defense halfway down the peninsula.

Getting to that new line was the problem. To begin with, because transport from Manila to Bataan was a disorganized last-minute concoction of jitneys, school buses, purloined oxcarts and anything else that could move, many of the fighting units had been separated and splintered into different groups.

* * * * *

In Torio's case, aboard a truck enroute to Bataan, he found himself sharing the truck with Filipino soldiers who were not Scouts but part of the U.S. Army Division, and many of them were from different regiments altogether.

Once they reached their line of defense, they were already fighting for their lives, and there hadn't been time to locate and unite with their individual regiments. They were all essentially under MacArthur and when he said fight, it was time to fight, never mind that a soldier wasn't with his specified regiment.

Basically, where you landed was where you fought.

In addition to the frenzied necessity of battle, the scarcity of basic supplies and food, the mosquitoes which infected them all with various diseases, and the general air of urgency which depleted their strength and willpower, there was a sense of confusion because soldiers were unable to connect and unite with the people they had practiced and exercised with during training.

Torio and most of his fellow soldiers were not only experiencing exhaustion but they were beset with fevers and chills from malaria, dengue fever and dysentery.

So when the command came for MacArthur's soldiers to retreat to a new line of defense, Torio had a choice of joining other soldiers on battered trucks and buses, or he could make his way through the woods with other soldiers. There just weren't enough vehicles for everyone, and soldiers who were uninjured and in fairly good shape were encouraged to walk the distance.

Torio started out with four companions through the woods, but the thickly wooded area, combined with the thick canopy of dense foliage above, created such a profusion of shadowed darkness it was impossible to see two yards ahead, even with flashlights. It didn't take long for Torio to find himself alone in his progress through the jungle.

The ground was moist from the torrential rains which poured in spontaneous bursts, creating mud so thick his boots sunk into the leaf-strewn mire and lifted with loud sucking noises.

But he had to move on. Now was not the time to sit on a fallen log and whine about his troubles. It was a matter of lifting one foot in front of the other, keeping his knapsack secure, and trying not to lose his flashlight. There were snakes, mosquitoes, and wild animals to worry about. As well, he had to be careful not to drop his rifle into the mud-sucking ground. If the mud got into the workings of his rifle, he'd be lucky if it still worked, and luckier if it didn't backfire into his face once he pulled the trigger.

Decaying leaves carpeting the wet ground often hid large fallen trunks of trees, and he had to avoid stumbling against one and falling on his face. The one time it happened, mud had gotten into his nose and mouth, and he had to stop, use some precious water from his canteen to clear his nose enough so he could breathe.

After three or four hours of travel, he heard voices up ahead, and he made as little noise as possible as he approached, bending low. Finally, he got close enough to see jeeps and trucks, front to back, surrounded by soldiers. It looked like one of the buses was stuck on the road and soldiers were trying to push it out of its rut.

His eyes were focused ahead and he wasn't looking at where he placed his foot, so before he knew it, he was rolling down a gully, bouncing against fallen logs and tree branches. He didn't fight it, relaxing his muscles and allowing his body to move in a path of least resistance. Broken bones resulted from rigid muscles during a collision or fall.

It wasn't a deep gully, perhaps only six or seven feet deep. He tested his body to see if anything hurt badly. All his limbs still worked. His neck and shoulders were fine. He got up slowly and managed to stand on his feet.

By now, he had recognized from the shouts that it was Filipino soldiers struggling with the bus on the road above him. He tested and found rooted bushes which could support his weight and pulled his way up the gully. At the top, someone saw him and gave him a hand up onto the road.

The man, as dirty and muddied as himself, asked him if he was all right. He nodded and thanked the man for his help. Torio asked, "*Ano ang balita?*"

"If you want a ride, there are buses and trucks up ahead, but they're pretty crowded and it's slow going. The roads are in bad shape."

Torio nodded. It was pretty much what he already suspected. He decided he'd get to his goal faster walking a straight line to his destination. He continued on his way. He saw some others making their way into the woods along the road, so he knew he wasn't alone in making this decision.

After about an hour of sludging through the wet leaves and mud, he came upon two soldiers sitting on a log looking out over a ravine. Both were Corporals and they stood up to salute him. They offered him their canteens, but he took out his own and took a careful gulp. He'd passed a stream several hours back and had refilled his canteen.

"Ease up, men. We're all in the same dugout now, let's not worry about rank until we get to base camp. I'm Torio."

"Pasqual." This one was short and muscular with one of his ears sliced in half, though the wound was healing well.

"Barniz." Somewhat taller than Pasqual, he had a bloody bandage wrapped around one wiry arm which needed to be changed, but Torio guessed the man didn't have any fresh bandages left and hadn't run across any medkits lately.

"I've got fresh bandages if you need a change."

"Might need it more later. This one's fine for now."

Torio nodded and joined them on the log. He took out his flashlight to study the ravine.

Barniz shook his head, "It's about 30 feet deep. We could get down, but it could be a problem climbing back up."

Torio looked across the chasm to the other side. "It's only about 15 feet across. Olympic jumpers have been known to jump up to 20 feet and more."

A scoffing laugh burst out of Pasqual's mouth. "*Aba*. And you're an Olympic jumper?"

Some yards away a tall tree grew on their side of the ravine, its branches stretching out over the ravine.

Pointing to the tree, Torio remembered watching his hero Johnny Weissmuller in the Tarzan movies, swinging from tree to tree. "We could tie a rope to that limb and swing from this edge over the ravine and onto the other side."

Again Pasqual scoffed, "*Seguro*. And you have rope on you?"

Torio looked around him. There were many fallen branches, many of them still green. "We could make one. Help me gather some of these branches."

Pasqual didn't budge from the log, but Barniz got up and helped Torio gather a dozen long branches and twigs.

Barniz watched as Torio took out his knife and cut off long thin strips of fibers from the limbs. When he had a dozen strips, He picked up two of them and began doing a reverse twist on the two strips until he had a thin long single rope. He tied off the ends and began on another set. Barniz picked up two of the long fibers and tried to follow Torio's moves, so Torio slowed down so Barniz could watch and learn by example.

By this time Pasqual was watching too. He watched Barniz's efforts and laughed when Barniz's ropes turned out uneven and lumpy.

"I bet you can't do any better."

So Pasqual picked up two strands and tried to follow Torio's moves. Surprisingly, his rope was tighter and more consistent than Barniz's. "Good thing I didn't bet you our next meal at camp. You would've lost."

"I need that food more than you do, *chibabo!*"

"I've got more muscles to feed, *maroyat!*"

Barniz picked up his knife and began stripping more strands for Torio and Pasqual to work on.

When Torio had enough twisted lengths, he tied them together in fishing knots so they wouldn't loosen, until he had a thin rope 25 feet long.

When he had two such ropes, he reverse twisted them together to create a thicker rope, and when he had three such double ropes, he braided them together until they had a sturdy rope. They tested it, tying one end to a tree and pulling on it with their combined strength. It held. It was sturdy enough to use.

Barniz punched Pasqual on his shoulder, "Good work, *chibabo!*"

"And you, *maroyat!*"

Torio hid his smile. He taught best by example and he had enjoyed sharing the process with these two fellow soldiers.

It had taken them more than an hour to make the rope, and now someone had to climb the tree.

Barniz punched Pasqual on the shoulder, "Hey, bet you your next meal that you can't climb that tree."

"What about you, *maroyat!* You weigh less than I do. It should be easy for you."

While they squabbled, Torio tied a large rock with one end of the rope and threw it to over the lowest limb. The rope was long enough for both ends to touch the ground. He took off his shoes, gathered up the rope ends and maneuvered the loop around the limb as close to the trunk as possible. Then his feet climbed up the trunk, his hands moving up the rope, one on top of the other, until he had reached the limb. When he reached the limb, he straddled it to look for the branch he wanted to use for swinging across the ravine.

By this time, Barniz and Pasqual were watching him in tense silence. A limb stretched out several feet to the side of and beneath the one he wanted to use, and he was able to walk on that limb, holding on to the upper one until he reached the place where he wanted to secure one end of the rope.

When he had done that, wrapping his hands with the cloth of his fatigues, he slid down the rope and landed in front of his two companions.

They were grinning and clapping, and he shook his head, "Didn't you guys ever see that Tarzan movie."

Torio next tied a short thick branch to the rope at head level as a handhold. It wasn't as safe as a foot hold, but it was easier to let go of the handhold than it was to jump off a foothold.

Pasqual offered to go first, and as he swung across the ravine, he yelled a Tarzan yell which sounded close enough to Johnny Weissmuller's yell, and Torio hid another smile. Once he reached the other side, Pasqual tied a heavy rock around the rope end and swung it back to them.

Barniz went next, and it took a few swings before he was willing to let go of the rope to land on the ground where Pasqual taunted him.

Torio was last and as he swung across the ravine, this time he couldn't hold back his grin.

The three men decided to stay together until they reached the new line of defense. Sometimes the trees were so thickly clustered and filled with underbrush that they had to use their bolos to clear a path. They took turns in lead position, but progress was slow.

Several hours later, they came across another gully, but this one was shallow enough, and they were able to climb down and reposition a log against the opposite incline to use as a handhold to get to the other side.

Half an hour later, Torio was leading when a wild pig came running out of the underbrush, squealing as he charged at Torio. Instinctively, Torio swung his bolo down at the pig and it collapsed, half of its head hanging from the neck and a great gush of blood pouring out.

Torio had saved several feet of rope and he used that to tie the pig's feet to a long pole which two of them carried while the lead man cleared a path for them to follow.

When they reached a shallow stream trickling in a wide gully filled with rocks, they decided to stop for the night. It was so dark their flashlights couldn't even penetrate more than several yards ahead of them. They built a roasting fire and positioned their wild pig above the fire, turning it around and around so that all sides were evenly brown and shiny with melted fat.

They ate well that night, and when it was time to sleep, they took turns keeping watch. Twice during Barniz's watch, fellow soldiers saw their fire and joined them. They happily accepted a meal of roasted pig and when the group was ready to continue their trek to MacArthur's new base camp in the morning, there were five of them, including newcomers Manuel and Tunoy. When Pasqual told the two newcomers about Torio's rope-making and vine-swinging feats, they all agreed he would be their leader, even if Manuel's Master Sergeant rank made him a higher level than Torio's Sergeant rank.

With remnants of the roasted pig to eat and plenty of water to drink, the five men coordinated their efforts and made good progress so that they reached their new base camp by late afternoon of the second day of travel. They traveled only ten miles, but it was ten miles of thick woods with heavy underbrush, leaf-strewn puddles of mud, deep ravines and rocky gullies.

As long as it had taken, they still arrived before the battered trucks and buses which had negotiated their way on narrow, winding, pit-marked roads which threatened the tires so severely they stopped more often than they moved.

Other soldiers who had started out in groups had lost track of each other in the jungle and they straggled in by ones and twos.

Torio watched them arrive, so exhausted and beaten by the arduous journey that when they came into camp, they hardly looked human – bearded, mud clinging to their clothes and bodies, uniforms in shreds, and expressions on their faces like the walking dead.

Not too many said it out loud, but it had been a badly organized retreat.

At camp, medical supplies were so low that only the worst cases of malaria were treated with quinine. Only the most weakened received extra rations beyond the 12-oz-a-day of rice and 3 oz of fish or canned meat which was the standard ration for the soldiers.

Somehow, Torio managed to remain fit for battle, even while chills and fevers overcame him at times. His naturally robust body enabled his system to maintain a strong immune system, sufficient to fight the ills which beset his less robust fellow soldiers.

It had only been one month since General Homma's troops had landed on Lingayen Gulf, and the struggle for survival was already more than many men could endure.

Torio wondered what would happen if the war lasted one year? Or two? Or three?

Little did he know the war would actually last nearly four years.

* * * * *

After Rissing's lunch with Juan, Paolo drove her and Ramon straight to the farm which Ignacio Fuentes leased from her. It was the opposite direction from the city limits, so they passed the Magsayan plantation and kept going for another two miles until they reached the farm.

The farm consisted of three hectares of land for planting crop (about 1-1/4 acres). Ignacio's main crop was sweet potato (*camote* or *lukto),* which he sold to the local markets and to a crop distributor in the city.

He had also allotted small parcels of land for banana and mango trees, as well as for corn. These secondary crops were primarily for the family's use, but when things were difficult, the family could sell any extras to the local markets.

Compared to labor-intensive rice plantations, the work of growing *camote* was simpler and the crop was easier to sell. It was considered a "poor man's" crop, but there were many poor people in the Philippines, so it had its value. In addition, the leaves served as fodder for the pigs the family raised... again for personal consumption.

When Juan had drawn up the agreements between Rissing and Ignacio ten years previously, Juan had explained all of this to Rissing and had supported Ignacio's choices. It had taken weeks of letters crossing between them, but they had finally reached agreement, and now that Rissing had met Juan, she would never doubt his judgment again.

They pulled into a narrow dirt road which led into a small clearing surrounded by banana, coconut and mango trees. The farm house was a *nipa hut* made of bamboo walls and roofed with nipa palm. Santol trees rose protectively around it.

The floor was raised only two feet above ground and she saw chickens roaming under the house and around the yard, picking at seeds and grub.

Ignacio was waiting for her outside at the small porch of the house.

"Manang Rissing, welcome to our humble house."

Ignacio was a thin man with thick black hair, sharp cheekbones and patient dark eyes.

Rissing accepted his deference as was her due. After all, she was the landowner of this house and without her agreement with him, he would be without land or home.

She introduced Paolo and then Ramon. To Ramon, she referred to the man as

"Manong Ignacio," a clue to her son on how to address the older man.

Inside, Rissing could see that it was a well constructed home and that Ignacio took great pride in its appearance. He confessed that he and his sons had renovated and added on to the original house which had been on the property. It had three bedrooms, a family room, and a kitchen. The add-ons were so skillfully rendered that she could just barely make out the size and layout of the original house. Rissing especially liked the kitchen, which was clean and organized, with all sizes of pots and pans neatly hanging from the ceiling and wall.

"Viktor, my 19-year-old, is the best cook in our family. But Lessie's pretty good too."

Rissing followed Ignacio out of a side exit and was happily surprised to see that Ignacio had planted a crop garden in this area beside the house.

Mango, coconut, santol and banana trees surrounded a quarter-acre enclosure where vegetables grew... okra, tomatoes, squash and neat rows of corn.

Her children were lined by age in front of the tomatoes.

Eduardo, 22 years old, was a good-looking man of medium height, with a vital energy in his movements. She could tell he took his role of eldest son seriously.

"Eduardo is getting married in two months. He's taking over his new wife's farm, because her father is too sick to keep it going on his own."

Victor, the good cook, was just as muscular, slightly taller, and resembled Eduardo except for a cleft chin and mischievous dark eyes.

Iglesia, whom the others called "Lessie" was 17 years old, slender, petite and rather plain, compared to her brothers. Her short hair was held back by two wooden clasps behind her ears. Her smile was sincere as she stepped forward to hug "Manang Rissing."

Turning 16 in a month, Romeo was by far the best looking of the bunch, with straight white teeth and a sun-tanned skin. Wiry and nearly as tall as his brothers, Rissing thought he would live up to his namesake and break a dozen girls' hearts.

Beside him, Ollie at 14 tended to be fleshy and stocky, but intelligence shone from his eyes which studied her without apology.

"Ollie wants to be a lawyer, someday. Mr. Delacruz says he'll help if he can. And finally, my youngest, Junior. When he was born, my wife finally talked me into giving my name to one of our children. Junior is the lucky one."

Rissing met Junior's eyes and knew she had found another JoJo. At 12 years old, he looked like a male version of Lessie, but his energy was pure mischief, mayhem and, no doubt, miserable punishment afterwards.

They all declared themselves happy to meet her and then dispersed to continue their various chores.

Back inside the house, Ignacio served Ramon and Rissing lemonade, "The elevation is too low here to grow lemon trees, but we farmers exchange harvested crops among ourselves as necessary."

Rissing would have preferred iced raspberry tea, but the lemonade was good, a perfect combination of sweet and tart.

"Your letter says you'd be staying with us a few weeks. We've prepared two bedrooms for you and your children, Manang, when you're ready to stay with us."

"Two? No, that's not right. I only need one for me and Flora. My sons have their *banigs.*"

"Please. My boys have cleaned up the storage room in the barn for them to use. I can stay with them..."

"No, no," Rissing interrupted. "This is your home and you're master of the house. Take back your bedroom, *kumpadre.*" While obviously Ignacio was not godfather to any of her children nor she a godmother to his, the fact that they shared a common interest – the farm – made it appropriate for her to signify their relationship this way.

Finally, Ignacio agreed to Rissing's suggestion. She and her children would return in two days time.

* * * * *

Without plan or intention, Rissing found herself enjoying her life on the farm. It was easy to enjoy her role because the farm was already so organized and well maintained.

She couldn't believe how her "luck" held out even to this experience.

Ignacio and his children respected her, and while she knew very little of farming *camote*, she had a practical mind which understood the necessities of their work.

The farm was small enough that Ignacio didn't have to hire outside help. His children were more than sufficient to do what had to be done. Even Ramon and JoJo enjoyed following the Fuentes sons in their labor, though it was mostly Junior they followed as he did the more mundane work, like feeding the pigs and chickens, pulling weeds from the garden, and cleaning out the barn.

Rissing had happily approved her sons' stay at the barn. It was made of bamboo, like the house, and the central storage area, which usually housed farm tools, surplus food supplies and seed, was spacious enough to hold *banig* space for the five Fuentes sons as well as JoJo and Ramon. The floor was five feet off the ground, not only to allow air into the room above, but to provide space beneath the house for a chicken coop.

JoJo liked to look through the thin spaces between the bamboo strips of the floor to look at the chickens in their nests beneath him.

Since their arrival, it had become his job to collect all the chickens every night and lock them inside their coop under the barn. Junior helped him collect the eggs every morning before breakfast.

Ramon had become responsible for feeding the pigs and making sure none had escaped from their fenced-in area behind the barn.

Sometimes Lessie helped the men in the fields, and sometimes she helped Rissing in the kitchen.

Rissing enjoyed her company. She was obedient and kind, ready to do Rissing's bidding to make her happy. Her thin face lit up easily with a smile and when she disagreed with Rissing, she did so in a gentle, polite way, her dark eyes anxious that she might cause offense to Rissing.

Ten days after Rissing's meeting with Juan, a beautifully handcrafted bamboo cradle arrived, with a note:

"*January 13,*
"*Dear Rissing,*

"*Here's a token to commemorate our friendship and to help welcome the latest addition to your family.*

"*Yours truly, Juan*"

Her previous babies had done well enough encased in the scoop made by the two ends of a *patadyong* tied to something strong and stable, with some kind of strong backing to support the *patadyong* so it wouldn't fold in on the baby. As flexible as it was, a person could sit on a chair and push the makeshift cloth cradle back and forth for hours at a time until the baby fell asleep.

Still, a gift was a reflection of respect and high regard, so she hurriedly scrambled a thank-you note which she sent back with the messenger who had delivered the cradle.

Then she went into her room, closed the door and allowed herself to shed some tears about what could-have-been and should-have-been. Except she did love Torio and she truly treasured their children. And yet, she thought to herself, if only...

On January 19th, 1942, Rissing gave birth to Antonia Maria Santos. The midwife, the wife of the farmer across the way, was surprised at how easy the labor and birth had been. To herself, Rissing credited her activity during the journey from Manila, as well as her activity at the farm, with the ease of the birthing.

She thought Tonia was the prettiest little newborn of all her children so far. She was a good baby, crying only when she was wet or hungry, and readily responded to anyone who picked her up. Little Flora felt it was her personal responsibility to keep an eye on the baby, and she was there to nag Rissing, tugging on her skirt, reminding her it was time to change Tonia's diapers.

Lessie fell in love with the baby and never tired of getting up in the middle of the night to watch Rissing feed her or help change her diaper. She found excuses to carry her while she cleaned house, the *patadyong* ends tied over the neck and under one shoulder, creating a perfect pocket for Tonia to snuggle in while Lessie sang to the baby.

Tonia loved it, smiling and burping happily along with the songs, and Flora, who was Lessie's shadow, learned to sing a few songs herself.

Rissing recovered quickly, and soon her busy activity on the farm gave her back the slim figure she had before her pregnancy.

She watched her children grow hale and hearty from their chores at the farm. She listened to Ignacio's troubles and worries about worms invading the sweet potato tubers during the upcoming summer. She learned a lot about farming and was grateful for it. someday she might need that knowledge.

By the end of January, she and her children had been fully integrated into the established routine at the farm. Torio was always in her thoughts, and she and Meling kept in touch several times a week to apprise each other of what was happening with their husbands in Bataan.

They heard about the hundreds of Filipinos who'd taken to the hills to fight as guerrillas or joined clandestine intel units in Manila. They discussed and worried about Inez, her children and Lucing in the city.

In mid-February, a young boy who'd recently left Manila with his mother and sisters delivered a letter from Inez to Rissing.

Rissing borrowed an oxcart from Ignacio, and with Lessie holding Tonia in the driver's bench beside her and the boys and Flora in the back, she trundled over for a visit with Meling.

They sat on benches outside, watching the children play. Lessie and Flora remained with the sleeping Tonia inside the house.

Rissing read the letter aloud to Meling:

"February 16, 1942

"Dearest Rissing,

I hope you, Meling and the children are doing well. It's dangerous here in the city, and there are many days when I wish I would have gone with you instead.

Lucing is staying at the University because she thinks she can help us better from there. She's helping the Japanese organize the compound. No, Rissing, she's not a traitor to our country. She's only trying to minimize the damage to her beloved University and the Americans being kept prisoner there.

Filipinos are basically free to move around the city, although the Japanese control the press, won't allow us to listen to foreign broadcasts, and won't allow us religious freedoms. Perry says they even beat and torture Filipinos who are suspected of subversive activities.

I'm not sure they're as bad as all that, but I don't leave the house because Perry says it's too dangerous. Perry is

Lucing's friend. When she went to the University to help out, she asked him to stay with us here at the house. He seems nice and is providing us food. I don't know how he does it, but we'd be lost without him.

Please keep us in your prayers, as I'll keep you in ours.

Love,
Inez

After reading the letter, Rissing looked up to meet Meling's eyes. Meling was holding back tears.

"That stupid girl! Of course the Japanese are beating and torturing Filipino subversives."

"It's war, Meling. They're fighting for their country the same way we're fighting for ours."

"And that's why they'll do anything they need to win."

Rissing nodded her head. Meling wiped her eyes and grasped Rissing's hand. Rissing squeezed her hand comfortingly. Together, they watched their children chasing each other around the yard.

Ramon and JoJo looked robust and healthy after two months of healthy food and work around the farm. Andrew, Meling's eldest, was less pudgy than before. His grandfather was forcing him to feed the stock and accompany his uncles with farm work.

Cita's hair had grown longer and she carried a brush with her at all times so she could brush it from her face. Carmen couldn't run as fast as the boys, but she tried her hardest anyway. Ricky was inside with Flora and the baby.

"Can you let me know when it's convenient to borrow the *calesa?*"

"Why? What're you going to do, Rissing? Go back to Manila and get Inez?"

Laughing, Rissing shook her head. "Of course not. I need to visit my lawyer again."

"Paolo's getting supplies in town tomorrow. Shall we go with him?"

Rissing had to think about that for a few moments. Did she want Meling to accompany her? Just thinking of Juan Delacruz made her stomach flutter and her heart beat faster. Did she really want her best friend to know she felt this way about a virtual stranger?

"You've been complaining how hard it is to get around with this baby. Why should you suffer a long bumpy ride to town?"

"Listen to you! You were further along when we rode that oxcart from Manila two months ago!"

"I had no choice, Meling. You have a choice. You can choose to stay home, put your feet up and relax with a *halo-halo* in your hand, or you can sweat with me in a bumpy buggy with hard seats to town."

Meling made a face at the thought. She didn't want the hard seat for sure. But she felt guilty.

"Can I ask you to watch Tonia and Flora for me? Lessie needs to tend the garden tomorrow."

Relieved, Meling raised both hands, "Bring all the children. Andrew wants to make *biku* tonight so there'll be plenty left for tomorrow. Ricky and Flora can play together, so that'll just leave Tonia for me."

That settled, Rissing took a deep breath and admitted that she wanted to see Juan alone. She didn't have an appointment, so there was a chance he wouldn't be available.

Still, something told her he'd make time for her somehow.

* * * * *

And he did. Juan's days after his meeting with Rissing resumed normality after a week. It had taken that long for him to get over his distraction. In a way, he'd been forced to focus on his work. Many of his clients were in near-panic. Everyone knew that it was a matter of time before Homma's soldiers focused on the other islands of the Philippines. He tried to assure them that fleeing to Mindanao wasn't a guarantee that they'd be safe just because it was the furthest island from Luzon.

After being scolded by one client that Juan wasn't attending fast enough to his family's needs, Juan forced himself to get back on business track. He'd been so busy since then that thinking about Rissing became a luxury he couldn't afford.

He was finishing a meeting with a client when Anna came in and handed him a note. He read it and felt shock from head to toe.

Rissing was here. To see him. Oh God. Had something happened? Was she all right? Her family?

He assured his client once again that all his requests would be attended to. Standing up, he apologized that something urgent had come up.

After the client left, he took a minute to go into his private bathroom to brush his teeth, wash has hands, check his appearance and prepare himself psychologically for Rissing's arrival.

The moment she walked in, he heaved a sigh of relief. She looked fine. Her glowing beauty was as he remembered – a gentle smile lighting up her face. Her body was slim again, and she rested a big bag beside the chair before walking up to him, hand extended.

By then he'd reached her. He ignored her hand and gave her a heartfelt embrace.

It surprised her, but only a little. She laughed and he let her go.

"I'm sorry. Not so businesslike, I know, but I was worried you were here because something's wrong. You're all right?"

"We all are, thank you. Meling sends her regards."

"And they're all right?"

"Thank you for asking. Yes. Meling wanted to come with me, but she's nearing her eighth month now, and we decided she was better off resting at home."

"And Tonia, the baby?"

"Happy and healthy."

"Ignacio and his family?"

Rissing was impressed at how he remembered all the important elements in her life.

"Doing really well. We're still staying with him. I'm impressed at how well he's running the farm."

He nodded. He must have run out of questions because he just stood there, looking at her, a big smile on his face.

She turned to her large bag and took out a small sack which she extended to him.

"I hope you like *manggang hilaw.*" She handed him the sack of green, unripe mangoes. He placed the sack on his desk.

"My wife loves them with *bagoong.*"

She blinked and a strange look came over her face. It occurred to him that she might think he was talking about his wife to make a point. Even to create a distance between them. It embarrassed him.

He stepped away from her and went behind his desk, gesturing with his hand for her to take her seat.

He told himself to relax. Not to second-guess her.

"Any news about your husband?"

"Just rumors." She leaned forward and asked more quietly, "Juan, that's why I came. Meling and I thought that you have so many more connections in Manila. Do you know what's going on there?"

Juan shook his head. "Rumors. Like you. My friends in Manila say the Japanese are strict about enforcing all their new rules. They've promised to give the Philippines national independence by 1943. They're acknowledging Tagalog as the official language, along with Japanese. Their problem is that they don't have enough overseers to implement their plans."

"Do you consider it life-threatening for civilians?"

"The city is occupied by soldiers caught up in the mania of war. Of course it's life-threatening."

Rissing took this information in. She suspected as much. But poor Inez and the children.

"You're not thinking of going back?"

Rissing expelled a breath and decided to trust him, "My sister-in-law Inez. She stayed and I'm worried about her."

Juan couldn't believe it. Was Rissing actually considering going back to Manila to rescue her sister-in-law? He stood up and bent forward to look into Rissing's eyes.

"I don't mean to frighten you... or maybe I want to make a point. But those manic soldiers I was just talking about? A beautiful woman like you shows up in their midst and you'll be captured, beaten and much much worse, Rissing."

"And they'll do the same to Inez if they capture her too."

Juan sat back down. "If they haven't already."

Rissing caught her breath and straightened.

Before she could raise any resistance, Juan resumed, "My point is. She's there. What happens to her is what happens to women in Manila who aren't smart enough to keep out of the streets. My point is. You're here. Relatively safe from all that. Why should you endanger yourself now?"

Rissing got up, slapping her hands flat on his desk.

"Because she's my sister-in-law. She's not good at taking care of herself. Much less her children. They're family, Juan, and I can't... NOT do anything if they're in danger!"

Juan stood up, hurried around the desk to grasp her shoulder with his hands.

"And you'd risk your life? What about your children? War is coming here too, Rissing. What if you're dead and they have no mother to take care of them when soldiers come to take the farm away. And kill Ignacio and his sons. Who'll take care of Tonia the way only you can?"

Rissing couldn't help it. Tears poured down her face and she soon found herself sobbing in Juan's arms. He stroked her back soothingly, regretting his harsh words. But he'd do it again. Anything to keep this strong-minded woman safe.

"You're not expected to save the world, Rissing. Only yourself. For your children's sake."

He handed her the hanky which Emiliana had tucked into his breast pocket that morning.

She took it and dried her eyes and blew her nose.

She nodded, "You're right, Juan."

He stood watching her as she sat back down and stuffed the wet hanky inside her bag.

"May I take you to lunch, Rissing? Let's forget about Manila and tell me more what Ramon and JoJo are up to."

They went to the same restaurant where they'd lunched before. She hardly touched her food. They didn't talk about Manila, but when she asked about what news he'd heard about the battles, he felt duty-bound to pass on that information.

"Homma's forces are suffering just as much as the Filipinos. Mosquitos and flies don't discriminate. Both sides are coming down with malaria, dengue fever, dysentery or beriberi. Medical supplies are low."

"Both sides?"

"Both sides."

Rissing listened with some distress. Ashamed that this morning, it was herself she was thinking about. What dress to wear. How to fix her hair. Just to make an impression on Juan. All this while Torio might very well be sick in some gully with malaria or any of those other illnesses. Or... and she caught a deep breath at this... dead.

Juan continued, "I can't justify my not joining any longer, Rissing. My brother has a heart condition so we've decided he should stay here and keep the business going as long as he can. But me... I'm clearing my calendar and joining a group of volunteers early next week. We'll make our way to Bataan to join the forces there."

"Not you, Juan!"

He smiled. "Why not?"

"Because. Because."

"Because I have a law degree?"

"Because you're you. Your mind is your weapon! You weren't meant for violence and jungles and beriberi."

"And yet I have two good hands, and I'm healthy. There are other men like me, untrained for war, but we could still make a difference, Rissing. You were ready to jump into enemy hands to save your sister-in-law. Why shouldn't I be ready to jump into enemy hands to save my country?"

And now it was Rissing's turn to admire his passion. His courage. His commitment.

"Mothers stay home to defend the children. Fathers... well they're supposed to engage the enemy to defend their families."

"If all the men in Banga felt like you, if the war comes here... if the Japanese come here, who'll defend them here?"

"I've considered that. But... that's still an if. Meanwhile, I'm needed now in Bataan."

Rissing nodded. Neither one of them could eat any more. The waitress packed up their food and Rissing added the leftovers package into her bag.

They walked up the street towards his offices, not touching but feeling very close to each other. Rissing kept thinking that if he went to war, he might never come back. She might never see him again. When Torio had left her, she hadn't been as concerned. She trusted in Torio's athletic strength and soldier training to protect him against any true danger. Juan didn't have the same assets. What good was his educated mind when facing a gun aimed at him from several yards away.

She saw Paolo waiting with the *calesa* ahead and she waved at him. He waved back.

At the entrance to his building, Juan pulled her inside and behind an alcove. Before he could think about it, he pulled her into his arms and kissed her with a passionate fervor. In that kiss, he put all the thoughts and memories which had assailed him during the days and weeks of her absence.

He knew he might never see her again. This kiss was a goodbye. A fare-you-well in whatever future life plays out. It said to her in the only action he could think of...*I love you now, and I'll love you for as long as I live, however short or long that may be.*

Rissing was shocked by his move. Yet, she too had dreamt about being in his arms. Kissing him like this. So she gave herself to his passion. Never mind she was married. And a mother. And that she had never felt this kind of passion for Torio. This was now.

And she knew it would have to last her for the rest of her life.

When he finally let her go, they looked into each other's eyes. There were no words to say. He turned, straightened his jacket and walked through the lobby without looking back.

Rissing was a turmoil of emotions. But she kept it in control as she walked out of the building. Walked to Paolo and the waiting *calesa.* Stayed in control on the long drive back to Meling's, where she stayed to have some *biku* they'd saved for her. She gave the leftover restaurant food to Meling and her family, and she managed to laugh and enjoy the meal with them.

She was still in control by the time she got to the farm and passed on an edited version of the news to Ignacio and his family.

But, that night, after Tonia and Flora were sound asleep, she relived the long kiss with Juan and gave in to the tears of loss which flooded her. Loss of what might have been, could have been and now would never be.

* * * * *

In late March, Paolo summoned Rissing late one night to tell her that Meling was in labor and the midwife had been summoned. By the time Rissing arrived, Meling had given birth to Francisco, a healthy 5 lb, 16 oz. boy.

Rissing helped with the baby and with refreshing Meling's clothing and bedding. She stayed up all night watching the two as if she were standing in for Felix himself. Like Torio, Felix wanted to have a large family. With this fifth child, he was well on his way to fulfilling this goal.

The next morning, she breakfasted with Meling and they listed all of Francisco's wonderful characteristics to each other.

"I think his nose will be *matangos*," opined Rissing.

"*Sus.* I hope not!" responded her friend. "People whose noses are *matangos* tend to be conceited and superior."

"My nose is *matangos!*"

"See what I mean?"

They laughed and giggled and shared stories about friends with pointed noses. Meling insisted that people with rounded noses tended to be more humble. Rissing disagreed that it was a racial trait. Most Africans had rounded noses, and they certainly weren't all humble.

By the time Meling had to breastfeed the baby again, Rissing got up, tired and ready for a nap herself.

As she walked toward the door, Meling looked after her, "*Maré,* any news from town?"

"Why are you asking me? You're the one who gets news from Paolo."

"He hasn't said anything to you?"

"No."

"What about Ignacio? He goes to town sometimes. Has he said anything to you?"

"What about?"

"Well, he's a man. Men don't really gossip much."

"*Siyanga?*"

"I suppose some men do."

Rissing came back in and sat down, meeting Meling's eyes. She folded her hands on her lap, "Just say it, *maré*, whatever you heard. If it's about me, *bale wala*."

Unable to meet her eyes, Meling sighed, "You're a woman alone. Living in a house with a single man."

From Meling's hesitancy in passing along the rumor, Rissing concluded, first, it was bad; second, it was about Rissing herself; and third, since it had to do with the fact that she was a woman alone and Ignacio was a single man, then it had a sexual component to it.

She saved her friend the trouble of spelling it out, "So now the neighbors are saying that Ignacio and I are living together in sin, is that it?"

"*Sus!*"

"Maybe that he was seeing me all along, and he's really Tonia's father?"

"How could you think that? No, Rissing. That's not the gossip. The gossip is that Juan Delacruz is the father and he's paying Ignacio to take care of you."

Rissing was shocked. She could only stare wide-eyed at Meling.

"Someone saw you having lunch with him that first time. And you were laughing together and practically holding hands. Then the baby was born and people found out he sent you a cradle. They say there's trouble between him and Emiliana and that's why he joined the army."

Finally Rissing released a heavy sigh. The last thing in the world she wanted was for Juan to be the victim of ugly gossip. Or Ignacio.

It was time to move on, and she knew it.

"Meling, now that Francisco's here and healthy, I'm moving on to live with Torio's aunt in Malinao."

"I knew I shouldn't have said anything."

"No, no, it's not that. I didn't want to leave until you'd given birth."

"But I still need you. Wait a few more months."

"I promised Torio we'd get to Malinao as soon as we could. His Tia Delfie's been waiting for us all this time."

Trying to change Rissing's mind was harder than pushing a baby back in once it was out. So Meling nodded and looked away. She couldn't imagine life without Rissing.

Tears rolled down her face, and she took comfort in watching Francisco's little mouth suckling at her breast. She knew she was being selfish and that Rissing had her own life to live, but it wouldn't be the same without her best friend.

Rissing bent down to kiss Meling's cheek. "I'll miss you too."

Then she was gone.

That night, when Rissing told Ignacio that she was ready to give him back his house, he was actually dismayed. He had come to appreciate her practical ability to resolve problems.

She was an intelligent, strong-minded woman and while he personally found her too aggressive and he would never have married her or anyone like her, he did appreciate her value. Especially when it brought him profit. He tried to talk her out of it, but Rissing made it clear that she had promised to stay with Torio's aunt in Malinao should the Japanese extend the war to Aklan.

It was only a matter of time, she felt, and soon Aklan would become embroiled in the ugly realities of war. In order to secure a strong occupation of the Philippines, the Japanese would have to infiltrate all the major islands. If the Japanese attacked Panay, Torio had insisted that Rissing and the children should be with his relatives.

As Rissing wasn't about to change her mind, Ignacio knew he had no choice but to agree. Lessie was in the kitchen, washing dishes and singing to Tonia, who was falling asleep in the *duyan* made from Rissing's *patadyong.*

Ignacio leaned forward, "Manang, can you take Lessie with you?"

Rissing frowned.

"If the soldiers come... Lessie's a young girl..."

And suddenly Rissing understood. If the soldiers came and conscripted the farm for their use, they might also conscript Lessie for their use.

Quickly she nodded, "Of course."

"I can give you money..."

"*Aba! Hindi bale!*" She's a big help to me, *paré.* I'm lucky to have her with us."

Lessie cried to leave her father and brothers behind. She loved her family and the farm. The night before they left, she walked in the garden, looking at the vegetables which she had tended with care and diligence. She gave careful instructions to Junior about weeding and watering the various plants in the garden. She talked to the pigs and chickens, telling them to grow and remain healthy while she was gone. She shed many tears, but, ultimately, she was glad to be leaving with Rissing.

She had been only 6 years old when her own mother had died, and she felt safe around Rissing, whose nurturing warmth filled a strong need in Lessie. When it came to female things, she understood that Rissing would always know what to do and would always guide her responsibly.

Perhaps the fact that Rissing was not her true mother alleviated any sense of resentment at being "told" what to do, or perhaps it was just in Lessie's responsible nature to accommodate herself to Rissing's needs, but she never felt any rebellious impulses to assert her independence. Rather, she appreciated and welcomed Rissing's guidance.

While Rissing could be blunt and even harsh in her leadership style, Lessie understood instinctively it was from a desire to help, rather than control. Happy to receive guidance from an older role model, Lessie loved and trusted Rissing with all her heart. Had it been otherwise, she would never have left her brothers and father in such troubling times. She knew, without anyone telling her, that anything could happen. They could lose the farm. Her family could be killed.

As for Rissing, as she told Ignacio, Lessie would be of enormous help to her. Her sons were basically capable of taking care of themselves, and Flora, at 2-1/2 years old, was already strong-minded and independent, but her little body wouldn't be able to match her determination and the journey would be wearying for the little girl. And Tonia, while sturdy and healthy, was only a few months old.

Still, she had promised Torio that she would travel to Malinao to stay with his Tia Delfie, and so she would do exactly that.

Ignacio owned a second smaller oxcart which he gave to Rissing for her journey, and Eduardo bought a skinny caribao to pull it. She worried about how sturdy the *carabao* was, but Eduardo assured her the animal was used to pulling more weight than the oxcart. They brought *camote* leaves to feed her in the event there wasn't enough grass or *kangkong* along the way.

The cart was half the size of Renzo's cart, but to Rissing, it was perfect. It was a slow and plodding mode of travel, but even her sons could take turns guiding the *carabao* on the narrow roads they would travel.

Ignacio couldn't help himself. He repeated his instructions to Lessie and Rissing: Never leave the oxcart for any reason. Theft in these desperate times was guaranteed. Don't pick up strangers, no matter how handicapped they may appear to be. Stick close to other travelers. There's safety in numbers.

More than once, he offered to send Eduardo with them, but Rissing assured him she would find a protector along the way. She always did. And she knew if she was in the most desperate and dangerous of situations, Kal, her beloved *kaluluwa,* and Santo Nino, would find a way to protect her.

On the third day after her decision, it was pre-dawn when Rissing, at the driver's bench, holding the reins, with Ramon beside her, and Lessie, with JoJo, Flora and Tonia in the covered cart, waved goodbye to the men staying behind at the farm.

They had three large baskets of fruit and vegetables in the cart, covered by their clothing, blankets softening the hard wooden platform between the large wheels, and the love and blessings of the Fuentes men. Rissing's heart swelled with self-satisfaction.

There was no question in her mind they would reach Tia Delfie's house in Malinao with speed and safety and relative comfort.

After all, the Japanese had not yet attacked this island of Panay, and the mayhem, chaos and panic in Luzon had not yet infected this area. She was confident that she could handle whatever problems surfaced along the way. As always, she affirmed that she was named Venturissa for a good reason, and she intended to live up to her name.

* * * * *

In fact, the Japanese attacked Panay on April 16th, landing on Iloilo City, a major city located in the central southern portion of Panay. Iloilo City was in ruins, sabotaged by the retreating Filipino troops.

The next day, two columns of Japanese troops converged at Dumarao, a municipality in the province of Capiz, whose copper mines were an attractive acquisition for the Japanese.

In order to prevent the Japanese from occupying Banga, the United States Army Forces in the Far East (USAFFE) burned down the Banga Rural High School, Banga Elementary School and Home Economics building. About 95% of all the permanent structures in Banga were burned down by the USAAFE and the Filipino guerrillas.

* * * * *

CHAPTER 11
A MATTER OF DETERMINATION
Bataan and Manila, Philippines, 1942

In early February, the Japanese had launched an amphibious landing on the narrow points of land in the southwest corner of Bataan. This area had been defended by a motley combination of sailors, Marines, airmen who had lost their planes, and Philippine Constabulary. MacArthur had asked for immediate reinforcement by his Filipino Scouts.

Their teamwork bond re-established, the Scouts joined the fray with experienced competence and infused the slap-dashed-together defenders with newfound determination. Acting in a coordinated surge of aggression, they were able to drive the Japanese back to the beaches.

There, Navy PT boats annihilated the fleeing Nippon soldiers with unremitting volleys of fire, and the Japanese retreated into caves along the cliffs at the water's edge.

* * * * *

Torio was one of MacArthur's 12,000 Scouts who responded to MacArthur's call to reinforcement. He believed in MacArthur and was proud to be a Filipino Scout under the

General's command. The moment he'd left the Army to join the Scouts, his training had escalated.   Standards were higher and more rigorous for the Scouts, and he personally liked that.

He enjoyed pushing himself above the norm expected of his Scout companions. While many of them were happy to simply meet all criteria, he was determined to go beyond... to set his own standards... be the best he could be, rather than the best the Scouts accepted.

Along with several dozen intrepid fellow Scouts, Torio volunteered to climb down the steep cliff walls into positions where they could toss dynamite sticks into the caves along the cliff walls.

He knew he could die, if not by enemy gunfire, but by other accidental means... losing a handhold on the cliff face, releasing a burning dynamite stick too late, or... even collateral damage from the resulting explosion within the cave.

He didn't volunteer in a rush of national loyalty or in a passion for glory.

He volunteered because he knew that this was something he could do better than many of the other soldiers, and because it was something a soldier would do.   Practically speaking, throwing a dynamite into a small cave would seriously injure or kill whoever was inside that cave, and it was his job to neutralize the enemy, and so he wanted to do his job as efficiently as possible.

There was no fear in his heart... only a surge of adrenalin, very similar to the surge just before diving into the water to win a race in a competition. He felt confident he could accomplish his goal, and his focus was purely on achieving that goal.

A length of rope was firmly secured around a large boulder above him and the other end was tied firmly around his waist. His foot slipped a few times along the cliff face, which was slick with moisture from the unpredictable downpours of rain. He took his time and made sure each foothold was solid before moving on to the next bracing position. Gunfire echoed all around him but he ignored that. He had chosen to descend beside a fissure which provided him some protection from each side of the cliff wall.

When he was four feet above the target cave opening, he secured himself against the cliff face, lit the dynamite, and tossed it into the cave opening. Then, as quickly as he could, he made his way up the wall, using his hands to pull himself up the rope, and his feet to provide solid support along the nearly vertical rise of the cliff.

The explosion inside the cave reverberated against his body, and he took a moment to breathe deeply and stabilize himself before proceeding to the top of the cliff where hands pulled him up to safety.

He repeated this exercise half a dozen more times, resting between each foray to gain sufficient physical strength. Once, he thought for sure it was the end for him. A

Japanese soldier from a neighboring cave had seen him making his way down the cliff face. The soldier's shots had missed Torio, but the bullets had cut through his rope.

Hanging on a rock jutting out of the cliff face, he held himself in place until a new rope was thrown down to him. Return fire from his team pushed the Japanese soldier back inside the cave, and his team pulled him up to safety just as a spatter of bullets splintered the rocks and vegetation Torio had used as cover.

As darkness slowly triumphed over light, the caves were quiet. There were no pleas for mercy or statements of surrender from the Japanese soldiers.

These were not cowardly men. Their country demanded that they either won their battle, or died trying.

Surrender wasn't even an option.

In the morning, the caves were quiet. If there were any survivors, they had managed to escape in the darkness of night.

* * * * *

By mid-February, the amphibious threat had been nullified.

However, at the new line of defense which Torio had left behind to join his fellow Scouts, Homma's troops continued the aggressive attack against the American-Filipino defenders. At one point, Wainwright's men broke through the Japanese line and separated the Nippon soldiers into two groups.

They wiped out one group, and the Japanese colonel leading the second group managed to fight his way out of the second circle and back to their front lines. However, out of the thousand Nippon men from the original group Wainwright had separated two weeks earlier, only 377 survived.

By this time, Homma had used up the 50 days allotted to him to conquer Luzon. He had lost more then 7,000 soldiers, either dead or wounded in the fighting in Bataan. Another 10,000 to 12,000 were down with the same diseases the American-Filipino soldiers were fighting – malaria, dengue fever, dysentery or beriberi. Homma knew it was time to pull his army back a few miles and ask Tokyo for reinforcements.

During the lull of nearly two months which followed, both sides strengthened their positions, laid minefields and reorganized their remaining armies. The reality was that sickness and malnutrition had paralyzed MacArthur's army to a standstill. The quinine supply was almost out, and food supplies were so low soldiers were walking skeletons.

The Japanese weren't in better shape. They could no longer take the offensive. Instead, they reassembled units to platoon strength to ambush patrols, burn supplies and steal food and weapons from their enemy.

U.S. President Franklin Delano Roosevelt decided to boost the morale of the American-Philippines forces, intending to inspire them to greater effort. However, his speech backfired. It only reminded the soldiers that the U.S.

weren't sending any more reinforcements. MacArthur was still in fortified Corregedor, refusing to leave. His men called him "Dugout Dave" behind his back, with fondness and ironic humor.

Finally, President Roosevelt ordered MacArthur to retreat to Australia, and on March 10th, MacArthur obeyed his President. He, with family and staff, on a PT-41 torpedo boat, glided through the Corregidor minefields to the open sea towards Mindanao. From Mindanao, 500 miles south of Corregidor, they transferred to a B-17, for a 1600 mile flight to Darwin, Australia. Australia was also under imminent attack, but MacArthur told the news reporters, "I came through, and I shall return."

From Australia, MacArthur retained "supervisory" authority of the forces in the Philippines, but Jonathan Mayhew Wainwright was promoted to Lieutenant General and given the overall command of all U.S. forces in the Philippines.

* * * * *

In Manila, Inez wasn't happy at all.

For three months, Perry had proved to be stalwart and trustworthy, leaving the house every morning to do his errands, and returning each night, albeit at unpredictable hours.

Inez had learned to set his supper aside each night, and without complaint or comment, whatever time Perry came home from his trips into the city, as soon as he got home, he found his supper and proceeded to eat it with fervor and appreciation. If Inez was still awake when he arrived home, he never failed to thank Inez after wiping his plate clean.

So one morning when Inez woke up and found Perry's supper uneaten and his bed undisturbed, her heart plummeted. She went to the basement to see if the man was working in the makeshift darkroom he had made for himself down there, but that too remained undisturbed. No new photos drying out on the line.

She made a point to remain cool and calm during the day, encouraging the children to do their errands around the house, and following through on her own routines of cleaning and preparing for the day's meals.

By now, she had come to realize that her children were timid and dependent by example. When she thought of Rissing's children, who were self-sufficient and were able to act independently of her guidance, she had to admit it was primarily because Rissing continually nagged at them.

Inez herself refused to nag at her husband or children, feeling that such behavior was contrary to how a genteel lady would act. If Benito failed to do something she expected, she accepted it as part of Benito's character and adjusted her own behavior to compensate for it. If her children failed to pick up after themselves, she would gently show them the acceptable and appropriate way to deal with such things. She would say, "Look, Julio, if you leave your dirty shirt here, next time it's time to do laundry, I won't wash it and you won't be able to wear the shirt again."

By contrast, Rissing's method was to glare at the offending son (usually JoJo) and bark, "*Huy,* who cut off your hands? Why can't you pick up your shirt and put it in the laundry bin like you're supposed to?"

Of course, Inez's way was potentially more rewarding (with loving attention given by Mama) than Rissing's way (nagging was irritating and so JoJo usually learned to avoid it by not doing anything Mama didn't like... or hiding when it came time for the nagging).

People can debate which style is the better one in raising children, but Inez soon realized that while gentle rewards feel good to the soul, nagging generated more urgency, so ultimately, Rissing's way worked faster and more efficiently.

Inez soon realized that timidity and dependence were detriments, rather than assets, in times of War.

* * * * *

After a week and Perry still hadn't returned from his latest foray, Inez realized they were running out of food. There was still rice in the small barrel in Lucing's pantry, but no meat and vegetables.

Lucing had made a stab at growing a vegetable garden, and she had *camote* and okra growing, but she had admitted to Inez that if it wasn't for Mrs. Mansillas next door keeping an eye on the garden, everything would be dead. All the okra was gone, but maybe she and the children could dig to see if there were any sweet potatoes left in the ground.

She didn't want to borrow any more food from the Mansillas. They too were scrounging for meals.

Two more days passed and still no Perry. Inez was very worried. There was no man in the house to protect them or to advise her on what to do about food.

Now she regretted that she didn't go with Rissing. Her sister-in-law always knew what to do, no matter what happened. She would have known where to get food.

So Inez was scared. She couldn't help it. She hadn't had a good night's sleep since that first night Perry hadn't come home. She'd tried to present a calm face to the children, but Julio had caught her crying a few times.

Now, she could feel tears welling up behind her eyes.

"Where's Uncle Perry, Ma?"

Julio's eyes were big and scared. He was so sensitive to her moods, quick to feel the very same feelings overwhelming her at any given time.

And what Julio felt was quickly telegraphed to three-year-old Cencia. They crowded up to her, waiting to be comforted.

She gathered her courage and put on a smile. "Have you both finished your chores this morning?"

"Why hasn't he come back?" Julio insisted.

"Is Papa coming back?" Cencia gripped her skirt tightly, her mouth trembling.

Inez took their hands and led them into the living room where she sat down. It was time for her to accept realities. Perry wasn't coming back. Something had happened to him.

"Both of you, listen. It's just us three now, and we all have to be very strong. I don't know when Uncle Perry's coming back. And Papa's fighting the Japanese so he'll be gone awhile."

"Why isn't Uncle Perry coming back?"

Inez wanted to tell them that Perry would be back... that everything would be all right. But she had resolved to become less timid and dependent... to be an example for them. She was determined to find her backbone and use it.

"We're fine without him. We're fine by ourselves. I'll go and get us some food..."

"Don't leave, Mama!" Cencia threw her arms around Inez, wailing sorrowfully. Julio looked at her in anguish.

Oh, her poor babies. Had she done them such a disservice in over-protecting them from the harsh ways of the world?

She stood up and pulled apart Cencia's hold on her. "Stop it, Cencia. Stop it right now." But her little girl couldn't stop crying.

Soon, Julio was wiping at his own tears.

Her children were crybabies. Both of them. But who was to blame if not herself. She herself was a crybaby. She remembered crying when Rissing told her the journey to

Aklan would be rough. She and the children had arrived in their Sunday best.

Rissing had tried to tell her, but she was scared and gave in to that panic. Like these children now, she had surrendered to tears.

Well, she couldn't afford that now.

Hardening her voice, she leaned down to look in their faces. "Listen to me. Both of you. LISTEN!"

Her voice had taken on a harsh edge, filled with frustration and anger.

Cencia stopped crying immediately, and Julio's eyes were round black wet pools.

"Julio, you're the man of the family now. Papa's away and Uncle Perry may not come back."

His voice protested squeakily, "But I'm only seven!"

"I don't care how old you are. Look at your cousin JoJo. He's younger than you! But would he be crying just because Uncle Perry hasn't come home yet?"

"But Uncle Perry..."

"Stop it. Stop making excuses."

They both stared at her, frightened at the anger lighting up her eyes. They had rarely seen her like this, and especially with them.

"I'm scared... just like you. But now I'm in charge and you two have to help me. I have to buy us some food, and you two have to stay here."

"But what if you don't come back."

Inez took a deep breath. Reassure them or....?

"I'm taking you next door to the Mansillas. They'll watch you until I get back. Okay?"

She leaned forward and kissed their foreheads. "I'm sorry I shouted at you. But this is very important. No more crying. Both of you. And me too. I've been crying too much, and sometimes I forget that it's hard to think when I'm crying."

She knelt down and hugged Cencia. "Let's all remember that from now on, okay? No more crying."

"But what if something hurts?"

Inez stood up, "If something really hurts, then it's okay to cry a little."

The Mansillas couple were both in their 70's, small, thin and their faces furrowed in wrinkles. Hosep wore thick glasses and had two upper teeth missing. Lima's hair was wiry and gray, wrapped in a tiny bun behind her head. She was nearly blind but she moved in quick bursts of energy.

Lima took Inez' hand and pulled her into the kitchen, "I just picked some tomatoes this morning. Take some home with you."

Hosep followed them, "If you're going to the market, you should go with Manang Maya. She knows where all the freshest vegetables are."

"Here, bring her some tomatoes."

Manang Maya's house was the tinest house on the block, five houses away from Lucing's house. Inez knocked on Manang Maya's door, a bag of tomatoes in hand.

A short, stocky woman with a round leathery face lined with wrinkles opened the door. She looked about 80 or 90 years old, with short hair which clustered in greasy white strands around her face. One of her eyes was cloudy with cataracts, but the other was shrewdly appraising and intelligent.

"Yah? Who are you?"

"My sister Lucing lives down the block. She's a college professor?"

The old woman took the tomatoes and waved Inez inside. "Yah, I know Lucing. She has a sister. Inez."

"That's me."

"Yah?"

"I'm... Hoseph said if you're going to market, I should go with you."

A quick study of her clothing and Manang Maya shook her head, "Not like that, you're not."

Inez froze in the entry way. She look down at herself. She was wearing a dress with a flowery pattern... an old one about five years out of fashion.

She followed Manang Maya into the tiny kitchen, just large enough for a counter and a small stove.

"What's wrong with my dress?"

"Not enough. *Sus.* This must be your first time to market. Come on."

Inez followed the old woman into a small bedroom across from the kitchen. It was cluttered with clothes strewn over the bed's headboard, hanging from hangers resting on curtain rods stretched over the window, and over the one chair beside the bed.

"You want to get kidnapped by Jap soldiers and raped into the bargain, what you're wearing will do it for you. You want to be safe, this is what you wear."

She rummaged through the dresses hanging in front of the window, pulled one out and threw it at Inez.

It was smelly, baggy and torn in a few places. It looked like it wouldn't survive the next washing, which is why it probably hadn't been washed in a while. Whatever pattern had graced the fabric was reduced to faded yellows and dull greens.

"Put it on."

Inez looked around for a bathroom.

"Go ahead. Take your clothes off and put 'em there, on that chair.

Remembering her vow to overcome her timidity, she took off her dress and set it aside, sliding the grey dress through her head. It was about two sizes too big for her.

Manang Maya nodded her head. "Better."

The old woman took her hand and pulled her back into the kitchen. "Wash your face. Get all that prettifying gunk off."

Inez couldn't believe it. What vendor would sell anything to her if she looked like a woman living on the streets?

"Do it, or go by yerself. I'm not gonna save your virtue if some Nippon gook takes a fancy to you."

Inez washed her face.

Manang Maya reached to a planter on the windowsill, took some dirt in her hands and wiped it on Inez's face. She took out the clips and pins from Inez's hair and rubbed some dirt on her hair.

Inez wanted to cry. Her care in dressing for this morning's foray destroyed in several casual swipes of this old woman's hand.

"Okay, now you're ready. My turn."

When the old woman came out of her room, she was wearing a bright yellow shirt over a blue and green *patadyong*, with a purple scarf wound around her neck.

"Let's go."

"What about your face?"

"Yah. Any Nippon wants my fat body, he's welcome to it."

Manang Maya's heavy body moved quickly on tiny little feet. Her toes peeking out of her sandals were colored a sloppy thick red. Inez was mortified to be seen with this woman and no doubt about it. Of course, she could only imagine how she herself must look.

"You walk too pretty and too smart. Stoop a little. Keep your mouth open like you're too stupid to close it. Take little steps. Stay behind me and do everything I do."

For a moment Inez wanted to laugh. Was this for real? She couldn't believe she'd let the old woman browbeat her into this silly charade.

Then they reached the market.

Japanese soldiers, rifles slung over their shoulders, walked in pairs and groups in the market, eyeing the merchandise and the shoppers.

Seeing them, Inez stiffened in fear. Ahead of her, she saw two soldiers stop a Filipina woman. She was slender with long black hair. Her dress was clean but simple, with many patches. She lowered her head and bowed to the soldiers.

One soldier reached to brush her hair away from her face and Inez saw the woman shrinking away from the touch. He said something to his companion, and they laughed. The woman tried to walk away but the soldier held on to her.

Manang Maya veered away from them, Inez close behind. She lowered her head so that her hair covered her face. Someone grabbed her from behind and spun her around.

She couldn't hold back a terrified "Uhhhnnnn" as she faced a Japanese soldier. He grinned at her, big crooked teeth revealed between his thin lips.

Manang Maya stopped and swung her big yellow plastic bag at the soldier, "Bad boy no grab my daughter."

She pulled Inez away from the soldier. A group of soldiers gathered around them, laughing at Manang Maya. Inez scurried away while Manang Maya berated the soldier in broken English, "Daughter sick with clap-clap from soldiers. You want clap-clap?"

The big-toothed soldier laughed, raising his hands in surrender, and the group around him laughed with him.

Manang Maya and Inez escaped behind a market stall. "Now you get it, right?"

Inez's heart was beating like a drum gone crazy. Was this really the way it was? A woman couldn't walk in a public market, with hundreds of people watching, in safety and comfort? The Japanese could kidnap anyone they wanted, and no brave Filipino would intervene or try to save the kidnapped victim?

They wove in and out between stalls, avoiding soldiers. Occasionally, Inez was horrified to see pretty women in flowery dresses, identical to the one she had put on this morning, flirting with the soldiers.

"Yah. Well, they gotta eat too, right?"

"How could they..."

"You get hungry enough, you'll understand."

Finally, they reached their destination, a little stall which plucked chickens hanging from the piped support of the cloth covering. Vegetables and fruits had their own baskets on the table underneath the canopy.

Manang Maya pulled Inez to the back where a big man covered by a white apron stood next to various sizes of meat hooks hanging on long chains above his head. Most of the meat hooks were empty.

The remaining assortment of meat hanging on the hooks didn't look too promising to Inez, although the flies had no problem swarming over the pieces. The early morning crowd had already taken the best pieces. The man nodded at Manang Maya.

"Chuy, this is my daughter Inez. If she ever comes here without me, treat her well."

Chuy winked at Inez and waited for her to make her selections. Inez chose the last two skinny chickens and added a few vegetables. Manang Maya, who had placed Inez's coin purse in her waist belt, handed Inez's purse to her.

When Chuy told her how much her groceries were, Inez couldn't help it. Her eyes opened wide.

Chuy shrugged, "Food in short supply. Costs more."

Manang Maya whispered, "Got enough?"

Inez counted out her money and nodded. She had brought just barely enough.

They made their way through the market behind stalls and in narrow pathways between oxcarts and wagons, avoiding the soldiers as much as possible.

By the time they made it back to Manang Maya's house, she was drenched in sweat, a mixture of fear-sweat, and humid-heat-sweat brought on by their fast walk home.

Safe inside Manang Maya's house, Inez collapsed on the kitchen chair.

The old woman studied Inez and smiled. "Yah, scared the crap out of you?"

Inez smiled back, "Yah!"

Manang Maya laughed.

After a while, Inez joined her. Soon, they were laughing like two silly schoolgirls sharing a secret.

She had been scared, yes. But the excitement of the risk, the suspense of eluding danger... she found herself feeling thrilled by it all. She had been determined to overcome her timidity and she had done it.

* * * * *

Face washed and dressed in her original clothes, Inez left some chicken for the Mansillas couple to thank them for watching Julio and Cencia.

The children hugged her happily, and still high from her adventure at the market, she laughed and returned their hugs with a feeling of victory.

Once she got home, that disappeared.

Perry lay unconscious on the floor, a small bag of rice in his hand, and blood seeping from a wound on his shoulder, just above his heart.

* * * * *

CHAPTER 12
A MATTER OF TRUST
Manila, Philippines, 1942

Lucing had been prepared for hardships when she volunteered to assist Captain Nokorazu. She knew it was a 24-hour-a-day job, and that many of the soldiers patrolling the grounds would resent and hate her. Her own people would probably hate her even more.

What she hadn't expected was how much she would enjoy her work.

On the day of her arrival, after the Captain had asked her to organize her desk, she thought it best to stay until he dismissed her.

Corporal Asahi had delivered dinner on trays at 6:00. They'd both eaten at their desks, and at 7:00, the Captain had looked at his watch, then advised her to report to work the next morning at 9:00.

"Do I report anywhere for breakfast?"

"Corporal Asahi will deliver a tray at eight o'clock."

"And my room?"

"Across the hall. Corporal Asahi will take you there when you're done here. I want to be clear, Dr. Trinidad. You are to make yourself available to me 24 hours a day. As you learn my routine, you'll find that I have established obligations.

"For example, I like to attend a 7:30 evening roll call of the internees. As much as possible, my mornings will be spent in meetings with my Lieutenants. My first meeting is at 9:30 and I expect you to sit at your desk and take notes. I'll trust you to organize your day accordingly, but when I need you, I advise you to be here and ready to work. I'm usually in the office beginning at 8:00 in the morning, but unless I tell you otherwise, you may come in at 9:00."

"Yes, Captain." She almost saluted but stopped herself. She didn't think he'd appreciate her mockery.

She'd been given a room next to the Captain's, across his office. It had a bed, desk and chair, and a small cabinet to hold her food. It was small but it had its own toilet and shower.

The next morning, she entered the office at 9:00 on the dot. The Captain was seated behind his desk, looking crisp and competent.

"Good morning, Dr. Trinidad. I found your list of office supplies. Corporal Asahi will make sure you receive everything on the list." He handed her a sheet of paper with the day's schedule printed in neat block letters. "Here's my list of things to do today."

He busied himself with paperwork on his desk, so Lucing took that to mean she should do the same.

At 9:30, a short tap on the door and a thin, sinewy officer came in. Lucing looked at the Captain's schedule. This was Lieutenant Orashi, the man in charge of repairs and maintenance of the buildings and grounds.

The Captain stood up and they exchanged salutes.

"Lieutenant Orashi, my Special Assistant, Dr. Trinidad, will be taking notes. Proceed in English, please."

The officer looked at her.

At her desk, Lucing stood and bowed to her waist. She straightened enough to note through her lashes that Orashi's hair was thick and unruly. His eyes were dark almond dots surrounded by smile crinkles. She liked the crinkles.

"The south perimeter of the fence has been repaired. We're still working on the northeast damages, but basically the fence is secure. We'll keep patrol guards at the weakest areas. As to the debris, my crew has cleared the Plaza and the inside of the Main Building. We're also removing the rubble in and around this Church so this building should be cleared by the end of today. The monks are helping us. They're sensitive about how the crew handles the Church and Seminary. They're not happy you've made your office here."

"I consider this Church to be the safest edifice on the campus."

"We've already got patients at the hospital and the internee doctors seem to know what they're doing. The nuns helping them are trained nurses."

"Good. It'll keep their minds and hands busy."

Orashi nodded and they continued to discuss the disposition of all the other buildings on campus. Lucing couldn't keep up with them, but she wrote down key words to trigger her memory when it came time to transcribe her notes.

Before leaving, "Crinkles" stopped in front of her desk, clicked his heels together, and inclined his head slightly. She got to her feet and bowed waist down until he was gone. That was interesting. Japanese soldiers expected Filipinos to bow to them; not vice versa.

The next visitor was Lieutenant Hiroku, a muscular man who was shorter than the Captain. He was in charge of the soldiers patrolling the campus. When the Captain explained to him that she would be taking notes, he gave her a once-over and otherwise didn't acknowledge her in any way.

He sported a shaved head and his teeth were very big. The Captain made a joke at one point, and Hiroku laughed. When he did, Lucing felt as if she were under a shark attack. Otherwise, he was very serious and stern, and his English was not as fluent as Crinkles' rendition.

He presented his report in a matter-of-fact monotone, but Lucing couldn't help but feel all he did was complain. His men didn't have enough food. The soldiers were restless to join Homma's forces in the field. The internees were undisciplined and out of control, and he wanted to know how much disciplinary measures were to be applied.

He left without so much as a glance at her.

Last but not least, the third visitor, Lieutenant Tomatzu, was big and fleshy... nearly six foot tall. Not fat... just big-boned. He not only inclined his head to Lucing when she bowed to him, he also smiled. Lucing liked him the best.

Tomatzu's eyesight was bad and at some point, he pulled out his notes and put on some glasses before reading his paperwork.

"With the Main Building cleared, we've told the people they can find places to sleep in there and they're responsible for their own living arrangements. We found a volunteer, an American businessman by the name of Truman Edwards, to organize them. We're keeping men separate from women, and children under 14 stay with the mothers. What kind of feeding arrangements do we have?"

"Tokyo wants it to be clear they are prisoners of war. We're here to keep them in a confined area. Guard patrols are meant to keep them from escaping that area... not to service their needs."

"Relatives and friends are gathering at the fences to give them food. And things like toothbrushes. Hand soap. Clothes. Most of these people have nothing but the clothes on their back."

"Set up an exchange area. Post guards to inspect the packages before allowing our internees to keep them. Have this man Edwards arrange all that. He should check with you before implementing his plan."

"I've spoken to Orashi and he doesn't have enough men in his crew to repair the toilets and bathing facilities."

"Make Edwards responsible for getting his own crew for that. Our soldiers are here to fight a war. Not to make life comfortable for the internees."

When Tomatzu had left, the Captain stood and moved to his window, looking out at the remains of the botanical garden below him which separated the Church from the Main Building. From what Lucing had seen, there were still some trees standing in the garden, but everything else was a mess.

After about ten minutes of silence, the Captain spoke… as if to himself. "Tokyo doesn't care about people. Tokyo just wants to win this war. The sooner the better. Win the Filipinos to our cause. Imprison the Americans and British and anyone else who isn't on our side. Tokyo doesn't care that when everything is done as they require, there won't be enough left in this camp or any camp for people to remember what and who they are. They'll be too focused on staying alive. Finding food. Finding shelter. Making sure their loved ones are safe. Tokyo doesn't have time to worry about human rights and dignity."

He turned and met Lucinda's eyes.

"Apparently that's my problem now."

She saw the pain in his eyes and felt it along with him. She wanted to cry for him. She understood him at once with a shining clarity.

Captain Nokorazu was a man of conscience. As Commandant of this camp, he had to act the devil's advocate, while his heart and soul were anything but.

* * * * *

Nokorazu heard himself voicing his thoughts. Regretted it immediately when he saw Dr. Trinidad's expression. What on earth was he doing sharing his innermost feelings with this stranger... this woman who was an enemy of his country.

America had spoiled him. Showed him how to be free with his thoughts and feelings in a way he never could in Japan.

He hadn't realized how much he loved that about America. This woman wasn't American, but she'd learned their ways. Probably from the American professors she worked with at the University.

From the moment she'd looked into his eyes and allowed her innate self-confidence and intelligence to show, he'd admired her. Respected her. But to trust her with such revelations about himself? He certainly never intended to do so.

Abruptly he sat down. "Please read your notes to me, Doctor."

Lucing understood, of course, that the Captain already regretted his moment of vulnerability.

She picked up her notes and summarized what each of the Lieutenants had reported. When she finished reading her notes, he nodded once, "Now tell me what you think of Orashi."

"He's a good choice to supervise onsite repairs to the campus buildings. He seems the type to take pride in his work and he'll work hard until he's finished the job."

"And Hiroku?"

"Takes himself very seriously. He probably has a big ego and he'll be more interested in impressing you than he is of having his men love him. He may be stricter than necessary, but at least he'll be good at controlling his soldiers."

"Tomatzu?"

"He's loyal to his country and so he's here fighting the enemy, but he's an excellent choice to supervise the prisoners. He'll never forget they're people and that makes him a fair overseer."

For some minutes the Captain simply stared at her.

She wondered if she had overstepped the boundaries again. She wondered if her comments were what he was asking for. Had she been that wrong in reading him?

Finally he grinned his half-grin. "Dr. Trinidad. If I were a different man, I would have you flogged for your presumptuous comments which reveal you as a self-serving judge of character."

Lucing's heart sank and suddenly she was very nervous.

"However, since I am what I am, what I say is that your assessments are fairly accurate. Your deportment during today's meetings with my staff has proven to me you know how to conduct yourself around my soldiers. Feel free to articulate your thoughts to me, but never to my staff and never within their hearing. Around my soldiers, speak only if you're spoken to. Trust no one, Dr. Trinidad. Never forget you are our enemy."

Lucing couldn't believe it. She had taken a risk and it had worked. She dared another step forward. "Will I have access to all areas of the campus?"

He opened the top desk drawer and handed her an identity badge. "This should give you access anywhere on campus. I trust your judgment to choose what areas are off limits to you."

Lucing looked at the badge. There was her picture, copied from the paperwork she had given him the day before. Beneath it was her title: "Special Assistant to the Commandant".

"My Lieutenants have been told that you answer only to me."

The Captain got up and reached under his desk, lifting a red Royal manual typewriter onto the desk.

"A 1930 model. Orashi found this in one of the offices that wasn't entirely destroyed.

Please use it to type up your notes, which I'll expect on my desk at the end of the day."

Lucing assumed she was being dismissed so she stood up and bowed low to the Captain. He might treat her as an equal, but she'd better remember who was boss here.

That lopsided grin appeared on his face.

"As those notes are for my eyes only, please feel free to include any additional thoughts which you feel are relevant, including your presumptuous assessments. Finally, Dr. Trinidad, let me say I think we'll get along just fine. I'll be lunching at the mess hall today, but Corporal Asahi will bring you lunch."

With that, he bowed, exited and was gone. Lucinda stared at the closed door, reviewing in her mind everything that had transpired that morning.

When the door opened, it brought her out of her introspection. Asahi place a tray in front of her: Fried rice, sausage and fried *ampalaya*.

"Thank you, Corporal Asahi-san."

The Corporal bowed his head, his chin touching his neck.

Lucing wasn't a person who listed food as a top priority of life. Half the time, when she was deep in her research work, she'd forget to eat. Many a day had passed where she'd look at the clock, discover it was already midnight, and she hadn't eaten anything other than *lugao* (soupy rice) for breakfast.

Still, she knew that there'd come a time when food would be scarce in this place, and she didn't want to think of this moment and regret that she hadn't eaten what was placed before her.

So she ate, even though she hated *ampalaya.* Her mother had forced her to eat it as a child, telling her it was a very nutritious vegetable. She'd been anemic as a child and often fainted during Mass. She wasn't sure the *ampalaya* had cured her, but it had probably helped.

She finished quickly and drank her full glass of water. She thought again about the Captain. What kind of man he was. How difficult his position must be.

She thought of Inez, alone in the house with Perry. Poor thing must be going out of her mind. She should at least send her a letter of reassurance.

Quickly, she jotted a letter for Inez. Then another one for Perry. She made the letter to Perry innocuous and simple... in case she got caught with it on her person.

"Hello Boy,

Hope you and the family are well. I'll be staying here on campus for a while.

I've made some friends: Crinkles... who likes to build and repair things. Shark... who's pretty fierce and territorial about what belongs to him. And Specs. He needs them to see but he's too proud to wear them in public.

Things are getting organized here but it will take some time. Be careful and thank you for taking care of my pets."

She didn't sign it. She had nothing to report yet, so this didn't really reveal anything. This was a test run. If it was found by a curious soldier, it would read like the ramblings of a schoolgirl. If it passed the test and Perry got it without interference, she could include important messages on her subsequent messages.

As the Captain had noted, Lucing was a woman with an ability to judge character for self-serving purposes.

The Captain had warned her that she wasn't to speak to the soldiers unless spoken to. However, she sensed that Asahi was inherently so humbled by the Captain he would treat anyone affiliated with his superior with the same deference.

She hid the letters in a pocket sewed at the bottom of her skirt and opened the door.

"Corporal Asahi-san, may this woman ask when the Captain is expected to be back at the office?"

He turned to her and bowed.

"Commandant back three hours." He showed three fingers at her.

So far so good.

"Is this woman allowed to take a walk for some fresh air, Corporal Asahi-san."

Asahi's brow furrowed. He took a minute to think about it. Pointed to himself. "Must stay with Special Assistant."

Lucing decided to be daring. "Excellent, Corporal Asahi-San. This woman would welcome your company on a little walk."

Before he could think further or talk her out of it, she turned and headed down the corridor. After a moment's pause, he was right behind her. She noticed there weren't any guards along the corridors of the building. There was one at the entrance, however, and she waited for Asahi to explain their foray to the guard. In all that Japanese, she heard "Special Assistant" so she stood at attention, her eyes downcast.

But there was no problem. They joined the crowd of internees clustered together along the plaza, whispering among themselves.

One woman complained, "I had to stay in line for half an hour just to use the toilet."

Lucing hurried past them, her eyes downcast. She suddenly felt lucky she had her own toilet and shower.

Arrivals were lining up in front of the main building for registration. She saw Filipinos and half-Filipinos accompanying Americans and British in line. Apparently Filipinos married to foreigners were being interred as well.

She veered away from the main building and headed for the football field. She needed to get to the UST Publishing house, which was located near the southwest corner of the field. A tall tree grew just outside the fence between that building and the Beato Angelico Building... a tree with a small cavity chest-high along the trunk facing the campus. She and her college sweetheart used to leave notes for each other in that cavity. She had told Perry about it, and it was to be their secret post office now.

There were people gathered on the field as well. Children were chasing each other around the groups. She walked slowly, but at times it was so crowded she lost sight of Asahi. Good. That would work to her advantage.

When she finally reached the area where the tree stood, she was relieved to see the bombings hadn't destroyed the tree. It still stood there, some of its branches burnt and denuded of leaves. But at least it still stood.

She saw Asahi turn his head to address a group of internees, and she took that moment to lose herself in the crowds. In another minute she'd planted the letter in the cavity. Several minutes after that, she was at the grandstand, where she found a seat and waited for Asahi to find her.

After a few minutes passed, she climbed to a higher position on the bleacher and stood to look at the crowd. She saw the Corporal alone in the distance, looking in all directions around him. She knew that at some point, he'd turn in her direction.

When he did, she waved at him. He ploughed through the crowd towards her, ignoring the angry people who shouted after him.

She climbed down to meet him just as he got there. Poor guy was scared. And really angry.

He grabbed her arm and pulled her through the crowd all the way to their building.

At the entrance, he released his hold on her and pointed inside. She climbed the stairs to the first level, and he followed closely behind. In front of the office, he chin-bowed to her.

"Special Assistant. So sorry to lose."

"No, Corporal Asahi-san. It's my fault. It was so crowded I didn't know where I was going." She bowed all the way from the waist and murmured, "I'm so sorry."

He opened the door for her. The Captain wasn't back yet. Thank goodness.

She settled behind her desk and resumed typing her notes. She doubted Asahi would let her leave the building again. It was going to be tough being a spy when her babysitter refused to lose sight of her.

* * * * *

Eventually a routine was established and Lucing adjusted with ease.

The Captain's meetings with the Lieutenants became three times a week to twice a week to once a week, so Lucing's services didn't require as many hours as before.

Homma recalled most of the soldiers to the field, so Lieutenants Hiroku and Tomatzu were deployed to join the forces in Bataan. Lucing worried about Tomatzu's eyesight in the field. Maybe he only needed specs for reading, and he'd be fine for long distance vision.

Orashi remained behind to become the Commandant's sole Lieutenant. Internees called him Number Two.

Since Tokyo didn't have sufficient administrators to run the camp, internee particatipon in self-government was a necessity. The Dominican authorities who still resided in the Seminary tried to negotiate with the Japanese on behalf of the internees, but many of the challenges were beyond their ken.

The volunteer Truman Edwards was made head of the internee government and half a dozen committees reported to him.

Most crucial was the Sanitation and Health Committee which was responsible for building more toilets and showers, laundry and cooking facilities, overseeing disposal of garbage, and controlling the flies, mosquitoes, and rats that infested the compound.

Other committees constituted a police force, a medical committee made up of abundant medical internees, and a committee responsible for providing meals for those who couldn't provide for themselves. People staked claims to land for growing vegetables and developed alliances to protect such claims.

A British missionary who spoke fluent Japanese, Hugh Trelaney, was made liaison officer between the Japanese and the internees, though the prisoners resented his easy camaraderie with the Japanese.

Monied internees built shanties, huts which provided privacy during the day where families could eat and visit and couples could be intimate. Those without money depended on friends to give them food packages to keep them going.

Some soldiers kept the charity packages for themselves, while other soldiers were more humane, defending victims from their more greedy counterparts.

By the end of January, most internees had come to accept the fact that rescue and freedom would be a long time coming.

There was insurrection in the city, and the patrol guards on campus were reduced even more as soldiers were reassigned to patrol the streets. Thanks to the overall cooperation of the internees at Santo Tomas University, including formation of their own internee police patrols, the need for soldiers on campus was diminishing every day.

Lucing's private guard, Asahi, was reassigned to the field, and Lucing found that as long as she kept her ID badge handy, she had minimal trouble in visiting her secret post office several times a week. She'd even met with Perry a few times for a hurried conversation. He told her he was making himself useful by joining a group of insurgents who were broadcasting secretly to the populace. He refused to tell her the leader's name. It would be death to be discovered as part of this insurgent group.

* * * * *

By mid February, the number of internees at the UST camp amounted to 3200 Americans, 900 British (including Canadians and Australians), 40 Poles, 30 Dutch, and individuals from Spain, Mexico, Nicaragua,

Cuba, Russia, Belgium, Sweden, Denmark, China and Burma.

They were teachers, doctors, business executives, mining engineers, bankers, plantation owners, seamen, shoemakers, waiters, beachcombers, prostitutes, missionaries, and others.

Many of them were intelligent and were only too aware of the depressing effects of their lifestyle conditions. They used their influence to create better conditions in the camp. They held contests for the cleanest quarters, offering food (a basket of vegetables from the garden), clothing or blankets as prizes. They published a newspaper, called it the "Internews" and featured heartwarming, self-affirming articles to bolster the inhabitants. They staged variety shows, and the multi-talented internees were able to set aside their intolerable lives for a few hours each week.

All this still wasn't enough for some. In early February, two young Englishmen and an Australian escaped from the UST camp. They were captured, beaten, tortured and executed on February 15th. The volunteer leaders and the monitors of the rooms where the men lived were forced to watch. No one else tried to escape after that.

* * * * *

In early March, some ill-begotten moon shed its unfortunate rays on Lucing and an ambitious Japanese soldier caught her passing a letter to Perry across the fence. It was a damning letter. She had found paperwork on the Captain's desk naming a dozen participants of an insurgent group. She had to get those names to Perry. Warn them of the danger.

By this time, the internees knew about the Filipina professor who was assisting the Commandant oversee the camp. Her American and British professor friends were internees themselves, and they had seen her walking the grounds freely, sometimes in the company of the Commandant.

There was disagreement whether she was a traitor helping the enemy, or a loyal Filipina cooperating with the Japanese to create a better situation for her own people. Others insisted she was exchanging sexual favors to protect a subversive relative.

Nevertheless, it was true that she enjoyed certain privileges, including free access to the University grounds. She wasn't allowed to leave the camp without a guard, and for that reason, Lucing never even thought of visiting Inez and the children. She would never ever risk bringing attention to them in their safe little house.

But she took chances for herself. Food was becoming scarce. The Japanese didn't hesitate to confiscate bags of rice, fruit and vegetables from the city merchants to feed their soldiers. Lucing worried about Inez and the children. she knew Perry was looking out for them, but if food wasn't available, what could he do?

The busier the Captain got, the less often he left his office. The kitchen delivered him food supplies, so it became Lucing's job to make meals for him. She'd hide a handful of rice in her skirt pocket whenever she cooked, and it wasn't much, but twice she'd managed to get a small bag of rice across the fence for Perry to deliver to Inez.

It was time for another delivery. She'd already arranged to meet with Perry that night while the Captain was attending roll call.

7:30 roll call was effectively curfew hour for the internees. 30 to 50 people were crowded together in small classrooms, segregated by sex, and Japanese administrators took the roll every day. Virtually all the buildings were occupied by internees, except the Central Seminary, the first two floors of the Main Building, and the Publishing House.

Edwards, Trelaney and some other committee members were exempt from curfew. So was Lucing.

She was careful not to abuse that privilege. At first, she timed her outings at 7:00 after the Captain left, walking along the Plaza, enjoying her time away from the stuffy office. She only stayed five or ten minutes after curfew, but as time went on, she extended her stay, so that by late January, the patrol guards were accustomed to seeing her stroll by as late as 8:30.

It was about 7:15 p.m. when she reached her post office tree.

She checked to see if there were any guards patrolling the area. Saw no one. She approached the fence.

Because the guards weren't able to patrol the entire perimeter of the spearheaded iron fence, they had placed bamboo mats over the fence to prevent friends and relatives from passing food, clothing and other objects to the internees. It felt too much like a zoo, where visitors fed the animals behind the cage.

Perry had managed to cut a small opening in the mat, enough that Lucing could pass her hand through to the cavity in the trunk of her post office tree.

The cavity was too small to hold a small bag of rice, so she generally had to set up a time for him to come by for a pickup.

Tonight was a pickup night. The rice was in six paper packets she'd placed in pockets at the hem of her long skirt. Once hidden behind the building, she emptied the paper packets into a cloth bag and waited for Perry to open the flap. That was her signal he was ready to receive her letter and bag.

His hand came through. She placed the bag of rice in it and his hand disappeared. She waited until his hand appeared again. She handed him the letter.

Quickly checking to see if any guards were around, she leaned close to the fence and whispered.

"Inez and the children?"

"I don't know, Lucing."

That didn't bode well. Her stomach lurched. If her sister and the children were in danger, she'd have to do something.

"We think they're on to us. I haven't been at the house in case they're following me."

Lucing thought she heard someone behind her. She turned. Saw no one.

"In case anything happens to me... can I tell someone about your letters. Where to pick them up?"

"Be sure they can be trusted. Now get out of here. Read the letter and get out of here."

"What letter?" A hand clamped on her bicep and Lucing knew she was in trouble. She tried to free herself and kicked wildly, jabbing her elbow against the man's chest. He grunted. A shot rang out and punctured the bamboo mat.

She heard Perry moan, and then heard his feet running down the street. At least he could still run.

She kicked the soldier who was trying to pull aside the mat, but he barely felt it and ignored her.   She turned and took off. Seconds later, a body thudded against her and she fell. She struggled to free herself, her right hand going to the hem of her skirt where she found a pocket. Empty. Wrong pocket.

A fist landed against the side of her face and a groan escaped. She could't help it. Tried another pocket. There. Her ID badge. And a letter. She pulled them out, kicking and trying to free herself. Another blow. Closer to her eye this time.

Just before she blacked out, she thought, "I'm gonna look a mess tomorrow."

* * * * *

Lucing opened her eyes and saw a familiar face hovering over her. She closed them again and tried to make sense of her situation.

The man was Filipino with kind eyes behind glasses, a round face and thick lips. She knew him from somewhere.

Ah. The medical director of the hospital. His name was... Ricardo... no... Rogerio Bonaventura.

She opened her eyes again and muttered, "Hi, Doccturrr Vvv...Bbbb."

The Japanese plans to occupy Manila included the plan to keep Santo Tomas University as intact as possible. But war being war, it had sustained its share of damage. The San Juan de Diyos Hospital had been repaired to functional capacity, with nuns serving as nurses.

When the Japanese arrived to take the city, Dr. Rogerio Bonaventura had sent his family to relatives in Cebu but he himself had refused to vacate the hospital. He would be needed, and it was as simple as that.

Here in front of him was proof that this place needed him. He looked at Lucing and wondered how she'd gotten so beaten up. He'd heard about her assistant work with the Commandant, but if anything, that should have protected her from... this kind of damage.

"Don't talk. How do you feel?"

"Grrroggggggy."

"That's the painkillers. You've got a few broken ribs, and you'll be black and blue for a few weeks, but you'll be fine."

Lucing looked around. It hurt to move but at least she could move. She was in her room. Not at the hospital.

A figure moved in her line of vision. The Captain... looking worried and really really angry. At her?

He threw her badge on the bed.

"That was in your hand, and that's why you're still alive."

She started to respond but Dr. Rogerio shook his head at her. In warning?

The Captain threw a crumpled piece of paper on the bed next to the badge. "That was also in your hand."

Lucing closed her eyes and took a deep breath. The letter. Thank God.

"I... I..."

"Don't talk." Dr. Rogerio stood up and faced the Captain. "Are you sure you don't want her in the hospital?"

"No hospital."

"I can keep better track..."

"No hospital."

"Sir." Dr. Rogerio bowed to the Captain. Picked up his bag and headed for the door. "I'll come by tomorrow to see how she's doing, Commandant." He closed the door behind him as quietly as possible.

Not that it made a difference to Lucing. She felt like hell. She kept her eyes closed. God, she was in for it now.

The Captain pulled up a chair and picked up the letter. He read aloud:

"March 11, 1942
"Dear Sister,

I pray for you and the children every night before I go to bed. I worry if you have enough food. If you are all safe and healthy.

I am very busy assisting the Commandant here at UST. Funny enough, I like my work. I feel useful and appreciated. The Commandant is intelligent, thorough, and fair. Our countries may be at war with one another, but he's not at war with me or even with the internees. He never forgets that we're all human and that sometimes we are all swept up in events beyond our control.

Please kiss the children for me. Be very careful.

Love, Lucing

"You risked your life for this?"

Lucing opened her eyes and looked into his. She tried to smile.

"My shisssterrr..."

He put a finger over her mouth. Stood up and gazed at her with cold judgment.

"As Commandant of this camp, it's my responsibility to maintain discipline here. You were caught disregarding rules about passing messages to family without going through the necessary protocols. Fortunately, the message appears... harmless enough. But let's be clear, Dr. Trinidad, as Commandant I will do whatever my job requires me to do."

"I dddhow that."

He lifted a finger to silence her. Sat down on the chair and moved closer to her. Bent towards her face. And spoke softly.

"Otherwise, between you and me, I'm just a man. There are a lot of things I don't know. I don't know that you're stealing rice from our supply and passing it on to your sister. I don't know that you search my desk for information to pass on to your insurgent friends. I don't know that you've been sending messages since the first week you came to work for me. I don't know any of this because as your discerning letter says, I have no war with you. Nor your sister."

Lucing's eyes were wide open now. He had known all along. From the very beginning.

"The problem is, Doctor, that if the wrong person knew these things and came to me about it, I would no longer be just a man. I would have to be Commandant of this camp. And I would have to do my job."

Lucing nodded. She understood.

"Just so you know. Private Takata was rewarded for his diligence in catching you. He wanted to join Homma's forces, so I've reassigned him to the field."

He grinned his lopsided grin. "That was smart of you to have a harmless letter ready... just in case."

He left the room then. As groggy and dazed as Lucing felt, her mind worked and whirled in a frenzy of thoughts. He had known all along. And had allowed her to get away with it. Emotions surfaced and roiled inside her. Tears dripped from her sore eyes.

Dr. Rogerio came the next day to approve her healing process. He left painkillers and instructions for the Captain.

The Captain cooked and fed her *lugao* filled with rich broth and small pieces of chicken for two days. They barely spoke to each other at such times. Hello and how-are-you. That was it. Fortunately, she could maneuver herself to the toilet, so that wasn't an issue. She couldn't stand long enough to take a shower, but oh well.

On the third day, after the Captain fed her, he undressed her carefully. Put the chair in the shower and arranged her on it. Washed her hair. Her body. Dried her with gentle pats of the towel. By the time he was done, her hunger for him was no longer anything she could control.

When he was carrying her to her bed, she asked him, "Why are you so kind to me?"

A lopsided grin, "You remind me of my Texas girl. Not as blonde. Certainly a lot smarter. And just as sassy."

When he laid her down on the bed, she pulled his face down and kissed him. He lay down beside her and showed her he was as tender a lover as he was a man.

* * * * *

Perry was fine. Inez had sent Julio to get Manang Maya, who was known in the neighborhood as the local *mangkukulam,* a healer or medicine woman. That amazing woman had taken one look at the wound. Announced, "No bullet. Went right through his shoulder." Had bandaged Perry swiftly and efficiently.

"Would you believe I was a nurse twenty years ago?"

Inez could and did. She decided she loved this old woman.

They had dragged the mattress from the wooden couch to the basement and made up a bed for Perry. When Inez asked him how he'd gotten shot, he'd answered, "Some idiot soldier saw me stealing some rice. Don't worry, I lost him."

She was on her way up the stairs when she saw Perry pull a piece of paper out of his shoe and hand it to Manang Maya. He was whispering directions to the old woman by the time Inez reached the top of the stairs.

She couldn't believe he'd risk his life for a small bag of rice like that. And she couldn't believe she was actually glad to see his brown face and crooked teeth again.

Two days after Perry's return, there was a knock on the door. The children hung on to her as she opened the door.

A Japanese soldier stood there, muscular and not too tall. He wasn't bad looking. Maybe early 40's.

Immediately she bowed to the waist. Julio and Cencia did the same.

He handed her a large bag. "Your sister wanted me to give this to you."

She took the heavy bag and looked inside. Rice. Fruit. Vegetables. Meat. And a sheet of wrinkled paper.

When she looked up to thank the soldier, he was walking hurriedly away. He hadn't even given his name.

She opened the sheet of paper. A letter from Lucing. She was fine and she enjoyed assisting the Commandant. In fact, according to the letter, the Commandant was an intelligent and fair man.

She sighed in relief. She hoped Lucing was right. Her sister had always been a good judge of character, but it was her life that hung in the balance now. And to be sending her food like this... Lucing must have acquired more clout than she had anticipated.

* * * * *

CHAPTER 13
REINFORCEMENTS
Malinao and Bataan, Philippines, 1942

The roads weren't as crowded as they had been on the journey from Manila to Balayan. People had entrenched themselves where they felt safest from the enemy and were staying put.

As the crow flies, Malinao was only about three miles distant from Banga, but it was across deeply wooded areas, mountains and rough terrain, and the road's course winded back and forth, and side to side. Traveling on the dirt roads and rough terrain would ultimately be nearly 13 miles.

Rissing wasn't as self-confident and assured of safety on this trip. She didn't have Renzo and Meling to back her up. She needed her Lieutenants to bolster her Captain status.

Yet, in a way, it was easier. She had less people to worry about. Her children were trained not to complain, not to make demands, nor to question her leadership. They trusted her completely, and even if they personally might hesitate at her orders, at least they ultimately obeyed.

She named the *carabao* "Clara." She had spoken to Clara the night before departure and explained to her that they needed her help.

They wouldn't be able to accomplish their goal without her cooperation. She'd asked the *carabao* to be strong and steady, promising that they'd give her plenty of rest and food.

Clara didn't discernibly respond one way or the other as far as Rissing could tell, but Rissing was confident that the *carabao* would cooperate.

They rested every three hours and as long as there was grass or other vegetation, Rissing let the *carabao* graze while they rested.

On the first day, they only traveled about five miles. The boys wanted to walk and she was actually glad to lessen the load for Clara, but that meant she wanted to rest long enough for Ramon and JoJo to recover from the walk.

On the first night, they found a small clearing not too far from the road protected by trees and ground flora screening them from the road. There were several small fire pits as well as trash receptacles, so Rissing knew that this was a common resting area for travelers.

She and the boys collected branches and twigs, made a fire and cooked some chicken steeped in lard to keep them from spoiling. They crushed tomatoes in water and added salt to the mix; added that to the rice; ate it with the chicken and it was a good meal.

Lessie and Ramon took first watch, sitting on the driver's seat in the oxcart. Whenever he got sleepy, Ramon jumped to the ground and walked around the camp, the gun weighing down his pants pocket.

Inside the oxcart, Rissing was able to get some rest with little Tonia, Flora and JoJo. After several hours, Lessie woke Rissing, and she and JoJo traded off with her and Ramon.

It was hard to keep her eyes open. She wouldn't let JoJo take the gun but she allowed him to carry the bolo knife. At the farm, he'd gotten proficient in killing chickens by twisting off their heads, and then using the knife to cut off the heads.

With the knife slung over his shoulder, he strutted around their camp like a vigilant boy soldier.

Half an hour after Rissing's watch, Clara gave a little snort and started moving away from camp. Rissing had unyoked her so she could be comfortable, tying a rope around her neck which she secured to the oxcart. Rissing's eyes flew open when she heard the snort. She saw JoJo running to catch the *carabao*.

By the time Rissing had stepped down from the cart, JoJo was shouting, "*Huy! Huy!*"

Rissing hurried to where Clara was now standing still. JoJo stood beside the carabao, holding Clara's rope in one hand. In his other hand, he held his bolo high, ready to strike at the intruder in their camp. He was shouting at the little dark figure. By the flickering light of the camp fire, Rissing could just make out that the figure was only slightly bigger than 7-year-old JoJo.

"JoJo, *maingat*."

She ran up to the little man, both hands held high. He was holding a wooden spear which was pointed at JoJo. She walked toward the little man and he backed away from her, dragging one foot.

The outside of his left leg several inches above his ankle had a two-inch gash crusted with dried blood.

"He was trying to steal Clara, Ma!"

She tried to speak calmly, "*Tahimik. Tahimik.*" If the little man didn't understand Tagalog, maybe he'd at least feel her good intentions.

By then, Lessie and Ramon were awake. In the oxcart, Lessie had her arms around Flora, whose eyes were wide open in fear. But, God bless her, she wasn't crying or screaming in panic. Tonia hadn't woken up.

"Ramon. Take Clara and tie her to the oxcart." Ramon jumped down and took the *carabao* away.

Without Clara to block the flickering campfire light, Rissing could see that the little man wore a loincloth, and he had patterned scars on his breasts and arms. He was dark brown with tightly curled, wiry hair, small round nose and dark shining eyes. Rissing had heard about people like him. He was a race which the Spanish colonists called a Negrito. Filipinos called them Aetas.

Her father had told her about them. They were aborigine-like nomads who didn't like to stay in one place, traveling through the forests and mountains. She didn't remember her father say that they were dangerous.

Rissing could see that he was scared too. He was still holding his spear, now pointed at Rissing.

She touched her chest, "Rissing." Pointed to him and waited to see what he would say.

After a few moments, he nodded his head, touched his own chest and responded in a high raspy voice, "Babaah".

Rissing pointed to JoJo and said his name. Then she did the same with Ramon.

By now Lessie and Flora were standing beside Rissing, so she introduced them too... even little Flora. He nodded the entire time.

"JoJo, put down your knife." She could see that his thin arms were trembling from the weight of the knife lifted high.

"Ma, he tried to steal Clara!"

"He's hurt. Maybe he just needed a ride. JoJo, put it down."

JoJo put the knife down but stood ready to grab it again, arms hanging by his side.

"Ramon, please get my medicine kit. Lessie, bring the leftovers from supper."

She didn't take her eyes off Babaah while her troops did as they were asked.

When Ramon handed her the medicine kit, Rissing pointed to Babaah's spear and pointed to the ground. He hesitated but did as she asked and placed his spear on the ground. Then she pointed to the wound on his leg and then at the fire.

Now she'd have to trust him. Rissing turned her back and walked to the fire, waiting for him. He picked up his spear and used it as support as he hobbled to the fire and sat down, his legs stretched before him.

JoJo picked up the knife and stood beside her, and she didn't say anything. If Babaah was going to hang on his spear, it was only right that JoJo hang on to the knife.

Lessie brought the leftovers which she handed to Babaah. The little man looked at the food and ignoring the utensils in Lessie's other hand, began to use his hands to scoop the food into his mouth with ravenous gusto. While he ate, Rissing cleaned the crusts of blood from Babaah's leg. He watched her pour antiseptic on the wound, but barely flinched.

Well, why would he? Someone who cuts his own skin and pours lime on it to create scars wouldn't flinch at a little antiseptic.

She wrapped a bandage around the wound and Babaah didn't resist that either. If anything, he probably would treasure his leg scar as just another token of his manhood.

He finished the leftovers quickly and nodded at Rissing. She was putting her medicine kit back together when little Flora ran past her and towards Babaah, extending a slice of mango in her little hand.

Rissing held her breath and JoJo lifted his knife in readiness. But Babaah grinned, took the mango from Flora and nodded his head at the little girl.

"Everyone back to bed. I don't think Babaah will try to steal Clara tonight. We need our rest for tomorrow."

"I'm not sleeping. I'm going to keep an eye on him, Ma."

"If you want to, JoJo."

"Me too," insisted Ramon.

She nodded. It would be good experience for them both to stay up if that was what they wanted to do. She didn't intend to discourage her boys when they were acting to protect and defend the women in their group.

Babaah shifted his position by the fire. Except, instead of facing the wagon and the fire, he was facing out, as if protecting the camp, grasping his spear in readiness. He didn't look like he'd be going to sleep either.

When Rissing opened her eyes in the pre-dawn of the morning, she saw her two boys seated a short distance from Babaah, supporting each other back to back, their little faces drooping to their chests, fast asleep.

Babaah, on the other hand, was wide awake. She sat up on the driver's seat, where she'd stretched out, and he turned his head to her.

When he saw that she was awake, he nodded his head and grinned at her.

They shared their breakfast of *champorado*, *tuyo*, and fruit with Babaah. JoJo loved *champorado* for breakfast. These days *malagkit* (sticky rice) wasn't always readily available. Before the war, her children often made *champorado* for themselves, cooking *malagkit* in coconut milk, sweetening it with sugar and adding chocolate powder to the mix. If coconut milk wasn't handy, dairy milk would do, or canned Pet evaporated milk.

Babaah was delighted with it, slurping loudly and nodding his head at her.

After breakfast, they yoked Clara to the oxcart and prepared to continue their journey.

Babaah watched them as Rissing tugged on the reins to signal Clara to move. Clara headed for the exit to the clearing and Rissing looked back.

The little man was still standing like a statue, staring after them.

She tugged for Clara to stop. "JoJo, scoot over to make room for Babaah."

"Ma!"

She gave him a look and he shook his head in disapproval. But he did what she asked.

Then Rissing looked at Babaah and summoned him with a toss of her head.

He grinned and limped his way to the oxcart. Got in beside JoJo, thumping the butt of his spear on the ground to signal he was ready.

Rissing smiled to herself.

They traveled for three hours and took their first break. They drank water and ate hard boiled eggs and fruit.

When Rissing pointed to Babaah's leg wound, shook her head in puzzlement, and lifted her shoulders, both hands palm up, the little man stood up in front of them and re-enacted the scenario of how he'd gotten the gash.

Apparently he was a quick healer, barely limping as he mimed running in place, spear held ready to strike. He pointed at the ground, made horns on his head with a finger of each hand, then threw his spear. Pretended he was the boar running full tilt to attack him, moved again to take his position as he used his left hand to depict the boar swiping at his leg. Used his hands to show that blood was gushing out of the leg.

He fell to the ground and used his hands to stop the flow of blood. Grabbed some vegetation which he held against the wound. Grimaced to indicate he was feeling pain.

Then used his hand to show other hunters passing by him, chasing after the boar. Finally, he waved goodbye after the hunters. Meeting Rissing's eyes, he shrugged his shoulders, hands spread out in puzzlement as Rissing had done.

Flora jumped up and ran to Babaah, clapping her hands in delight at the reenactment. The little man giggled and nodded his head at Flora.

Glancing at her boys, she could tell Ramon and JoJo had been taken in by his antics as well.

From what Rissing could make out, Babaah had been hunting with his group, had gotten sideswiped by the boar, and when the rest of the hunters had gone chasing after the boar, they hadn't come back to get him.

Maybe they'd lost him. Maybe they assumed he went back to their camp. But he ultimately ended up alone and had gotten lost.

What puzzled Rissing was why he would choose to travel with her and the boys, complete strangers, instead of trying to catch up with his people. His wound looked at least a day old. Maybe he thought it was too late to catch up. Or maybe it was easier to accept Rissing's invitation to join her group until he felt strong enough to wander the woods looking for his people.

It didn't matter why he was willing to join her group. She'd gladly welcome his company.

In the scheme of things, he was just one little Aeta in a world gone amok with warring Japanese and Filipinos, but he was reinforcement for her troops... the protector she had told Ignacio she would find to accompany. Here he was, and she intended to take whatever God, or Santo Nino, or her *kaluluwa* sent her.

* * * * *

At Bataan, by the end of March, only a fourth of the original 80,000 MacArthur defenders were combat-effective, not only because of battle injuries, but by crippling disease and malnutrition. To add insult to injury, American and Filipino troops were put on quarter rations (1000 calories, or eight to 10 ounces of rice a day, plus an ounce or two of fish or canned meat). Men were so desperate they were forcing themselves to eat rotting chunks of dead animal flesh.

A series of debilitating events further crippled the American/Filipino forces. While an occasional submarine carrying food or ammunition did surface at Mindanao or Corregidor, the Japanese held the key bases in southern Luzon and the majority of such ships were destroyed before reaching the Filipino garrisons. Japanese Navy aircraft began daily bombings of Corregidor, and, most damning of all, Homma's troops were reinforced with 21,000 fresh troops, 150 new field guns and 60 bombers.

On March 26th, to add to the dismay of the troops, the Japanese bombings of Corregidor knocked out power for freezers containing 24,000 pounds of carabao meat. The troops attempted to transport the frozen meat from Corregidor to Bataan for immediate consumption by the soldiers, but Japanese air attacks foiled this move and the meat spoiled.

From Australia, MacArthur, per President Roosevelt's orders, radioed Wainwright, "Under no conditions should Bataan be surrendered. Any action is preferable to capitulation." Meanwhile, Japanese troops moved toward Mount Samat, the dominant position which commanded view of the battlefield below.

April 3rd was Good Friday for the Catholic Filipinos, and anniversary of the death of Emperor Jimmu, ancestor of Hirohito, for the Japanese. A five-hour air and artillery bombardment, followed by a massive assault of armor and infantry, barraged the center of the American/Filipino line. There was no hope of a successful defense against this barrage. The emaciated American/Filipino forces were outmanned, outgunned and seriously outmatched.

By nightfall, the crude roads and trails were clogged with thousands of Americans and Filipinos staggering away from the defense line.

Japanese tanks and infantry pressed on, while Zeroes swept the ground with ruthless strafing runs.

On April 7th, Japanese aircraft attacked an American field hospital which had large crosses painted on the roof, killing 89 and wounding 101. A large portion of the hospital's drug supplies were destroyed in this attack.

As the front crumbled and morale plummeted, American demolition teams at Mariveles, on Bataan's southern tip, blew up the remaining ammunition stock piles and set fuel supplies afire. 2000 people, including 104 nurses, managed to escape to Corregidor by small boats and barge.

* * * * *

Torio was one of the 2000. When it got dark and most of the battle noises had subsided, he climbed a tree and tied himself with some of his handcrafted viney ropes to the tree so he wouldn't fall once he'd fallen asleep. He slept until light filtered through the leaves of the trees... enough to see where he was going.

There was still water in his canteen so he took enough to fill his stomach. He had no food so the water would have to do.

He avoided the trails and roads because he knew those would be the focus of aerial strafing runs.

He was on the run. He didn't know how fast the Japanese soldiers were moving, but he figured that they'd be fueled by the thought of victory, adrenalin pumping them with the speed and blitzkrieg frenzy of conquerors in an impossible battle.

As he ran, his breath rasping, his body struggling to find strength enough to fuel his malaria-ridden, malnutritioned body, he bypassed fellow soldiers struggling through the thick jungle beside him. Many were badly wounded, managing to move at a half-run. Occasionally, Torio stumbled on someone whose life had run out.

When he stumbled on an outgrowth and landed on the ground, his face inches from the face of the soldier crumpled on the ground, the soldier whispered, "Help me."

He sat up and gauged the man's injuries. He had a scalp wound and one ear had been torn off. His left bicep had taken a bullet. Torio tore off the man's sleeve and used it to wrap the head and bicep injuries. There wasn't time for anything else. Then he helped the man stand.

Together, they adjusted themselves so that Torio supported the wounded soldier as they negotiated their way around the trees. After a while, Torio could feel the soldier's weight dragging them down. The soldier had stopped moving his legs beside him. He stopped and checked the soldier's vital signs.

Dead. He'd been carrying a man who'd probably been dead for the last ten minutes of his own struggle down the wooded slope.

He knelt on the ground, wanting to scream. Wanting to cry. The sounds of battle had slowly moved closer as the added weight of the wounded soldier had slowed him down. The burden had endangered his own life.

But, no, he didn't have time for regret. He had to conserve his energy. Five minutes later, he stumbled on another soldier. This one's legs were shot up, and he was barely conscious. His voice croaked to him in pain, "Help." At least it wasn't a head wound. Unless he'd lost too much blood, this one might survive.

How could he walk away and not help a fellow soldier? If that were him on the ground, wouldn't he want someone to stop and help him? This poor man probably had a wife and children. Just like him. He probably wanted to outlive this war and get back to his family. Just like he did. And no doubt, just like his own life, despite the setbacks and challenges which had beset his daily routines, that life was heaven and paradise compared to this. Compared to now.

So Torio helped the man up, wrapping the soldier's arms around his own neck, and half-carried, half-dragged the wounded man on his own back. At least it was downhill. He could tell from the sounds of battle – gunfire, shouts and screaming – that the Japanese were still gaining on him.

He didn't know how much longer he could carry this dead weight on his back. Dead weight. As he thought this, a blood-spattered American soldier passed him. Stopped. Turned to him.

"*Siya ay patay.*"

Torio stopped. Released his hold on the man's arms around his neck. Let the body slide to the ground. He knelt on the ground beside the wounded soldier and looked down at the man. He was exhausted. His knees wouldn't work on their own, and he had to use his hands to push himself up.

As he straightened, the soldier's eyes slowly opened. He was alive. Glazed in raw pain and a desperate determination to survive, those eyes burned into Torio's soul and branded him forever.

He looked down at the soldier, numb with hopelessness. Carrying this wounded man had depleted his reserves, but at the moment he'd picked up the man, he'd committed himself to the responsibility of keeping him alive. How could he just walk away now?

He felt a hand on his shoulder. Again he heard the soft American voice behind him, "*Patay na siya.*"

Realization flooded through him. This American soldier was right. He had to be practical. Chances were the wounded soldier wouldn't survive. For him to shoulder the responsibility of keeping him alive... it was beyond his ability. He had to accept that.

The soldier on the ground saw Torio's dilemma. Nodded his head once in understanding. And closed his eyes. Those blazing lights no longer shone their plea at him, but he still felt the burning brand in his soul.

The American soldier pulled at Torio, and he allowed himself to be led away. He followed the American, head bowed. He didn't want this American to see the tears flooding down his face.

"My name's Jack. We need to get out of here. Now."

Though the American had a bandage around his thigh, he moved easily enough. Torio guessed the man was early 40's and had seen battle before this one. He wore Lieutenant stripes and had an air of authority which Torio immediately respected. Like everyone else, he'd probably lost weight, but he moved in a way which suggested strength and competence. This man was a much better companion than a wounded one he'd have to carry on his back.

They passed more wounded soldiers asking for their help. Jack gave them a quick once-over check, then shook his head at Torio. If the man wasn't strong enough to move on his own, he wasn't strong enough to survive without medical help.

They headed downhill towards Manila Bay.

Torio took a deep breath and followed the American. He forced himself to keep up. He would not be a burden which the American would be forced to leave behind.

After several miles, someone stepped out behind a tree, pointing a gun at them. He was a freckled, red-haired American who looked fresh out of school. Like Torio and Jack, he was mud-splattered and bloody, though Torio didn't see any wounds on him. His eyes were young and panicked.

Jack nodded at him, "Easy, soldier."

The young boy-man lowered his rifle and saluted Jack.

"I'm Jack. This is Torio."

"I'm… Billy. From Iowa."

Fear oozed out of Billy's pores like sweat on a hot Manila day. Torio recognized it. But he also recognized that this young man's fears were different from his own. Billy hadn't lived life yet. He was afraid for himself… that he'd die and never taste the enlivening rush of life again. That he had never yet experienced the greatest pleasures and the greatest joys. That it would all just end.

Torio felt sympathy for Billy. His own fears weren't about pain or death. His fears were about loss… that he'd never see Rissing or his children again… that they'd die because he wasn't there to protect them.

Unlike Billy, he'd tasted some aspects of the pleasures and joy of life. He'd fallen in love with an exceptional woman. He'd gotten married and fathered children. He'd saved the life of a drowning boy. He'd established a history for himself, and this young boy-man… he hadn't experienced any of that yet.

So he reached over and grasped Billy's shoulder tightly, "Come with us."

After traveling for half an hour, they took a break and sat in an area thickly clustered with trees. It was late morning and Torio was starving... as he had been the last two days. He suspected the other two were hungry as well.

Torio took out his knife and punctured through a rotting log, scraping through the log until he saw white larvae squirming inside the log. He picked up a few and tossed them into his mouth, chewing vigorously. He'd gotten over his squeamishness long ago.

Billy stared at him in horror. "What're you doing?"

Torio grunted, "Protein."

Jack took out his knife and skewered a larva which he slowly put into his mouth.

Nodding, Torio scraped out another area of the log. "I just pretend it's shrimp."

Jack skewered another larva and offered it to Billy. "Go on." Billy slowly used his fingers to retrieve the larva. It wriggled between his two fingers. Jack and Torio stared at him expectantly. Billy put the thing into his mouth.

After crunching down on another piece, Jack advised Billy, "Chew and swallow as fast as you can."

Billy chewed and swallowed. Seconds later, he turned his head and threw up on the ground beside him.

Jack and Torio looked at each other. They didn't laugh. They'd been there themselves.

Hours later, they cleared the trees and reached the beach. Someone was shouting, "If you can get to Miraveles, there are still ships there." Some soldiers were running along the beach towards Miraveles in the distance.

There weren't planes here yet. Most were clustered around Mount Sumat in support of the offensive to take that commanding position.

Torio and his newfound companions stared at the panic and chaos before them. Along the beach itself, they saw dozens of soldiers getting into fishing vessels and small boats. It was very apparent that there wouldn't be room for all the soldiers on those boats.

A few hundred yards away, two soldiers were trying to get on a barge, but those already on the barge were shouting at them.

"No more room. Get off."

Corregidor was everyone's destination – the island where McArthur and President Quezon had claimed as their last bastion of defense. At its shortest distance from the Bataan Peninsula, it was only seven miles from shore. If he had to, Torio knew he could swim it. The problem was... Manila Bay was famous for its shark-infested waters.

Billy whispered, "Oh, God. There's no room for us."

Jack looked at Torio, "We could build a raft."

"What're you talking about? We don't have time!"

Jack and Torio ignored Billy's protest. They turned back into the forest. After a while, Billy ran after them.

After some discussion, Torio and Jack had agreed on the construction of the raft.

They'd collected six logs between six to eight feet long, each one about 14 inches in diameter. Torio had three long lengths of rope in his pack... woven on nights when he couldn't sleep. He'd often thought of his friends who'd sailed through the air with him Tarzan-style.

He hadn't seen Pasqual and Barniz again once he'd integrated into the battle, but he thought of them on those sleepless nights as he twisted the fibrous lengths of tree branches together... just like he'd taught them. He'd done it calm his mind, as well as to resupply his pack.

Now, it was proving crucial. Jack had a length of rope in his pack which they used to supplement Torio's hand-woven ropes, and Billy gathered some long vines which they used to bolster their raft even more.

The raft consisted of three logs tied to three logs crosswise beneath it. They'd taken time to cut seats on the lower logs so the upper logs would rest more firmly on them and not roll around.

The lower set of logs were positioned far enough apart to support the upper set of logs. The upper set of three logs were gapped only enough to create an upper platform about five feet wide. They had chosen the longest logs for the upper platform, so it had a usable surface almost eight feet long.

Three two-inch diameter poles had been embedded upright atop the length of the central upper log. They attached their packs and shoes to the four-foot length of the poles. If the waters got too rough, they could hang on to those poles for support.

To facilitate movement of the raft, Torio had tied some twigs and branches together to create three paddles, each with four-foot long handles.

The gaps between the logs could be a problem in Manila Bay's shark-infested waters. They'd have to be careful not to let any body parts dangle into the water. For now, they tossed branches and leaves onto the surface of the raft to create a bedding of sorts. They didn't have time to secure these smaller pieces so they'd probably float away when the first wave hit them.

Yes, the raft would float, but that was about it. A man lying down could fit on the raft comfortably. Three men sitting down would weigh it down considerably. But they had no choice. They'd used up nearly two hours to look for logs and build this flimsy raft, all the while the sounds of battle got closer and closer.

When they were finally finished, they dragged it to the beach. As they got ready to push it into the water, Billy pointed, "Look, there's a boat."

Sure enough, a boat, scraped by the water to the color of the sand, was held in place with big rocks against its sides.

Billy ran towards the boat. After a while, Jack ran after their young companion and helped him move the rocks. Together they pushed it into the water. Jack waved his paddle at Torio, "Come with us. This is a lot safer than that raft!"

Torio waved his paddle back at them. "I'm okay!" Torio pushed the raft into the water. Yes, it was less sturdy than a raft, but logs floated no matter what. Boats sunk.

He attached his paddle to the raft with a long vine so he wouldn't lose it in rough waters.

When he was in deep enough water, he clambered onto the raft. It took some moments for him to find the centerweight of the raft. When he did, he located a gap on the raft large enough for his paddle. Since he didn't have someone to counter his movements, unless he was dead center, the raft would move either to the left or right... not straight ahead, which was where he wanted to go.

Behind him, he could see more soldiers emerging out of the jungle. There were no more barges or boats. There were logs that littered the beach. He saw soldiers grabbing the logs, pushing them into the water. For them, there wasn't time to build a raft.

When he saw Filipino and American soldiers falling along the shore, he knew the Japanese had reached the edge of the jungle. He turned away. There was nothing he could do.

He concentrated on controlling his raft. It took him a while to figure out what angle to hold the paddle, how much force to use to propel the raft, and to find a position comfortable enough to maintain a steady, rhythmic movement of the paddle.

Torio's intuitive ability to merge his consciousness with the water made all this seem effortless. However, just as a tightrope walker can make walking on rope seem effortless, that didn't mean it was easy for anyone else.

It wasn't easy to move a raft forward with a single roughly made paddle. Once Torio placed the paddle in the water and felt the flow of water movement beneath the raft, he knew immediately it was too short and too flimsy to be truly effective. It would have no effect against any significant underwater currents.

Still, the currents were moving him away from shore... away from the enemy, and for now, that was good enough.

After some time, he heard shouts behind him and turned his head to see Jack and Billy on their small boat. They were paddling frantically towards him and shouting his name. He turned his head and watched their boat move towards him. It moved like a pregnant cow instead of like a flying fish.

Billy was shouting, "Torio! We've got a leak. We're sinking!"

If they had made it this far, about a mile from the beach, it couldn't be a large leak. A single man might still have made it to Corregidor if he took time to bail the water out. But two men were too heavy. If he'd been in the boat with them, it would have taken in water a lot faster.

They finally pulled alongside him, and he helped Billy onto the raft. Jack managed to clamber on by himself. The raft shifted and rocked as the two men found their places on it, but it stabilized after a while.

They all stared at the boat slowly filling up with water.

Billy's voice was defensive, "It was a good boat. You couldn't really tell it had a leak."

Jack agreed, "It's repairable."

Torio grabbed the rope on the boat and tied it to the back of their raft. "If it slows us down too much, we'll let it go."

Torio placed Jack and Billy on each side of the raft. He took position in the front to maneuver the direction of the raft with his paddle. After some experimentation, they managed to figure out how to use their paddles to control the movement of the raft.

With the other two helping Torio, the raft made faster progress in the water, though they couldn't totally escape the strong currents. Some distance away from them, they heard men shouting at each other on one of the barges. Apparently a boat was sinking, and four men were trying to clamber up the barge, which was already so full that water was sloshing onto the deck.

The men on the barge were trying to push the four men off.

"The barge can't hold any more."

"For God's sake, just let us hang on!"

One of the men lost his hold on the barge and fell into the water. A moment later he was screaming, "Sharks! Sharks!" One minute Torio was looking at the man's head bobbing in the water, and the next... the man was gone.

An arm floated to the surface of the water, and the water turned red around the barge. More men on the barge were shouting now, until they successfully shoved the other three men into the water. The barge slowly moved off, leaving the three behind.

Torio stood and waved his arms. "Here! We can take three men."

Billy turned to him in dismay. Torio ignored him. Jack took up the shout with Torio, "Hurry! Here!"

The men in the water began swimming towards the raft. Many soldiers had plunged into the water at the shore, hoping to swim to Corregidor. Torio knew that most of the sharks were having a feast in the shallower waters by the beach. He hoped that the first man already under attack by the sharks around the barge was enough distraction to keep any others in the area busy.

Meanwhile, Torio and Jack used their paddles to maneuver their raft closer to the men. Two men were swimming swiftly towards them, only yards away. The third man was making slower progress.

Jack helped the first man onto the raft, a middle-aged Filipino with muscular arms and legs. He was taking deep gulps of breath. "The third guy... his left arm's shot pretty bad. He can't swim too good."

That was all Torio needed to hear. Without hesitation, he dove into the water and headed for the third man. He moved like a seal towards the flailing man. If the man was wounded, the scent of his blood would attract sharks towards him. If it hadn't already.

He reached the man, grabbed him around the chest, and used his powerful side stroke to propel them in the water. His swimming muscles, so in tune with the water, automatically adjusted to flows and currents and ebbs, and before he knew it, they had reached the raft, where the others pulled the third man up and into the raft.

Billy helped him onto the raft and he lay on his side, the raft bobbing and rocking with all the bodies now moving on its platform.

Billy bent down, "Torio, there were sharks out there."

He nodded and sat up. "I know." In fact, he could see at least a dozen shark fins surrounding their raft now. Billy stared at him in dismay.

"We're fine." He turned his head and took stock of their situation.

There were now six men on their little raft. The weight was such that the first layer of logs was completely submerged. He wished there had been time enough to build railings for the raft.

The three rescued soldiers, all Filipinos, were sitting up now. Everyone shifted and moved to make sure there were no tempting body parts in reach of the hovering sharks.

The first man on the raft spoke up first, "I'm Pancho. Retired boxer from Manila. I joined up the day I heard about the Pearl Harbor attack."

The second soldier nodded at them, "Private Bunso Trujillo." He saluted to Jack, whose Lieutenant stripes were in full sight, and to Torio, who wore Sergeant stripes. Torio's stripes had been obscured by dirt and blood, but a dip in the water had washed off some of the discoloration.

Jack nodded at him, "At ease, soldier."

Bunso, a young man in his early 20's, was skinny with a long jaw. His dark hair straggled over his forehead. His eyebrows were thin and virtually non-existent; however, his dark eyes had a luminous quality of innocence.

The last soldier, the one Torio had rescued, looked at Torio with deep gratitude, "Thank you for saving me." He was also early 20's, slender, frail and handsome... a mestizo who was probably mostly of Spanish heritage. Funny enough, he reminded Torio of Rodolfo, the young swimmer he'd rescued so many years ago.

Torio nodded in acknowledgement.

"I'm Enrico... Rico Florencio. I was studying to be a doctor when the Japanese attacked. My parents were against my joining, but..." He shrugged, "... I want to defend my country as much as any other Filipino."

"I'm Jack. This is Torio, and the freckle-face over there is Billy." He took a deep breath. "As ranking officer, I'm taking charge.

You all can see this raft is just barely big enough to hold all of us."

Pancho asked, "What about that boat tied to the raft?"

Billy answered him, somewhat protective, "It's got a leak."

Torio turned to Billy, "It can hold someone who isn't too heavy... if that someone bails out the water as it builds up."

"Okay. I can do that." Billy turned to the three new men, "Do any of you have a helmet in your pack?"

Rico shook his head, "I lost my pack with the boat."

Pancho reached for his pack, "I've got mine. I tell you, they pound it into your head that if you lose your pack, you lose your life."

Jack looked at his team. "Let's move this raft."

Torio took central position with his paddle, using it to guide their direction. Jack and Pancho took each side of the raft with the remaining two makeshift oars.

Billy got in the boat and started bailing out the water. The wounded Rico with a useless left arm stood at the center pole, their lookout man, keeping an eye for sharks, keeping them apprised of other boats and barges in their vicinity. That left Bunso, who stretched out on a tiny area of the raft to rest up before his turn to take over paddling.

They worked together well, a small force of soldiers, but one trained to follow orders, aware of the fragile balance in the tiny raft which could make the difference between life and death for each one of them.

It went well until they were two miles away from the shores of Corregidor. It was late afternoon by this time. That was when the big wave struck.

* * * * *

CHAPTER 14
HOLDING PATTERN
Manila, Banga and Bataan, Philippines, 1942

When she was 11 years old, Inez had decided to use her older sister's nail polish to beautify her fingernails. The results were disappointing, with smears of red appearing not only on her nails, but also on her fingers, and even on her wrist when she hadn't given them enough time to dry.

She was in tears when she showed the results to Lucing. But Lucing had laughed and used nail polish remover to clear away the smears around her nails and hands and wrists. A short time after Lucing's work, little blisters formed on her skin wherever Lucing had rubbed nail polish remover.

It turned out that acetone tended to irritate and cause blisters when coming in touch with Inez's skin. She'd been disappointed to discover this when she was 11. Now, at 28 years old, she was happy she knew this fact about herself.

After the success of her first shopping run, Inez had approached Manang Maya for a second run. The old woman simply refused to take her, and Inez had accepted that decision.

In the days and weeks that followed, the more she thought about it, the more she realized she had to learn to fend for herself. Who knew if Lucing would come back. And what if Perry got shot again, and this time it killed him? And Manang Maya herself was in her 70's. It wasn't right that she would let the old woman take risks that she herself wasn't willing to take.

So this time, she was prepared when she asked to go with Manang Maya on her next run.

"Too dangerous. You nearly got raped last time. Tell me what you want and I'll pick it up for you."

Inez stood her ground, "I have to learn how to take care of myself, Manang Maya. I can't always count on other people to take care of me. If I can't take care of me, how can I take care of my children?"

She was referring as much to Perry as she was to Manang Maya. After Perry had sufficiently recovered from the gunshot wound inflicted by the Patrol Guard at Santo Tomas University, he'd decided it was too dangerous to stay with Inez and the children. He limited his visits to once a week, when he'd bring food, if he could, or money if he couldn't get food. By late March, because of the scarcity and exorbitant cost of food, she'd used up all the money Lucing had in her safe. Instead of paying Perry to help her out in Lucing's absence, Inez was now receiving money from Perry. He claimed that one of the insurgents in his group was a very wealthy man who was using his money to help the group and their families.

Because of the children, Inez wasn't too proud to take the money. She hoarded it carefully until she had enough to buy a chicken or some canned meat.

"We haven't had meat in two weeks."

"There are families who haven't had meat in months. There are soldiers who haven't eaten anything... not even rice... in days."

Inez straightened her back and glared at Manang Maya. "There's nothing I can do about that. Right now, at least there's something I can do about feeding my children."

When Manang Maya wasn't downgrading her appearance to the world, even with her one cataract-ridden eye, she emanated a warmth and trustworthiness which made people want to be around her. Inez loved this woman dearly, because she'd witnessed her strength, courage and unfailing compassion for everyone around her. She was often so loaded with supplies when she did her market rounds it was amazing she could make it back at all. Once, soldiers had taken all the food she'd been carrying in her big, multi-colored, homemade bags on the way home from her shopping.

"Manang Maya, can I show you something?"

"There's nothing you can show me that will change my mind."

"Maybe there is. Look." Inez pushed down her skirt and underwear to show Manang

Maya her stomach area. Blisters popped up like bubbles of all sizes on her skin.

"I've got these blisters even lower, like down there and on my thighs."

"*Sus.* What's that? I have medicine..." The old woman was already moving to her bathroom.

"It's nothing. It'll be gone by tomorrow." Manang Maya's eyebrows rose high.

"If I put nail polish remover on any part of skin on my body, I get blisters like this. If a soldier doesn't believe I'm diseased, once he sees the blisters on my thighs and stomach, he'll believe it. He won't rape me."

Manang Maya stared hard at Inez. For some moments their gazes locked. Finally, a laugh burst out of the old woman's mouth and Manang Maya chortled so hard tears were coming out of her eyes. Inez smiled to see the old woman so delighted at her idea.

"Okay. Maybe you're clever enough to pull this off. You can come." Then she got sober, "But remember, Inez, even if they don't rape you, they can still kill you."

* * * * *

Her first shopping trip with Manang Maya had been at an open market filled with stands and covered carts crowding the street of shops. Food was already getting scarce then, but there was still a hustle and bustle among the people who came to do their shopping.

Now, a month later, the market plaza was nearly empty. There were two stands side by side. One had several dozen *calabasas*, most of which were half rotting. The second stand had a cart half filled with old bruised bananas.

Occasionally, they had passed soldiers along the streets they'd taken to reach the market, but in the marketplace itself, no soldiers lingered. In fact, there were only five or six shoppers walking around.

An old woman whose business suit had seen better days handed over a sheaf of pesos for a bag of the *calabasas*.

Inez walked just a little behind Manang Maya, hanging on to her skirt with thumb and forefinger. Manang Maya had one of her colorful outfits on. Long green skirt with questionable stains on the hem; a dirty white blouse which had been washed too often with colors, and her assorted shopping bags over both shoulders. Inez herself wore a colorful, old, long-sleeved shirt over a long dark skirt. She had blisters on her face and arms, as well as areas of skin beneath her underwear. During their walk, a soldier had taken a look at her. Then looked away and moved on.

"It's so empty."

"Nippons take most of the food. And our own military needed their share. Takes a lotta food to feed a lotta soldiers. There's not much left to sell."

"Then where are we going?"

"Black markets. Some of our merchants who sell to the Nippons save enough to sell in their shops. If you got money, you can buy what you need. If they got what you need."

They turned into a narrow alley where they could hear people talking through their open windows on the second stories of the buildings.   It was smelly and the alley was filled with pools of filth and debris.

"But if there's no food left, where do they get the food?"

"They've got people squeezing crops out of farmers and raiding abandoned military supply buildings.   Heard about one couple. They picked up nearly 200 cans of meat from this one bombed-out building.   On the main ground floor, nothing but a mess of furniture and supplies.   But in the basement, shelves of canned goods."

Someone threw a bucket of water out an open window.   It splashed on the ground behind them.

Manang Maya glanced back, "Dirty water."   She grinned at Inez, "At least it wasn't piss or worse."

They stopped in front of a scratched-up, dirty green door.   Maya did a complicated set of knocks.   The door opened and a small boy, about seven, grinned at them.   "Hello, Manang Maya."

The old woman patted his head, "How are you, Chin?"

"Very well, *salamat po*."   He smiled at Inez and sat down on a stool under the stairwell.   She followed Manang Maya through a narrow corridor leading to the back.

"He opens that door when someone knocks out the right sequence.   Earns food for his family that way."

At the end of the corridor was a metal door. Manang Maya repeated her complicated set of knocks.

It opened. There stood the big guy Inez had met on her first shopping run with Manang Maya.

"Hello, Chuy."

Inside it was neat, organized and clean. "Want canned meat, Missus? Cheap now. Got plenty."

Inez glanced at Manang Maya. Aha! So that story was true.

She wanted a chicken. But when she learned the cost of one chicken was equivalent to 10 cans of meat, she went for the meat. She'd have to be inventive to make different meals from that, but food was food.

On the way back, they were stopped by a group of soldiers. The leader, a pock-faced overweight man with thinning hair, put his hand on her shoulder and moved her tangled hair away from her face.

When he saw the blisters, his hand jerked back. Inez lifted her head, her mouth dribbling spit and her eyes half-shut. She gave him a stupid smile and he quickly stepped away from her.

His friends laughed at him as he turned to hurry away from her. From the sound of it, a few were even taunting him to have his way with her. But the poor Japanese soldier scurried away like a rat fleeing from a burning building.

Manang Maya and Inez stayed in character until they reached the old woman's house. As soon as the door closed behind them, they looked at each other and burst out laughing. It seemed as if they couldn't stop. When they finally did and changed back into their regular clothes, they looked at each other and collapsed in another bout of laughter.

It was good to find something to laugh about.

Late one afternoon, three days after her second run and about a month after his first visit, a soft quick knock sounded on the door. With Julio and Cencia standing on each side of her, she opened the door. The same Japanese soldier who had given her a bag of food before stood there. He looked down at Cencia and Julio. Nodded once. Handed Inez the bag and turned to walk away.

"Who are you?"

He didn't even bother to turn around.

"Why are you doing this?"

He kept walking. Inez stared after him, until he disappeared down the street.

She closed the door and opened the bag. Inside was a bag of rice, some canned fruit and vegetables, and a handful of candy in red shiny wrappers. At the very bottom was a letter from Lucing.

"April 17, 1942

Dear Inez,

I miss you and Julio and Cencia. So much has happened since I last saw you. I wish I were there with you, but otherwise, my life here is so much better than so many other people's lives. They have done nothing to deserve their miserable conditions except to be in the wrong place at the wrong time.

Inez, please don't give up hope. I tell you without hesitation that not all Japanese are bad. I know one such man who has promised me that he would get this letter to you, and I trust him to keep his word.

Know that I am well. I pray that Perry continues to watch over you and the children. Kisses to the little ones and please stay safe and healthy.

Love, Lucing

Inez was so happy to hear from her sister than tears flooded her eyes.

"Mama, what's wrong?" He placed a hand on her back protectively, and his eyes were ready to cloud with anger at whatever was causing her tears. Suddenly she realized how much he had changed.

Julio's question was not coming from a child who was insecure and afraid of the answer. It was coming from a boy trying to be a man. Through all the challenges in their lives since the war had begun, her son was discovering the clay of character which would shape him into someone who challenged life, rather than one who became victim to it.

She was so proud that her eyes flooded anew. "Nothing's wrong. Look, a letter from your Aunt Lucing! Let's read it together."

She read the letter to them, and after a dinner of fried rice and Spam, they opened a can of peaches for dessert.

Throughout it all, she kept thinking to herself... *Who was that Japanese soldier? What was his connection to Lucing that she could trust him with her letter?* She was determined to find out. And she actually had an idea of how to make that happen.

* * * * *

After Juan turned over all his cases to his brother, cleared up household matters at home with Emiliana, assured his children how much he loved them, and notified his clients of his intentions, Juan was ready.

The biggest hurdle had been his wife, Emiliana. She was undeniably an elitist... convinced that war belonged only to soldiers who didn't have education and mental acuity enough to do anything else than hard labor. She herself had continued to study with private tutors until her education was equivalent to at least two years of college-level studies.

During their arguments, he couldn't help but compare his wife with Rissing. He kept saying to himself, "Rissing would never say that to me. Rissing would never think that. Rissing would understand what I'm doing."

Finally, along with two other lawyers, one judge, and four shopowners he'd known all his life, he signed up at the local recruitment center, an abandoned office building in the oldest part of town. The soldier behind the desk was a man who'd survived the Spanish-American war 45 years previously with only one leg intact.

It wasn't the perfect setup. The guns and uniforms the recruiter gave Juan and his group were recycled, but everything fit well enough and the weapons worked. This was right after President Roosevelt's announcement that there would be no more American reinforcements, so everyone knew these were desperate times. No one complained.

After they signed up and were entered into the system, they were hurried to the basement of the old building where another old soldier, this one with a patch over one eye and a hand missing, showed them the basics of their weaponry and gave them common sense rules of survival, the most important one being, "Keep your head down."

Then they got on a *bangka* which took them later that night across the water to the Bataan peninsula where they joined the American-Filipino troops. They had been warned that the Japanese ships patrolled the waters relentlessly, but they made it without incident, thanks to the two fishermen brothers who knew the sea well enough to maneuver in the darkness of night.

Once they reached the battle front, survival became the prime directive. It didn't take long for them to get separated from each other, and after a week, Juan, no longer in touch with any of his original companion volunteers, was as hungry, sick and starving as the rest of his fellow soldiers.

He thought to himself he was lucky that at least he was still alive.

It was his strong moral code and ethical standards which had prompted him to sign up. He had wanted to live up to the high expectations he had of himself. He had wanted to be the kind of man who could be proud of himself all his life.

Most of all, he had wanted to be a part of his country's war. There was no doubt about it... he'd gotten his wish.

* * * * *

CHAPTER 15
SURRENDER
Bataan and Corregidor, Philippines, 1942

Torio and his fellow soldiers found that the most stable position on the boat was stretched out across the platform. They were essentially at the mercy of winds and currents, so they had to counteract the power of both elements if they wanted to reach Corregidor.

They each took turns as watcher, boat scooper and raft rower. Jack was diligent in timing their rotation. The boats and barges had long passed them by.

Once they passed an area where bodies floated on the surface of the water, and they could only watch as sharks pulled at them for an underwater feast. Torio was ashamed to admit it, but he was glad those bodies kept the inevitable sharks occupied.

Another time, they almost lost Pancho after one sizeable wave. Rico had fallen on him when the wave hit, and Pancho had lost his hold of the raft. He went tumbling into the water, but he'd quickly made his way back to the raft where the others pulled him up to safety.

After that, the group had taken time to attach themselves more securely to the raft somehow. The wear and tear on the raft had loosened some of the vine-ropes Torio had used to tie the logs together, so the logs were no longer as tightly secure as when they had started out. They did their best to repair the damage, but the raft wasn't going to hold together much longer.

And then the big wave hit them. The raft tipped on its side, and they all fell into the water. When it righted itself, the logs battered against each other and Torio, Jack and Pancho were still clinging to what remained of it. The leaky boat had capsized and sunk and there was no sign of Enrico, who had been boat scooper at that point.

What remained of the raft were five logs... the two end logs from the first tier, and the three logs from the 2nd platform tier. Except one of the outer logs at the end of the 2nd platform tier was attached to the raft only at one end, and the other end swung out on its own, tossing and swinging at cross-purposes to the raft.

Torio dug into his pocket and retrieved his knife. Made his way to the recalcitrant log and cut off its remaining ties to the raft. He watched it float away from the raft. It had gone only a short distance, when Torio saw Billy's head surface beside it, and an arm grabbing onto it for dear life. Torio watched as the currents took the log and Billy away from them. If he jumped in the water and tried to recapture the log and Billy, he could well go swirling away from the raft faster than he could save both of them and swim back.

352

A hand clutched at the raft beside him, and Torio grabbed on it and pulled. When he saw Enrico's head surface, he pulled Enrico's shirt and helped him onto the raft. Enrico, gasping for breath, still found words to thank him. The poor kid's arm wound was bleeding badly.

When the raft stabilized, there were five of them on its remnants. Bunso was gone. The boat was gone. Only three packs had remained attached to the poles on the raft, and Torio's pack was one of them. One of the paddles remained attached to the raft. Another had been torn away, and only the handle remained of the third paddle.

Jack turned to him, "Bunso?"

"Gone."

"Billy?"

"On a log headed that way." Torio pointed away from them.

They were alone now. They could see land several miles away. Torio knew he could swim that easily enough.

Without paddles to control it, the raft itself was at the mercy of whatever currents guided the flow of water. They could even be swept out to the South China Sea.

He studied the water. There weren't any sharks in their immediate vicinity.

He considered their situation carefully. They had no paddles, but they still had their arms and legs. He slid into the water, hung on to the raft with his left arm, and used his right arm and legs to propel the raft towards Corregidor. It was better than nothing.

After a minute, Jack slid into the water on the other side of the raft and did the same, hanging on to the raft with his right arm. Pancho hung on with both hands to the back of the raft and paddled with his feet.

The currents were still too strong but at least they weren't being swept out to sea. It was late afternoon when their feet finally touched land, and they pushed the raft to the rocky shore, got on their backs and lay panting against the rocky ground. The unconscious Rico was still on the raft, unaware of his free ride to Corregidor.

They had landed on the mountainous side with tall cliffs overlooking the water. The raft was resting on some rocks, slanting down towards the water.

A fierce voice shouted at them, "Identify yourselves."

Jack sat up, raised his hands and shouted back, "We're soldiers from Bataan. We escaped."

After a pause, the voice continued, "You can't climb up here. It's too steep. You'll have to make your way around the bend... where that rock sticks out like a fat nose. There's a landing field about a mile away on that side surrounded by a wire fence."

They discussed whether to get back in the water with the raft and maneuver themselves around the "fat nose" bend... or whether they could just carry Enrico along the rocky shore.

Pancho didn't want to get into the water again, so he and Jack decided to walk along the shore. Before they did, however, they helped Torio dismantle the raft. Then Torio took the central log with the poles, bolstered another log against the poles to hold it in place, and tied those two logs together to make a wide enough surface to hold Enrico's slender form.

Torio took some salvaged length of rope and tied it around his chest, and then tied each end of the rope to the slender new raft, leaving just enough space between him and raft to give him swimming room. Enrico, conscious now but too weak to maneuver the rocky shore, got on the slender raft while Torio towed him along the water.

There were no sharks this close to land, and Torio actually made better time than Jack and Pancho on foot. He went to shore at intervals to wait for the two men to catch up. At one point, Torio had enough time to catch six fish, which he had gutted out, cleaned and cooked just in time for Jack and Pancho to join them at their meal.

Several hours later, Torio swam ashore in sight of the wire fence. He scouted ahead to look for a gap in the fence, and when he found it, he returned to wait with Enrico for the other two.

It was getting dark when Jack and Pancho arrived, but they wasted no time in finding the gap Torio had found. They all went through, their arms in the air. Minutes later, two soldiers in a jeep found them and took them in to headquarters. Enrico was taken to the hospital in Malinta Tunnel, Jack was reunited with his unit, Pancho was assigned to the Philippine Army, and Torio was sent to the U.S. Army unit at Fort Mills who were defending the bay against the Japanese.

They had escaped the final Japanese offensive in Bataan, but they were back in the thick of war in Corregidor.

*　*　*　*　*

When General MacArthur retreated to Australia on March 10th, Jonathan Wainwright was promoted to Commander of U.S. Army Forces in the Far East, and Major General Edward King Jr. took over the command of Bataan.

By Easter Sunday, the Japanese stormed the upper slopes of Mount Samat, which provided a commanding view of the battlefield below. King threw most of his slim reserves into a desperate counterattack, but the outmanned and outgunned American/Filipinos were no match for the Japanese.

On April 6th, six days after the final Japanese offensive, Major General Edward King, Jr. sat down at a field table across from General Homma's operations officer, Colonel Motoo Nakayama, and asked for a 12-hour stay to collect the wounded. Nakayama refused. King asked, "Will our troops be well treated?" Nakayama answered, "We are not barbarians." King laid his sidearm on the table and surrendered the remaining 76,000 men of Bataan.

But Corregidor, "The Rock", had not yet given up.

Corregidor Island consisted of 65 miles of paved roads and trails and nearly 20 miles of electric railroad track. It had a school where children of both Filipino and American servicemen studied. Its water and food were hauled by barges from Mariveles or Cabcaben, Bataan. The fact that it was dependent on outside sources for its water and food made it very vulnerable, despite its otherwise impressive fortifications. The defense installations for Corregidor alone had cost the US government more than $150 million.

It was fortified with 56 coastal guns and mortars, supplemented by 14-inch guns on its three neighboring islands: Caballo, Carabao, and El Fraile. Fort Drum on El Fraile resembled an oversized pillbox, sporting 14-inch and 60-inch guns, and was nicknamed the "concrete battleship" by the soldiers.

On Corregidor, Fort Mills had direct access to the Malinta Tunnel, and the official headquarters at this point was deep inside the tunnel.

Malinta Tunnel was a 1400-foot tunnel with an elaborate network of bomb-proof underground passages reinforced with concrete. Not only did the tunnel house the staff headquarters, it had a communications center, an ammunition dump, a hospital and, of course, it served as a sturdy bomb shelter.

* * * * *

Torio did everything and anything he was asked to do at Fort Mills. He was at times a watcher, and divested with some authority as a Sergeant, he was otherwise tasked with organizing and advising civilians during defense of the fort.

Having vanquished Bataan, the Japanese now aimed their sights on Corregidor itself. When the bombings focused on Corregidor, the civilian cooks fled the island and the fort asked for volunteers to cook for the officers. Torio was quick to volunteer, claiming that he had experience as Mess Sergeant back in Manila.

He hadn't been, of course, but he knew how to cook well enough to satisfy the desperate conditions in Corregidor. He maneuvered himself into a position where he could eat three meals a day... mostly canned foods at that, but sustenance enough to give him strength through the remaining days of battle.

When the Japanese subjected Corregidor to continuous artillery barrage, day and night, Torio was back in action. They found a civilian to take over the cooking stints, and he was given guard duty beside the cannons. As guard, it was his responsibility to oversee the firing of the cannons.

One day when he was on guard by the cannons, Japanese planes zoomed in to bombard the fort and took out one of the cannons beside him. All the other soldiers retreated to take shelter inside the tunnel, but Torio didn't feel like dying inside the tunnel.

He wanted to see the sky above him.

So he ran to a working cannon, loaded it, and fired it. He continued this until finally, the Japanese zoomed away and it was quiet again.

Next morning, Torio was given command of the cannons.

The attack on Corregidor was relentless. Shellfire from more than 100 Japanese guns rained down on the island survivors. Fires raged over the surface of the island, generating smoke thick with black cinders.

Fissures widened in Malinta Tunnels' concrete walls and the sick and wounded were crowded together so closely that the air was thick with dust and fetid with the stench of death. Fatigue, hunger and terror demoralized everyone, and no one knew whether they'd last the day or not.

Torio survived it all. He still considered the tunnel a death trap, so he refused to join the others there during strafing. Instead, he stayed in the jungle with a few others and they did what damage they could from their hidden places.

One day, bombardment was so intense it reached Malinta Tunnel itself. Torio was outside among the trees. When the firing stopped, there was smoke coming out of Malinta Tunnel itself.

He ran inside the tunnel and helped moved people outside. Back and forth he went, and a few times, he saw that someone he had taken out two trips before had died.

There weren't enough nurses and doctors to tend to everyone.

He lost track of time, and finally he himself collapsed beside the body of a soldier whose head was caked in blood.

When he opened his eyes, he found himself inside the crowded, blood-stenched Malinta Tunnel, on a makeshift floor bed beside other makeshift beds filled with wounded men.

He sat up and looked around him. It was organized chaos. The more seriously wounded and sick were in beds, some areas cordoned off with plastic curtains. There was no pretense at sterility... not when so many of the soldiers on the beds were still wearing their dirty, torn and blood-drenched uniforms. The smell was sickening.

The tunnel walls loomed above and around him, and he felt himself overcome with a sudden surge of panic and fear. It was a greater panic and fear than he'd ever experienced before... not even in the heat of battle when guns were blazing all around him and he saw his companions taking bullets and falling lifeless on the ground.

A nurse came hurrying to him, "I'll be with you in a minute."

He looked down at himself. He was shirtless, his body covered in blood. "This isn't my blood. Where's the way out?"

The nurse pointed and he took off as fast as his legs could take him. He knew surrender was inevitable.

He knew it was just a matter of time.

* * * * *

On May 2, Corregidor's last big gun emplacement took a direct hit in its magazine. Ten-ton mortar barrels flew into the air like matchsticks. Ammunition exploded into the fortress, shaking apart its very foundations. From the nearby island of El Fraile, Fort Drum, the "concrete battleship," was now the only effective defense against the Japanese barrage.

Added to the bombardment, the Japanese had blocked all potable water and food supplies from reaching Corregidor.

Three nights later, Homma's troops landed on Corregidor. Tanks rolled ashore and artillery zeroed in on the mouth of Malinta Tunnel.

Before noon on May 6, nearly a month after King surrendered at Bataan, Wainwright cabled President Roosevelt, "With broken heart, and head bowed in sadness but not in shame, I report to Your Excellency that today I must arrange terms for the surrender of the fortified islands of Manila Bay."

Then he radioed MacArthur in Australia, "I have fought for you to the best of my ability from Lingayen Gulf to Bataan to Corredigor. Goodbye, General."

A young Army radio operator from Brooklyn, New York, tapped out Corregidor's last message: "Everyone is bawling like a baby. They are piling dead and wounded in our tunnel... the jig is up."

Because Wainwright feared that the Malinta Tunnel, sheltering all the survivors – civilians and soldiers alike – would become a slaughterhouse, he agreed to surrender all his forces to the Japanese. The next day, he radioed the commanders of all units in the Philippines to capitulate. They reluctantly did so over the next five weeks, but not before several thousand of their troops had vanished into the hills, to survive and resist, as best they could.

* * * * *

*** TO BE CONTINUED IN BOOK 2 ***

* * * * *

Please be on the lookout for Book 2 of the
"BLACK CLOUDS IN MANILA" series:

Book 2: "A PEOPLE UNDEFEATED"

GLOSSARY OF TAGALOG WORDS AND PHRASES

aba	whoa; an expression of wondering surprise
abala	trouble; inconvenience; bother
adobo	Filipino dish featuring chicken and/or pork, vinegar and soy sauce, etc.
ako	I; me
alamang	small shrimp used to make a dip called *bagoong*
ampalaya	bitter melon; belongs to the gourd family of vegetables which include *upo* and *patola*. *Patola,* when allowed to shrivel and dry, becomes loofah for body scrub.
ang	the (an article to specify a noun or adjective)
anuman	whatever; anything
aray or aruy	Exclamation: "Ouch!"
arigato	Japanese: thank you
arroz valenciana	Spanish dish featuring chicken, sticky rice, coconut milk, etc.
aswang	similar to a vampire... but worse. They come out at night but not only suck blood... they eat human flesh, including entrails and

	organs, like liver, and even the foetus from a pregnant woman.
ay	when combined with noun or adjective, it suggests verb form equivalent to am/is/are
ay apo!	Exclamation: "Oboy!" *Apo,* if the accent is on the first syllable "A", is a term of respect to an honored old man or grandfather, but if the accent is on the 2nd syllable *po,* the term *apo* refers to a grandchild.
baboy	pig
bagoong	small salted shrimp, especially the small ones called *alamang.* Could also be small fish like anchovies or *dilis,* or *dulong,* the smallest fish found only in Lake Buhi in the Philippines, or fish roe (fish eggs). *Alamang bagoong* is usually used as a dip for green mango or any sour fruit, or put in that famous Ilokano dish, *pinakbet,* and also used as a condiment for *kare-kare,* a stew with peanut sauce.
bahay	House (or *casa* in Spanish); a house is not always a home, and a home is not necessarily a house.
bale wala!	"It doesn't count!"; "It's nothing!"
bangka	boat; skiff
banig	a sleeping mat woven from *buri*

	palm tree
banyo	bathroom; shower room; wash room
barangay	Filipino town; village; small community
baro at saya	Filipino national formal wear for women; made of pina cloth or *jusi*, banana fiber cloth... even synthetic clothing materials, such as lace, silk and other luxury materials
barong tagalog	Filipino national formal wear for the men; made of pina cloth or *jusi*, banana fiber cloth... even synthetic clothing materials; counterpart of American coat and suit over fine trousers of the same clothing material, complete with neck tie
bida	hero; heroine; leading man or lady
biku	Filipino dessert featuring coconut milk, sticky rice, sugar, etc.
bobo	Also *tanga;* vernacular pejorative for mentally challenged or unlettered, i.e. idiot; stupid
butiki	lizard; gecko
calesa	horse-drawn carriage
camote	sweet potato; or "*kamote*"
carabao	Asian water buffalo, national

	animal of Philippines
centavo	Spanish: *sentimo;* counterpart of U.S. "cents"; in the 1940's, the rate of exchange was 1/2 (1 cent = 2 centavos); at today's rate of exchange, 1 U.S. cent = 44 Philippine centavos; since 100 centavos = 1 peso, then U.S. $1 = 44 pesos.
champorado	Filipino morning porridge, made with *malagkit (*sticky rice) sweetened by sugar, cooked in coconut milk with chocolate stirred in. Dairy milk could be used as well.
chibabo	fat one; chubby
cuidao	a command to take care; be careful
"Dahil Sa Iyo"	"Because of You" – Filipino Kundiman-style love song popular for serenading women
dilis	anchovies, sometimes dried and eaten with plain rice; other times used to make a dip called *bagoong*
"Dios mio, nunca"	Spanish: "My God, never!"
"Diyos Ko!"	"My God!"
dulong	the smallest fish in the Philippines found only in Lake Buhi,

	sometimes used to make a dip called *bagoong*
duyan	hammock; swing
gabi	*evening; night*
guapo	handsome; good-looking
hacendero	owner of a hacienda
hacienda	An entire estate composed of a large tract of land, with all the improvements thereon, including the mansion or a house where the *hacendero* (owner) lives; might include a plantation for raising crops, trees, mills to process the crops, etc; or might include a ranch with cattle, livestock and horses raised for income purposes
hai	Japanese : yes
hala	an exclamation equivalent to "Hey!" or "Go ahead!"
halo halo	Filipino dessert featuring shaved ice, sweet beans and fruit, etc.
hapon	as an ordinary noun, accented on the first syllable, "ha," this means afternoon; as a formal or primary noun, accented on the second syllable, "pon," it refers to the Japanese as a people or as a single person.

hayop	beast; monster; animal
hilaw	unripened
hindi	not; no
hindi ba?	right?; isn't that so?; isn't it?
hindi bale!	"Never mind!" "It's not important!"
ho	A coarser term for "po"; a term of respect for an elderly person or a person of authority, even if younger.
hoy	hello; hey there
Huwag	don't
huy	to catch someone's attention: "Hey you!"
ichi	Japanese: one
iha	daughter; young female child
ihi	pee; urine
iho	son; young male child
ikaw	you
inay	mother; mommy
ingat	caution; care; prudence
itak	a bolo knife or any large knife
itay	father; daddy

jusi	Chinese: silk; fine transparent woven fabric made from silk and *pina* threads
kaagad	right away; immediately
kababayan	Refers to one or all persons who are natives of one country, so all Filipinos are *kababayan* to each other
kagat ng langgam	"bite of an ant"; pain so minor it's not worth mentioning
kain	eat
kalaro	playmate; companion
kaluluwa	a ghostly spirit; an elfin spirit
kami	we; us; ourselves
ka	you; used as a subject pronoun
kang	your; used as a possessive pronoun
kangkong	a type of grass in Philippines; also refers to a type of swamp spinach, a very nutritious green leafy vegetable which grows on water. Filipinos like to add it to *sinigang,* a tart soup made of vegetables, like okra, eggplant, radish, string beans or *sitaw.*
kanji	A mixture of Japanese/Chinese symbols, or ideograms, to represent places, objects or living

	things.
kanya	His; hers; possessive pronoun
kanyang	"*kanya*" + "*ng*" = its; his; hers
karaskaras	sloppy; reckless, every which way
kare-kare	A Philippine stew made from peanut sauce with a variety of vegetables, stewed oxtail, beef, and occasionally tripe; sometimes also with *bagoong*
kayo	you; all of you
kilikili	armpit
kubeta	Toilet; privy
kubo	Nipa hut; a small house usually in the forest or fields
kumadre or mare'	someone who is godmother to one's child; may be used to denote courtesy to a close female friend
kumpadre or pare'	someone who is godfather to one's child; may be used to denote courtesy to a close male friend
kung	if; when
lagundi	Filipino medicinal herb or plant used for treating cold, coughs and other respiratory ailments
lamggam	Ant

lechon baboy	roast pig
lelang	grandmother
lelong	grandfather
lola	grandmother
lolo	grandfather
longganisa	Filipino sausage
lugao	rice porridge
lukto	a variation of *"camote"*; sweet potato
lumpia	Filipino roll, fresh or fried, filled with fruit, vegetables, meat or shrimp... or a mixture of any or all of these
mabuhay	As a toast: "Long may we live!"; life; to be alive
mag	to (usually followed by verb)
mag-alala	to worry; to be concerned
maganda	beautiful; pretty; attractive
"Magandang gabi"	(*maganda* + *ang*) with *"gabi"*: literally, "beautiful the night", implying the verb form "is"... or "good evening"
"Magandang hapon"	(*maganda* + *ang*) with "hapon": literally, "beautiful the afternoon", implying the verb form "is"... or

	"good afternoon"
"Magandang umaga"	*(maganda + ang)* with *"umaga"*: literally, "beautiful the morning", implying the verb form "is"... or "good morning"
mag-ingat	to watch out; to look out
magmadali	to hurry; to rush
mahal ko	my beloved; my dearest
maingat	as a command: "Be careful"; "Take care"
malagkit	sticky rice
malaki	large; big
manang	a respectful title given to older sister or other female relative; to denote courtesy to an older woman in a respected position
mangga	mango
manghihilot	One who restores dislodged bones, ligaments, and joints due to falls or accidents without surgery... usually by massaging slowly the affected body parts with oils and balms
mangkukulam	medicine man or woman; a healer
manong	a respectful title given to older brother or other male relative; to denote courtesy to an older man in a respected position

maraming	many; much
maroyat	skinny; thin one
mas mabuti	better yet; even better
masarap	delicious; tasty
masuwerte	lucky; fortunate
matangos	pointed; sharp
mga	the; some; approximately
musuko	Japanese: son; male child
na	already (if it follows a verb, e.g., *"tapos na"* – *"finished already"*)
naku	Oh my; wow
nanay	mother; mom
ng	of; by, with; from
ngayon	now; at this moment
Ngunit	but; otherwise
nipa hut	a small hut made of bamboo and roofed with nipa palms
"Noli Mi Tangere"	"Touch Me Not" – title of a famous novel by Dr. José Rizal, considered the ideal hero by the Filipinos
oo	yes (pronounced "ough-ough" as in "ought")
oho	"*oo*" + "*ho*"; "yes sir" or "yes

	ma'am"; a coarser term of respect than "*opo*" when saying "yes" to an elderly person or someone with authority, even if younger
opo	"*oo*" + "*po*"; "yes sir" or "yes ma'am"; saying "yes" to an elderly person or someone with authority, even if younger
orinola	chamber pot
palengke	an open market square; shopping area
palikuran	toilet; privy
pansit	Filipino dish made with rice noodles and shrimp or chicken, with vegetables
papag	a bed made of bamboo, on which *banigs* are placed
papayag	please; approve; agree
patadyong	rectangular cloth used as a wraparound skirt; also used for other wraparound functions, like a sling, an apron, a hammock, a bundle container, etc.
patay	dead
payat	skinny; thin one
pina	a fabric hand-loomed from pineapple leaf fibers

pinakbet	Filipino popular dish of Ilocano origin featuring vegetables like string beans, *sigarillas*, okra, squash, eggplant, etc., with *bagoong*, shrimp or pork
po	a more respectful term of respect than "*ho*," used to address an elderly person or a person of authority, even if younger; "sir" or "ma'am"
pugot	mindless; headless
Pumunta	go; visit; to get to
"*Que deliciosa, iha!*"	Spanish: "How delicious, daughter!"
sa	to
sakana	Japanese: fish
salamat	thanks; thank you
sari sari	various; miscellaneous. A "sari sari" store is one containing miscellaneous things.
sayas	A woman's dress featuring butterfly sleeves
seguro	as an exclamation: "Sure"; "you bet"
si	when combined with noun or adjective, it suggests verb form equivalent to am/is/are (i.e.,

	"Maganda si Rissing" translates to "Rissing is pretty.")
"Sige namam!"	"Go ahead"; "So go!"
Simpatico	sympathetic; in sync with
sino	who (am/are verb implied)
"Sino ito?"	"Who's this?"; "Who's this one?"
siya	he; that one
siyanga	"Is that so?"
so desu	Japanese: I understand; okay
sundalo	soldier; military man
"Sus naman!"	"Oh, Jesus!"... "sus" is contraction for Jesus.
taba	fat; fat one
tahimik	peace; quiet; calm
tahimik na	be calm now; be quiet now
tainga	ear
talaga	truly, really, very; surely
tanga	Also *bobo;* vernacular pejorative for mentally challenged or unlettered, i.e idiot; stupid
tapis	a *patadyong* type of wraparound skirt which is usually accompanied

	with a built-in sash for tying around the waist; the cloth used to make the skirt
tapos	done; finished; complete
tatay	father, dad
tocino	Filipino bacon
tuba	alcoholic beverage made out of coconuts
tuyo	fried and dried small fish
ube	Filipino purple yam
ulam	viand; article of food served during meals
umaga	morning; morn
unggoy	monkey
utos	command; order
utot	fart
uy	hey
wala	none
"Walang anuman"	"Think nothing of it"; "it's nothing whatsoever"; equivalent to, "You're welcome"
yerba buena	a plant whose dried leaves are used for tea

yung	the; those

* * * * *

SONG TRANSLATIONS

LA PALOMA	THE DOVE (Julio Iglesias Version)
Cuando salí de la Habana *¡Válgame Diyos!* *Nadie me ha visto salir* *Si no fuí yo.* *Y una linda Guachinanga* *S'allá voy yo,* *Que se vino tras de mi,* *Que sí señor.* *Refrain:* *Si a tu ventana llega* *Una Paloma,* *Trátala con cariño,* *Que es mi persona.* *Cuéntale tus amores,* *Bien de mi vida,* *Corónala de flores,* *Que es cosa mía.* *Ay, chinita que sí!* *Ay, que dame tu amor!* *Ay, que vente conmigo,* *Chiquita, a donde vivo yo!*	A song reminds me Of that yesterday When she silently left One afternoon She went away to another place Taking her sad melody with her All that was left as my companion Was my loneliness A white dove sings to me At dawn Old melancholies, things Of the soul It arrives with The morning silence And when I go out to watch it It flies back home Where does it go to? For it doesn't want to hear my voice anymore Where does it go to? For my life extinguishes When she's not by my side If she would like to come back I'd go and wait for her Each day, each early morning

	To love her more.

* * * * *

BAHAY KUBO	MY HUMBLE HUT (Translated by Roberto Verzola)
Bahay kubo, *kahit munti,* *ang halaman doon ay sari-sari* *singkamas at talong,* *sigarilyas at mani* *sitaw, bataw, patani* *Kundol, patola, upo't kalabasa,* *At saka mayroon pang labanos, mustasa,* *sibuyas, kamatis, bawang at luya.* *Sa paligid-ligid ay puno ng linga.*	My humble hut May look tiny, But the veggies around it Sure are many. Yam, beans and eggplants Wing'd beans and peanuts, String, hyacinth and lima beans, Winter melon and loofah, Bottl' gourd, squash, etcetera. There's more, amiga. Radish, mustard, yeah. Onions, tomatoes, garlic and ginger If you look all around Sesame seeds abound.
COUNTING SONG *Isa, dalawa, tatlo...*	COUNTING SONG

Ang Tatay mong kalbo... *Umutot parang bumbo...* *Kanyon de rapido*	One, two, three... Your father's bald... And farts like a drum... As fast as a cannon...

* * * * *

Made in the USA
San Bernardino, CA
22 April 2014